Stolen

Also by Carey Baldwin

Stolen

A Cassidy & Spenser Thriller

CAREY BALDWIN

WITNESS
IMPULSE
An Imprint of HarperCollinsPublishers

STOLEN. Copyright © 2017 by Carey Baldwin. All rights reserved. Printed in the United States of America. No part of this book may be used or reproduced in any manner whatsoever without written permission except in the case of brief quotations embodied in critical articles and reviews. For information, address HarperCollins Publishers, 195 Broadway, New York, NY 10007.

Digital Edition FEBRUARY 2017 ISBN: 9780062495549

Print Edition ISBN: 9780062495495

WITNESS logo and WITNESS IMPULSE are trademarks of HarperCollins Publishers in the United States of America.

HarperCollins is a registered trademark of HarperCollins Publishers in the United States of America and other countries.

FIRST EDITION

17 18 19 20 21   LSC   10 9 8 7 6 5 4 3 2 1

air, snake between her breasts, she took it all in, and a gasp agonized its way up her throat.

She was naked.

Bound around the waist, chest, and ankles to a chair.

It all seemed so . . . unreal. But the scrape of splintered wood beneath her bottom, the shivers that wracked her body from the frigid air, told her this was no dream. This wasn't another one of her ubiquitous nightmares.

If she closed her eyes now, she'd never wake up.

Her throat burned with the urge to scream. But sensing that might give him pleasure, she clamped her teeth together, stuffing her fear down deep. She inhaled a fortifying breath through her nose. Wiggled her freezing fingers. But when she tried to shift her arms into a more comfortable position, she found that they, too, were tied to the chair, just up to the elbows. He'd left her hands and lower arms free, giving her enough slack to cross her palms in her lap and cover herself. Tears of gratitude for this small kindness welled in her eyes.

Maybe *he of the knife* had a tiny, shriveled semblance of a heart.

He proved he did not by dragging the jagged blade across her neck again—a shallow retracing of its former path that produced exquisite pain and more hot red blood. The need to cry out shook her body so hard the legs of the chair rattled against the floor. Then he pressed the knife's point into the hollow of her neck— that spot that ought to be reserved for a lover's kiss. It was as if this monster could not decide whether he wanted to kill her with a long, decimating swipe or by a swift, stabbing impalement. She didn't know whether he was deliberately prolonging her agony or working up his nerve.

A spasm of fear knotted her toes. Her vocal cords trembled from the impossible effort of restraint. Finally, she opened her mouth, releasing a hysterical noise.

He wanted to hear her scream? Let him hear her laugh instead. Her pulse bounded harder against the blade, but she no longer feared the consequence.

Whether he revealed himself to her or not, she suddenly didn't care. It didn't matter who he was. It only mattered who *she* was. Relief flooded her entire being, drenching her in joy.

Her death would be a victory.

Because it answered, once and for all, the question that had haunted her since the age of eight.

She was not a murderer.

Chapter 2

THE JOLT OF touchdown, the roar of the plane's wheels grinding against asphalt, and the oily smell of exhaust woke FBI Special Agent Atticus Spenser. But it was the sound of a soft, familiar voice murmuring beside him that made him want to open his eyes. Savoring the anticipation, he resisted the temptation.

"'In wildness is the preservation of the world,'" Caity whispered.

"You've sure got a way with words," he said appreciatively, stirring in his seat.

"Not me. Henry David Thoreau."

"'He'd be a poorer man if he never saw an eagle fly.'" Spense would never be as classy as Caity, but he did his best to impress.

"Walt Whitman?" She sounded pleased with him.

Too bad he had to let her down. But hey, it was still a classic. "Nah. It's a line from 'Rocky Mountain High.'"

Her laugh sounded like a pretty bell. "The John Denver song?"

"Best I could do off the cuff." He'd waited as long as he could stand it to open his eyes. Now, from beneath sleepy lids, he took in the profile that made him feel like he was nineteen again and just about to dive off Acapulco's famed La Quebrada cliffs—only for that, he'd been prepared. The waves beneath the rocks rose to a safe depth mere seconds at a time, which is why he'd studied and practiced a full year before taking that life-and-death leap. But when it had come to Caity . . . he'd just jumped.

With her exotic dark hair, surprising blue eyes, and sexy, full lips, Dr. Caitlin Cassidy was beautiful by anyone's standards. But he'd known plenty of smoking hot women, and none of them had ever mesmerized him the way she did. He couldn't explain why he was willing to risk anything to be with her. What he did know was that so far the fall was exhilarating.

Though he could hardly take his eyes off her, Caity's attention seemed fixed elsewhere. She stared out the window, fingers pressed against the scratched, plastic pane as a terminal, topped with white fabric peaks, came into full view. The Denver airport had been designed to remind visitors of both the snow-capped Rockies and Colorado's Native American history. No doubt Caity had been recalling her beloved mountains when she'd quoted Thoreau.

Hard to believe how much things had changed in just a few short weeks. The last time Spense and Caity had flown into Denver, she'd sat with her back ramrod straight, her jaw clamped, and her hands fisted miserably in her lap—anticipating a tense reunion with her mother. Today, her eyes were bright, her body relaxed, and her smile eager. This time, Caity had things all squared away with her mom. Now *he* was the one with a black cloud hovering above his head—a devastating piece of family news he had yet to deliver.

At the Bureau's behest, he and Caity had boarded the first flight from Dallas to Denver, and that meant he hadn't had a chance to touch base with his mother in Arizona after finishing up their last case. But that was his problem. He didn't want anything to diminish the gleam of happiness in Caity's eyes. "You glad to be home?"

"I wish it weren't under these circumstances, but yes."

Said circumstances were another assignment—an important one. But fortuitously, Caity's mother lived in Boulder, just about thirty minutes down the road from Denver. So they hoped to sneak in a short visit or two while they were here.

Her gaze lighting on him at last, Caity said, "The year we moved to Colorado was the worst year of my life."

Not hard to figure why. That was the year she'd turned eighteen—the same year her father had been executed for a murder he didn't commit. She and her mom had fled from Phoenix to Boulder to escape the gossip and the harsh memories, but her father's ghost had dogged their steps. Caity's mother, Arlene, had coped with his death by denial—whereas Caity had raged against the injustice, creating a distance between them that had once seemed too far to bridge. But now, thanks to Caity, and yes, thanks to him, too, her father's name had been cleared. The Cassidy women had finally put their differences aside and were hoping to forge a new and improved relationship.

"It's the first time in years I've felt as though I'm coming *home*. I can't wait to see Mom."

The sincerity in Caity's voice made his throat grow tight, reminding him that the news he must deliver to his own mother would change her world forever. The prospect sat like a concrete block on his chest.

Perhaps sensing his thoughts, Caity reached over and squeezed his hand. "Spense, I've been thinking . . ." Her voice died out as though she was reluctant to broach the subject. "Since you can't go to her, why don't we fly your mom out here? She can stay with mine in Boulder."

He hated to intrude on Caity's family reunion, but he'd feel a hell of a lot better delivering his news to his mother in person. Hesitating only a moment, he said, "You sure? I know you need time with your mom . . ."

"I'm positive."

No doubt his mother's visit would mean less chance for Caity and her own mother to regroup, but Caity's smile was genuine. This wasn't Caity grudgingly making a sacrifice. This was Caity looking out for him, because that was just how she was.

"I'll bet they'll have a blast together."

"It's a deal. You clear it with Arlene, and I'll book Mom's flight."

Interrupting their conversation, a tanned, toned, feminine arm reached across the aisle, flapping a pen and a piece of paper at him. His shoulders jumped. *Oh yeah.* There were other people on this bird. Reluctantly, Spense turned away from Caity toward the overly enthusiastic limb. It belonged to an attractive woman, about late twenties.

She beamed at him with bright green eyes, her cheeks flushing. "Can I have your autograph?"

"You talking to me?" He started to say ma'am but stopped himself. According to Caity, women hated to be called ma'am. "You must've mistaken me for someone else. I'm not a celebrity."

She waved what looked to be her boarding pass harder. "Oh yes you are. I recognize you both." She smiled, though less vivaciously, at Caity. "She can sign, too, I guess."

Spense tried to straighten and stretch his legs, but the seat was too damn small for his six-foot-four frame. Too bad real life wasn't like television where the FBI profilers flew to every crime scene on a luxury jet. As he lamented his lot, a charley horse galloped up his leg. He winced. How long was this plane going to taxi?

"Ladies and gentlemen, thanks for your patience. We're stacked up a bit. Please keep your seat belts on until the captain turns off the fasten seat belt sign and gives you the all clear to stampede," an irritatingly cheery voice announced.

Spense rubbed his tight calf muscles.

The green-eyed woman thumped him on the chest with her pen. "Ma'am, please . . ."

The irritated expression on her face made him wish he'd heeded Caity's warning. And it wasn't the woman's fault these seats were designed for Tom Thumb. He should've been nicer. "Sorry. We'll sign." He handed the woman's boarding pass to Caity who smiled big and autographed it with a flourish before giving it back to Spense.

He signed, then looked up to find the woman in the row ahead peering curiously over her seat back at them. "Who are you?"

He handed the paper back to its owner. "Nobody, ma'am."

Another devastated look. Someday he'd learn.

"That's Atticus Spenser and Caitlin Cassidy—the FBI agents

who caught all those serial killers," Green Eyes said. She ticked off several monikers from their recent cases.

Impressive. This woman knew her psychopaths. Though they hadn't granted any interviews, *Forensic Facts* had featured Spense and Caity yesterday. Maybe the woman had caught the broadcast.

"I'm not an FBI agent." Caity hurried to correct the woman's misconception. Caity didn't like to take any extra credit. She wasn't a glory basker. Though to his way of thinking, her credentials were every bit as impressive as his—more so in fact. "I'm a psychiatrist," she explained.

"But I saw it on TV. Kourtney Kennedy from SLY news went on and on about how you solved that Angel case in Hollywood."

Kourtney.

That pain-in-his-ass celebrity newscaster, not *Forensic Facts*, had been to blame. "Dr. Cassidy may not be an FBI agent, but she's a very important part of the team," Spense supplied.

Still, the woman continued to side-eye Caity as if she'd hoodwinked her into accepting a worthless autograph. "I don't get it. Are you FBI or not?"

An unpleasant itch developed on the back of his neck, but Caity smiled, apparently not the least bit annoyed. "I'm a civilian, a private citizen contracted with the FBI to help with specific cases. Agent Spenser is a criminal investigative analyst with the BAU—the Bureau's Behavioral Analysis Unit."

The plane hung a left, and Spense groaned aloud. The "snow-capped peaks" of the terminal were getting farther away. Apparently they were going to take another turn around the runway.

The woman thrust her hand over her heart. "I just realized what this means. There's a serial killer in Denver!"

The plane changed its mind and turned back toward the terminal. Thank goodness.

"Not that I know of." The first hint of impatience finally crept into Caity's voice. Her initial approach to others was always warm and respectful, but Spense knew from experience that however lightly Caity treaded, she was a force to be reckoned with when challenged. It was best not to mess with her.

"There's a serial killer in Denver! You're just not allowed to tell me! I know I'm right!"

Spense heard a number of gasps and saw heads turning. All neighboring eyes fixed on them.

Caity raised her palm in a stop sign. "We don't know of any serial killers in the area." Then, keeping a remarkably straight face, she added in a low voice meant just for Green Eyes, "But if you're keen on meeting one, I can always put you in touch."

The woman's jaw went slack.

The plane rolled to a stop. A bell dinged, diffusing the tension in the air, and the race to de-board was on. It appeared the threat from crazed killers was nothing compared to that of other passengers getting ahead in line. Spense stood up and popped open the overhead bins on either side. He passed Caity her carry-on and then asked their "fan," "May I get your bag?"

"Oh, no. I checked mine. But can I have your phone number?"

Spense made his voice polite but firm. "No can do."

"I don't see a wedding ring," she insisted.

Spense threw Caity a wink. "I'm taken just the same."

The woman's lips became puffy . . . make that puffier. "If you won't give me your number, the least you can do is tell me why you're in Denver. Serial killer or no serial killer, there must be something big going on for the two of you to get called in."

Chapter 3

Thursday, October 24
12:20 P.M.
Denver, Colorado

"DO YOU THINK she's still alive?" Caity whispered as they rushed toward the gate's exit.

"Don't know," Spense said. Now that they'd cleared a space between themselves and the big ears of surrounding passengers they could speak freely, but to be safe, he kept his voice low. Discretion had never been more vital.

At the conclusion of their last case, the president had called to thank them, and he'd issued a request. He'd said he would consider it a personal favor if Spense and Caity would join a task force formed in Colorado to find a missing coed. On Tuesday morning, Laura Chaucer, the twenty-one-year-old daughter of Senator Whitmore Chaucer, had gone missing. Spense hadn't believed anything could make him give up a Tahitian vacation with Caity, especially not after they'd finally declared their love for each other, but a young woman in trouble and a plea from the president of the United States had been impossible to ignore.

As for whether or not Laura Chaucer was still alive, they could only hope. For now, they'd operate on the assumption they were here to rescue rather than search and recover, but he wasn't optimistic. In a missing person case the first forty-eight hours were vital and that critical marker had already passed.

Beyond the security checkpoint, Spense stopped short to avoid barreling into a man dressed in a black uniform. He held a placard that read "Cassidy & Spenser." Shooting a look over his shoulder at Caity, Spense asked, "I forget your birthday or something?"

"No."

"Because it sure isn't mine, and I can't remember the last time the Bureau sent a driver to pick me up at the airport."

The look on her face made him regret his quip. Her father had been executed on her eighteenth birthday, and he'd just carelessly reminded her of that black day. But the darkness in her eyes vanished almost as quickly as it had appeared, and she smiled at him, as if he were the finest version of himself instead of a thoughtless ass. He hoped she knew he'd rather rip his own heart out than hurt her, and just in case she didn't, he'd tell her so later. But right now, there was a man with a sign to deal with.

Spense dropped the bags. Offered a hand to the driver. "What the hell's up?"

"You're Agent Spenser?" he asked, though his tone and pointed address told Spense he knew the answer already.

"Yeah, and this is my partner, Dr. Cassidy . . ." Spense angled his head, checking out the man's name tag . . . . "Mr. Crawford."

"Jasper."

"Nice meeting you, Jasper." Caity stuck out her hand. "Pardon our surprise, but we weren't expecting you. The Bureau doesn't usually . . ."

"The Bureau?" Now it was Jasper's turn to look confused, but he made a fast recovery. "You mean the FBI."

Impatiently, Spense shifted his feet. They didn't have time to waste on small talk, and he wasn't going to put Caity in a limo and go for a joy ride without verification this guy was legit.

"You're right, I wasn't sent by the Bureau." Jasper rolled the word around on his tongue, seeming pleased to be speaking their language. "My employer asked me to FaceTime him as soon as you arrived."

Spense said nothing while Jasper put the call through and handed him the cell. The man who appeared on the screen was immediately recognizable.

"Agent Spenser, Dr. Cassidy, I'm Whit Chaucer."

"Senator," they answered in unison.

"I hope you don't mind, but I took the liberty of sending a driver to take you to the task-force meeting."

"That wasn't necessary, but thank you," Spense said, annoyed that local law enforcement had given the senator their flight information. He knew the Bureau's Denver field office would never have done so.

"I'm incredibly grateful you two agreed to join the team. I've arranged to have Mr. Crawford at your disposal for as long as you need him."

Spense had no intention of letting the senator's personal spy chauffeur them around, and he was about to say so when Caity jumped in. "That's very kind, but we won't be able to take you up on that offer. We need to be ready to go on a moment's notice."

"Crawford can be ready on a moment's notice." Senator Whit

Chaucer was used to getting his way. Spense understood the man was high on the food chain, but the last thing they needed was the father of the missing girl trying to call the shots.

"We're grateful for the lift today, but in the future, the Bureau will provide a car for us," Spense said with finality.

The senator nodded. The close camera angle accentuated his bloodshot eyes, haloed with purpled rims as though he'd cried all night. Worry had drilled the expression lines on his face into deep trenches, giving him a very different look than the man Spense had seen on television stumping for the senate. Spense wished he could reassure him that Laura would be okay, but platitudes weren't an option for those charged with telling the truth. The best he could offer up was a sympathetic look.

He could hardly blame the guy for trying to take control in a situation that would make anyone feel helpless. If Spense's loved one were missing, he'd probably be barking orders and refusing to take "no" for an answer—even though he certainly knew better. He chose his next words carefully, mindful not to mention Laura's name in public. "I hope you understand, sir. It's just that we've got the best chance of bringing her home safely if you steer clear and let us do our jobs."

"Of course," Chaucer said. "But if you change your minds, the offer stands. Meanwhile, I'll let you get to your meeting. And it goes without saying, I'm at your disposal whenever you're ready for me."

It was a good sign the senator had the self-restraint not to in-trude on the upcoming task-force meeting, even though he could've easily exerted his influence to be present. Maybe he planned to let them do their job without interfering after all, which was a smart play if he wanted his daughter back alive. After a polite good-bye,

Spense disconnected the call, and then he and Caity followed Crawford to a limo with blacked-out windows.

Crawford swung the bags into the trunk while Spense opened the rear passenger door for Caity to get in first. He saw her shoulders stiffen, and when he touched the small of her back, felt resistance. She let out a quick breath before climbing in. Spense followed, then grunted aloud. He wasn't fond of surprises. And there, waiting in the limo, was a big one.

Chapter 4

Afternoon
Somewhere in the Rocky Mountains

THIS WASN'T THE first time Laura had awakened with a pounding head and a hole in her memory. The sun, peeking beneath her eyelids, carried a glow that told her she'd slept past noon—and that was no first either. But the deep ache in her bones, the shredded feeling in her stomach, like someone had taken a potato peeler to its lining, was beyond anything she'd experienced before. Her mouth was so dry she barely had the saliva to swallow, and when she attempted to do so, she gagged on her own bile. This was shaping up to be one mother of a blackout.

Hang on. Breathe.

Once the nausea passed, she braced herself on her elbows, lifted her shoulders, opened her eyes fully, and cried out—the noise screeching violently out of her chest as if propelled by a demon. She'd been expecting to find herself in bed, sheets tangled about her feet, or maybe kicked to the floor. A single worn sheet did cover the lower half of her body, but she wasn't in her bed. Instead, she lay naked on a cold floor surrounded by a pool of foul-smelling liquid.

She cringed and rolled away. She'd been sleeping in vomit and feces . . . and something else . . . that looked like blood.

No. No. No.

She touched her forehead. Sweaty hair stuck to her face, but she was cold . . . really, really cold. She saw that her hands were trembling, and then, without warning, her entire body began to shake violently. She couldn't control her limbs. They jerked open and shut, jackknifing at the joints. Panic travelled over her in waves as tangible as the convulsions. Her head slammed against the floor, but God took no mercy on her—the head bang didn't knock her out. She remained fully conscious through every excruciating muscle spasm until, after what seemed an eternity, the seizure passed. Nothing like this had ever happened to her before. What the hell was going on?

Get off the floor, Laura.

If she could manage to stand up, she told herself, everything would be okay. She'd look around and realize that this had all been one of her bad dreams. Or maybe a hallucination. After all, she'd seen things that weren't really there before. But . . . that was so long ago, and she'd been heavily medicated at the time. Dr. Webber had said the hallucinations were caused by an interaction between her antidepressants and her sleeping pills. Once he'd changed her meds around, the visions had stopped. At the moment, she couldn't remember much about the recent past, but one thing she knew for sure: she'd tossed out all of her pills the day she left DC for Denver.

There was no way drugs could be the cause of all this because she hadn't taken any.

Get up, Laura! Now!

Lurching to her feet, she looked around. Her eyes filled with tears. Everything was still there: the puke on the floor, the blood, and the stench that permeated the air, bearing shameful witness to her incontinence.

Hallucinations didn't smell—at least not the type she'd had in the past.

This was *real*.

She'd been passed out in a pool of her own bodily fluids, and she had no idea for how long. It might've been hours or even days.

Shuddering, she dragged her gaze around the interior of the room. Its bare walls brought a glimmer of recognition. She remembered seeing this cabin before . . . before . . . before what? She yanked at her damp hair, as if that could stimulate her memory. And maybe it worked because she now recalled the flicker of a candle. A table. Her hand went to her throat. Her heart, already racing, kicked into overdrive. With her fingertips, she sought out the razor-thin scars that had long marred her neck and felt new wounds—ones that were still moist and excruciatingly sore.

Dead ahead was the table she remembered, as well as a chair with her silk scarves—the ones she wore to cover the marks on her neck—wrapped around its arms.

Another flash of memory: He'd tied her up.

But as she studied her arms, she didn't find any telltale ligature marks.

Because he'd used her silk scarves.

Unlike rope would have done, the scarves had left no trace, no physical evidence, but she *remembered* being bound. She *remembered* . . . a knife.

He'd held a knife to her throat.

Gripping her abdomen, she doubled over, barely managing not to throw up.

She closed her eyes and recalled her mouth being stuffed with a damp, stinky rag.

The pieces were slowly falling into place. He'd drugged her, taken her from her room and brought her here to this remote cabin. That must be what happened.

It was *him*.

It *must* have been.

Her legs tried to buckle, but she didn't collapse. He would not bring her to her knees. She would not cower naked on the floor. She retrieved the soiled sheet that had covered her, wrapped it around her shoulders and body, and in the process noticed her purse where it lay open beneath the table. Rifling through it, she located her wallet. It still contained the five hundred dollars in cash she'd withdrawn from the bank on Monday to loan to her friend, Harriet, who was in a tight spot after falling out with her mom. Laura had never learned to drive, but she had a Colorado state identification card. It was there, along with her Holly Hill student badge. Only her cell phone appeared to be missing.

With clumsy hands she removed a compact of powder from her bag. She opened it, took a bracing breath, and inspected herself in the mirror. It wasn't the haggard look in her blue-gray eyes, it wasn't her bone-white complexion or even the vomit and blood matting her long black hair that made her want to climb out of her own skin. It was those fresh marks on her neck. There, just above her old scars, she touched the new wounds—each one a nearly perfect match to the scar below. She bowed her head, not to pray, but to think. The cuts were fine and shallow. Too superficial to be the cause of all the blood on the floor . . . and yet she didn't seem to have any other injuries. As shaky and weak as she felt, she could still stand, still walk, still think. Like everything else, it made no sense . . . unless all that blood wasn't hers.

It was impossible, at least for her, to tell how long the blood had been soaking into the floor. Had someone else been brought here before her? The thought made her gag, but she forced herself to breathe through the moment and focus on her own survival.

She should catalogue any and all information available to her.

The wounds on her throat were covered in a thin yellow pre-scab. How long would that healing process have taken to kick in? She didn't know, but she guessed it to be longer than a few hours but shorter than a few days.

When you're fighting to survive, you never know what little thing will turn out to be important.

Her counselors at wilderness camp—a survival therapy program that had been one of her parents' desperate schemes to fix her—emphasized that point until she had been sick to death of hearing it. How she'd hated that camp.

It had been just one more confirmation that she was broken.

But now, a flicker of hope began to build inside her. Because of that stupid survival therapy, she had skills. She knew more than most people about staying alive. Despite her dire circumstances, she wasn't completely helpless—and she had her parents and those relentless counselors to thank. Irony, it seemed, wasn't always a bad thing.

She decided to take inventory of what she knew—or thought she knew—so far. Between one and three days ago, someone had drugged her, kidnapped her, stripped her naked, slashed her throat, and left her to die in the middle of nowhere. As her brain clicked into gear, her pulse slowed. She ticked off the terrifying facts like she was reciting a grocery list.

Good.

That meant she was pulling it together.

It meant she was going to get through this.

Then suddenly, her chest contracted to the point she could barely breathe, as a thought pushed its way to the surface, shattering her confidence into a million pieces.

Maybe *he* hadn't left her to die in the middle of nowhere.

Maybe her monster was still with her.

Chapter 5

AT FIRST GLANCE, Caitlin hadn't recognized the man in the back of the limo. He'd changed over the years. His face had grown slightly fuller, more lines cracked around his cunning blue eyes, and his blond hair exposed a touch more of his forehead—but that wasn't the reason it took her a moment to know him. She simply hadn't expected to see Dr. Grady Webber in Senator Whit Chaucer's limo.

She hadn't expected to see Grady anywhere.

Ever again.

Never would've been too soon.

Still, here he was.

She searched her brain for a reason. Among the cobwebs draping the farthest recesses of her mind, that place where she'd vanquished all things Grady, hung the flimsy recollection that he and the senator knew each other.

She ducked her chin to conceal the displeasure that must be written all over her face. Then, teeth gritted, she climbed in, choosing a seat directly facing Grady. He was still built like a running back, and he still dressed like a *GQ* model. His long legs stretched across the aisle of the limo, and he politely bent them to make room for her. He appeared handsomely distinguished in an expensive gray silk, Hugo Boss if she had to guess—he'd always been partial to that designer.

Their eyes locked.

"Dr. Cassidy, I presume?"

Her face went white-hot. "Hello Grady," she said, trying to add enough enthusiasm to her voice to hide her annoyance at his subterfuge. Why pretend he didn't know her unless he wanted to make it seem like a bigger deal than it really was once the truth came out? And of course the truth would come out because she had no intention of keeping her past relationship with Grady Webber a secret from Spense.

They'd fought too hard to develop mutual trust to risk losing it now.

For years she and Spense had battled one another professionally, with her working to protect the rights of accused innocents while Spense did whatever it took to get the bad guys off the streets. It wasn't until recently, when they'd been forced to work *together* on the Man in the Maze case, that they'd realized they'd been on the same side all along: justice. It hadn't taken long for theirs to develop into much more than a working relationship—so maybe those sparks between them all these years hadn't been about competition after all. In any case, over the past few months they'd been through the fire together. He'd saved her life more than once, and she'd saved his. He'd earned both her trust and her heart, and there was no way she would deliberately mislead Spense—not about Grady—not about anything.

Spense found a seat next to Grady, and she turned her mind back to the job. She wasn't sure why Grady was here, in the senator's limo, but she could guess what he might have to do with the Laura Chaucer missing person case.

As Spense settled in, his gaze swept over Grady with a deliberateness that told her Spense hadn't missed a thing. Grady's false greeting had put him on full alert.

Waving her hand between the two men, she said, "Let me introduce you two. Dr. Grady Webber. Special Agent Atticus Spenser." She paused, waiting for Spense's stock response: *Call me Spense.*

Instead, a long, tense silence followed.

As she watched the two men, she couldn't help comparing. They were both tall, muscular, and undeniably handsome, but the difference between them was striking. Whereas Grady looked like he'd stepped out of the pages of a fashion magazine, Spense could've made the cover of a G-man calendar. His dark hair was cut short, FBI style, and his build was powerful in a way that didn't just make you want to stare—it made you feel safe. His eyes were plain brown, but when he turned them on you, pencils dropped, lattes spilled, and thoughts became decidedly unladylike. He turned those eyes on her now, and she realized he was waiting for her to speak.

"Grady was chief of psychiatry at Rocky Mountain Memorial— the hospital where I did my psychiatric residency." Had she left it at that, it might've seemed to Spense that Grady simply hadn't remembered her. But Spense was too clever, and she was too honest.

She had nothing to gain by glossing things over. She straightened her back and said, "I'll fill you in on the rest later."

Grady turned to Spense. "Forgive me. Caitlin and I know each other well. I was simply trying to respect her privacy, not knowing how much of her personal life she'd want aired in a public setting."

Some things never changed. Grady had just taken the upper hand by letting Spense know, before she had the chance to tell him herself, that they'd been more than colleagues. In a flood of unpleasant memories, she recalled how manipulative Grady could be. The only way to deal with him was to refuse to play his games. "Consider my private life officially off limits. As you suggested, I'd like to keep things professional. I presume you had some sort of medical involvement with Laura Chaucer."

"I wouldn't dream of making you uncomfortable, Caitlin. Let's talk about the business at hand." The barest hint of condescension threaded its way into his polite words. "I was Laura's psychiatrist from the time she was eight years old until a little over a year ago when Whit—Senator Chaucer—got elected to the senate and the family moved to DC."

"Isn't that privileged doctor-patient information?" Spense asked.

"Not when the patient in question may be a danger to herself or others. In that case I have a duty to act in my patient's best interests, and in the best interests of the public. Whit's asked me to provide any insight I can into Laura's disappearance—and I consider it my responsibility to do all I can to help find her."

Spense arched one eyebrow. "A danger to herself or others. Which is it and why?"

Up until now, she and Spense had understood Laura was believed kidnapped or worse.

"Let's get into that at the interview so I don't have to repeat myself for the task force." Grady slid his eyes toward the driver. The privacy window was closed, but he had a point. This probably wasn't the place.

Spense tapped the window, signaling Jasper, and the limo pulled away from the curb.

Glad she'd chosen a conservative button-up blouse instead of a V-neck sweater, Caitlin crossed her arms over her chest. She could feel Grady's eyes on her. Her stomach soured like it used to do when she was one of his students.

Long after she'd ended things with this man, whom she'd once considered her mentor, he'd continued to behave as though he had exclusive rights to her body. He'd touch her bottom during rounds and stare openly at her breasts in front of the other psych residents. It was all so miserable she decided to transfer to a different teaching hospital. But in the end, it hadn't been necessary. A beautiful young intern arrived at Rocky Mountain Memorial and Grady turned his interest to her.

Caitlin tried to warn Inga, but she said she could handle herself, insisting Caitlin mind her own business. And despite Caitlin's concerns, Inga had seemed very happy to be on the receiving end of Grady's attentions.

Then, six months later, when one of his colleagues questioned the appropriateness of the chief of psychiatry dating an intern, the couple married, and Inga transferred to another hospital, thereby putting an end to any accusations of moral turpitude on Grady's part.

"How's Inga?" Caitlin asked, genuinely interested. Inga was bubbly and sweet and smart, and Catlin had always liked her.

Grady stared out the window, then back at her with moist eyes. "I'm afraid Inga passed a few years back." His Adam's apple bobbed in a hard swallow. "Terrible thing—she went out hiking one morning and didn't come home. Fell off a cliff and broke her neck—I lost the love of my life in a freak accident."

Chapter 6

Afternoon
Somewhere in the Rocky Mountains

SHE HAD TO get out of there.

On shaky legs, sometimes grabbing the cool log walls for support, Laura made her way around the cabin's perimeter, searching for her clothes and more importantly, her shoes. If *he* came back, and she had to make a run for it, she wouldn't make it far in bare feet. Then she spied her pumps and willed her legs to carry her toward them. Over in a corner, stood her favorite navy blue high heels, side by side, toes perfectly aligned. Next to them, the green dress she'd worn to her dinner with the editor from the *Mountain Times* lay neatly folded, her bra and underwear on top, all very ladylike.

Though she had little time to lose, she was too weak to move quickly. She lifted her dress, preparing to slip it over her head and cast her eyes down at the soiled sheet draped across her shoulders.

She froze.

Her torso was stained with blood. Her skin was pale and cool to the touch. And though it seemed to her that her heart might stomp straight out of her chest, when she pressed her fingers to her wrist, her pulse was strangely weak—barely detectable.

A painful, wet breath rattled out of her chest.

She could barely stand.

It hurt to breathe.

Her stomach seemed to be cannibalizing itself.

Why was she so very sick?

The cuts on her neck couldn't have bled much, or else she'd be dead by now.

She hadn't taken any meds . . . yet she felt as though she were in a trance.

At dinner on Monday, the last clear thing she could recall, she hadn't even had a beer—only tea. She swiped her tongue back and forth across her teeth, trying to scrape away the bitter flavor embedded in her taste buds. Had he used a knockout drug on the rag he stuffed in her mouth?

Her head tilted up and just that slight stretching threatened to rip the skin on her neck apart. Still, she kept her gaze upward, as if the answer might descend from above—but in her heart, she knew heaven would not save her.

She had to figure a way out of this on her own.

She brought her chin level again, easing the pain. Her feet rooted themselves to the floor, and she gazed helplessly out the window like a ruined mannequin, waiting for someone to come and either mend her broken body or dump her in the trash.

Move!

She took a step forward.

She refused to leave her fate to someone else. If only she could get her thoughts together, she could make a plan. She blinked rapidly, and somehow, it helped jolt her mind back into gear.

Think!

Her gaze settled on the windows, some of them cracked.

If *he* knew she was alive, if he was coming back to torture her, he would've tied her up or locked the door and boarded the windows. And if he didn't plan to return, surely, he would've finished her off. In either case, he wouldn't risk letting her escape. He must have believed her dead, or at least so close to death there was no point wasting any more time with her. The longer he stayed in the cabin, the greater the chance he might be caught.

He thought she was dead!

She was absolutely sure of it.

And that meant he wasn't coming back.

Her mouth formed a wobbly smile. Wind sang an Ode to Joy through the cracked, glass windowpanes. She could see God's beautiful, green world outside. She crossed to the door as fast as her unsteady legs would take her. With only a gentle tug of the handle, it sprang open, bringing to her the fresh scent of mountain air and the sound of birds warbling. But then . . . she looked back over her shoulder.

From the corner of the room, her pumps stared at her accusingly.

Kidnappers don't carefully fold their victim's clothes.

She let the dress she'd been holding fall to the floor.

Kidnappers don't line shoes up toe-to-toe and heel-to-heel.

Her hand flew to her heart, as bit-by-bit, her newfound happiness faded.

She was the one who had the habit of arranging her shoes just so—it was almost a compulsion if the truth be told.

She shook her head violently.

As if she could've done all this.

As if she could've cut her own throat.

No!

She did not!

True, at the age of fifteen, she'd sliced similar, shallow cuts into her neck in a so-called "cry for help" that had landed her in a mental hospital for months. But help was the last thing she'd wanted at the time. She'd longed for death's repose. She'd been desperate to put a stop to the nightmares, to the blackouts, and yes, to the therapy sessions with Dr. Webber that had only left her more confused.

She'd truly wanted to end it all.

And that was the difference between now and then.

Then she'd wanted to die.

But not anymore. She might not have the answers but at least she'd begun to ask questions. And she'd developed a theory, a terrible one about a monster who had to be stopped. That was the reason she'd set up a meeting with the newspaper editor on Monday. She'd needed to talk through her theory with someone who had no stake in the past. No bias against the truth.

She absolutely did not want to die.

She *needed* to live if she were going to expose the monster.

There's no one else here, Laura.

It didn't matter. She could never have done this to herself. She wouldn't have tried to kill herself when she was just beginning to take back her freedom. Not when she was getting so close to finding out the truth about what had really happened to her—and to Angelina—thirteen terrible years ago.

Chapter 7

Thursday, October 24
12:55 P.M.
Task force headquarters
Highlands Hotel
Denver, Colorado

SPENSE COULD TELL from her forced smile and stiff posture that Caity didn't much care for Dr. Grady Webber—and Caity liked everyone. If Webber was on her blacklist, Spense figured he must've done something despicable. And the presumptuous way Webber spoke to Caity made Spense want to hoist him up by that fancy collar of his and scramble his Ivy-League face.

Caity sent him a warning look.

He relaxed his jaw, stuck his hand in his pocket and rearranged his miniature Rubik's cube instead.

Then, all self-control, he aimed an equanimous look at Webber. "You, wait here."

They'd just arrived at the Denver Highlands Hotel where a task force consisting of detectives from the Denver PD and agents from the local FBI field office and the Colorado Bureau of Investigation had rented three adjoining suites. Using a private venue as a command center provided another layer of confidentiality to the proceedings and had the added benefit of preventing any one agency from gaining home-turf advantage. One suite had been set up as a waiting area for potential witnesses, another as a war room, and a third as an interview room/kitchen. This case, involving the missing daughter of a United States senator from Colorado, didn't seem to be plagued by the usual funding problems.

Webber checked his watch. "I'm on the clock. The longer you keep me cooling my heels the more it's going to cost."

"Cost whom?" Caity asked.

"Whit Chaucer, of course. Naturally, I want to do all I can for Laura. But my time is valuable."

"Everyone's is. We'll call you back as soon as possible," Spense assured him, though he wasn't about to rush anything up for the arrogant jerk.

"Really, Caitlin." Webber turned his back to Spense. "No need to give me that disapproving glare. I'm sure you're getting paid for your expertise, as is Agent Spenser."

Caity's lips thinned.

She had a beef with this guy. Spense was one million percent sure of it.

"No one's judging you, Grady. Spense and I need to get our bearings and meet the team before we bring you in. That's all there is to it."

"Yes, but have you considered including me, officially, as part of the task force? Surely I have as much or *more* to offer in terms of psychiatric expertise as you. After all, I trained you."

What a condescending creep, Spense thought.

Caity smiled broadly. One thing about her, she didn't rattle. "You played a small part in my general psych training, yes. But, to my knowledge, you don't have any hands-on experience with the criminal mind. And, as I'm sure you'll agree once you think about it, you're too close to Laura to be objective. You're far more valuable, in this instance, as a witness. So take a seat and maybe try some of those cookies over there. We'll call you as soon as possible. Meanwhile, you can take comfort in knowing you're going to be well compensated."

"She's got a little sass on her, but she's one hell of a shrink. Of course, you'd know that, since you trained her and all." Spense patted a cushion on an overstuffed, orange sofa.

Muttering something sotto voce, Webber took a seat.

Spense opened the adjoining room door and ushered Caity into the business end of task-force headquarters. He wasn't sure what to expect. Sometimes, headquarters atmosphere, no matter how grave the case, seemed more akin to a dugout or a men's locker room—with off-color jokes flying and foul wind breaking. It was no disrespect to the victim, just guys blowing off steam. In this instance, however, Spense was glad to see both genders well represented. He knew what a tough climb women in law enforcement faced, and to be chosen for this task force would be a feather in anyone's cap.

Along the back wall of the war room, a few institutional size corkboards had been set up. One was blanketed with photographs of Laura, some recent, some dating back to her childhood. Pictures of her parents and other folks Spense didn't recognize covered another. There were also giant area maps and a whiteboard with so many arrows and indecipherable scribbles it looked like it belonged in a college physics class.

The low hum of many people talking at once made Spense's skull vibrate. Since childhood, his brain went haywire when there was too much sensory input. But over time, he developed his own tricks for coping. Now, without thinking about it, he fiddled with the cube in his pocket. Soon the buzz became a calming, white noise, incapable of disrupting his thought process.

His fog cleared, he assessed the room. The urgency in the faces of the officers bending over notebooks and staring at computer screens told him higher command had cranked up the burner on this one. Not to mention the place boasted more body odor than a hot yoga class.

This was one serious-ass command center.

A silver-haired guy in a polyester suit that was rumpled enough to match the slump in his shoulders, caught Spense's eye and approached.

The man pushed his Coke-bottle glasses up, then stuck out his hand to Caity. "Jordan Hatcher—detective sergeant—Major Crimes. Welcome to our humble abode, Dr. Cassidy." He dragged his glance from Caity to Spense and offered a firm shake. "You, too, Agent Spenser. Just in case there's any doubt, let me put your minds at ease. This operation is going to be by the book. No sloppy chops allowed on my watch. I welcome inter-agency input. Any man on my team who doesn't play nice—all you gotta do is say the word and he'll be back on patrol in time to lift a cold one at happy hour with the crew he thought he'd left behind."

A bit defensive for introductions, but Spense suspected he knew the reason behind the chip on Hatcher's shoulder. Thirteen years ago the Piney Trails PD had taken heat for their handling of a different case involving the Chaucer family. Hatcher had been part of that team. They'd been accused of contaminating the crime scene, mishandling evidence and generally botching the investigation.

Spense and Caity needed to understand everything possible about not only the current case, but about that earlier one as well. Even with thirteen years intervening, it was rare for a victim to disappear twice. It didn't matter if this time Laura *might* not have been kidnapped—as Webber had implied. The more they learned about what happened thirteen years ago in the small Denver suburb of Piney Trails, the better they'd be able to judge its relevance to Laura's disappearance on Tuesday.

And if it did turn out the two events were linked, they just might have to solve one of the most baffling cold cases in Colorado history in order to bring the senator's daughter home safely.

"Good to know you've got our backs." Spense nodded his understanding. It stood to reason Hatcher would want to get it right this time around. Here was a chance to not only rescue a missing coed, but for Major Crimes to thumb its nose at those who'd impugned its integrity. In a way, these guys had been given a do-over. "I'm sure everyone will cooperate. After all, we have the same goal: finding Laura alive. So how about we get down to it?"

By way of an answer, Hatcher stretched the corners of his mouth with his fingers and whistled. "Attention everyone."

It only took a minute for a hush to overtake the room. Then the detective sat his fists on his hips. "As promised, we've got some extra help, courtesy of the BAU. Agent Spenser and Dr. Cassidy are here to shed light on the psychological issues surrounding the disappearance of Laura Chaucer, but they've indicated they're willing to help out in all aspects of this investigation—everything from boots on the pavement to interviews to research. They've volunteered to help wherever needed." His gaze swept the crammed room. "Damn there are a lot of us. And that's a good thing, but maybe best to hold off on individual introductions for now. If you've got a piece of information you think might be useful to our profilers—that would be the ideal time to introduce yourself. Meanwhile, let's get back to work."

A smattering of applause broke out, about as loud as the sound of one hand clapping. Spense shrugged it off. It wasn't uncommon for the feds to be perceived as a threat, or for their presence on a task force to be interpreted as a sign the locals had been deemed incapable of doing their jobs. And in this situation resentment would be doubled. Any of these detectives who'd worked the old kidnap case were likely carrying baggage too big to fit in the overhead compartments. "Ready when you are," Spense said.

Hatcher led Caity and him to a round, linoleum table that looked like it belonged in his granny's kitchen. Carrot-colored sofas out front, pea soup tables in the war room—it seemed someone had brought in additional furniture from the local rental center. Another indicator of extra budgetary resources.

Hatcher pointed out a group of files and documents piled haphazardly on the table. "I don't know if you've been briefed already . . ."

"Just the bare minimum—we packed our bags and flew in from Dallas right after wrapping up our last case," Caity said.

"Then, I'll start at the beginning."

"Great." They knew only basic details from what the director of the FBI told them on the way to the airport. But of course they'd heard of Laura Chaucer before. She'd been kidnapped as a child, and it had made national news—a cold case that confounded police and provided fodder for the gossip rags even to this day. "As I understand it, Laura Chaucer was last seen at the Wildflower Café on Monday evening, October 21."

"That's right. She had dinner with Ronald Saas, the editor of the *Mountain Times*—that's a local newspaper here in Denver. Saas is also a community advisor to the *Holly Hill Gazette*, the campus newspaper. Laura enrolled as a freshman at Holly Hill College in late August. By all accounts, she was eager to score a spot as a cub reporter. Not sure what you know about the college, but it's not only pricey, it claims one of the top journalism programs in the country."

"So the editor of a local newspaper . . ." Caity scribbled something in her pocket-sized notebook.

"Ron Saas," Hatcher repeated.

"Was the last person to see Laura before she went off the radar?"

"No. He was the last person to be seen *with* her. Her bodyguard, Ty Cayman, was the last person, as far as we know, to see her before she disappeared."

"I didn't know Laura had a bodyguard." Spense tugged his lower lip. This was quite a wrinkle. If she had protection . . .

"What the hell was the bodyguard doing while Laura was busy disappearing?" Caity finished his thought for him.

Hatcher swept some of the strewn papers together and tapped them into a neat pile. "I misspoke. Technically, Cayman isn't her bodyguard *anymore*. But he says he followed her to the Wildflower Café where he observed her having dinner with Saas and engaging in animated conversation. Afterward, Cayman tailed her back to her off-campus apartment. After watching her enter her home, he continued to stand sentry until all the lights went out, and she was, presumably, in for the night. Then Cayman headed home with the plan to return around five a.m.—per his routine."

"Okay, so she was last seen by Cayman on Monday night, entering her own apartment. He kept watch until she turned out the lights. Did he check in with her by phone to make sure she was good for the evening?" Spense asked. The dots didn't connect.

"He made no contact with her."

"Why not?"

"Because he wasn't supposed to be following her. As I said, technically, he wasn't her bodyguard. He used to be, but she told him to take a hike before she moved from DC to Denver."

"Then why *was* he following her?" Caity frowned.

"He worked for Daddy—not Laura. The senator kept him on the payroll as a secret watchdog. Chaucer wanted protection for his daughter whether she liked it or not."

Caity leaned forward, a look of comprehension on her face. "And she *didn't* like it. I'm guessing this Cayman had been on her for a long time. That she may have been fed up with being kept on Daddy's leash."

"The Chaucer family hired Cayman as Laura's personal bodyguard after the first time she disappeared, at age eight." The flush on Hatcher's face suggested discussing that old kidnap case made him uncomfortable. He'd better learn to deal with it. Laura's disappearance, once it was made public, would bring it all back into the spotlight.

From what Spense knew of the matter, the Piney Trails police had indeed screwed up. At the time, Whit Chaucer, a wealthy businessman and city council member was already highly regarded among the town's elite, including the police chief—and the uniforms at the scene had been deferential rather than commanding.

After calling 911, Chaucer summoned a caterer to bring in food for the family and the officers. With people traipsing, unsupervised, through the home, the crime scene had been contaminated. But that flotsam had floated too far out to sea to be dragged ashore now. Spense said nothing about it, and pasted on a neutral expression. "You were one of the first uniforms on scene. What can you tell us about the kidnapping?"

"Thirteen years ago, eight-year-old Laura Chaucer disappeared from her home along with her nineteen-year-old nanny, Angelina Antonelli. On the morning of October 14, Whit Chaucer found a ransom note warning him not to contact the authorities or his daughter would be tortured and killed. Tracy, Mrs. Chaucer, was terrified of the consequences to her daughter, but despite her pleas not to, Whit had the good sense to call 911.

"I was a beat cop in Piney Trails at the time—my partner and I took the call. Later, Piney Trails got an assist from the Denver PD and the CBI got involved. Many of us here in this room had a hand in the investigation—when we heard Laura had gone missing again, we wanted in. So if you're hungry for cold case details, we can dish 'em up hot."

"Mid October." Spense hadn't remembered the dates surrounding the first case.

"So this isn't a coincidence. It's an anniversary," Caity said. "I understand a ransom was paid. Is that what led to Laura's safe recovery?" She emphasized the words *safe recovery* as if to remind Hatcher that no matter what else had gone wrong, the authorities had achieved an all too rare victory. They'd brought a kidnap victim home alive.

"Probably. We orchestrated a ransom drop with marked bills. We took every precaution. Did it by the book, but things didn't go as planned . . ." He coughed into his hand. "We had eyes on the bag containing the payoff. Then a small fire broke out in the trees that concealed our men, and they had to put it out or risk a major forest fire—not to mention their lives. During the ensuing chaos, the money disappeared. We never got a bead on the kidnapper. Once the fire was out, we initiated an area search based on a tracking chip sewn into the lining of the bag. We later located it—empty—a few miles up a trail leading into the Gore mountain range. Laura was found nearby, huddled behind a bunch of boulders, less than fifty yards from a park-service cabin. She was covered in blood. Turned out not to be hers. Thank God. She was unharmed except for minor scrapes and cuts."

"I don't remember reading about a cabin," Caity said.

"That's because we held the information back from the press. Not even the family knows."

"So the cabin is a test of guilty knowledge." Caity nodded. "Got it."

"Did Laura give a statement after she was found?" Spense asked.

"Chaucer allowed it, but only after his buddy, Dr. Grady Webber, talked to her first and gave the go-ahead. Laura had no memory of anything that happened after being tucked into bed by her nanny the night of October 13. Last thing she recalled was arguing with Angelina, because she'd refused to let her watch a scary movie on television."

"Was that the routine, for the nanny to put her to bed?"

"Either the nanny or Chaucer. Apparently Mrs. Chaucer liked to retire early."

"Earlier than an eight-year-old?"

"Tracy Chaucer suffered from migraines and an assortment of other ills. Took pills—and by her staff's reports, boozed more than a little."

"What about the blood they found on Laura?" Caity steered them back to the track Spense had jumped.

Hatcher grimaced. "Angelina's. A few yards from where we recovered Laura, we located a corpse, thinly covered in leaves. Angelina had been stabbed over one hundred times."

"And he—the kidnapper—Angelina's murderer—has never been apprehended," Spense said. Just tying things up. It was a well-known fact. Led to a public outcry and the belief that shoddy police work had left a deranged monster prowling the streets of Denver.

"Here's the thing. We think Angelina was not an entirely innocent victim. Experts later determined the handwriting in the ransom note to be similar to samples from Angelina's diary, and the note included several idiosyncratic phrases, also consistent with her journal entries."

"So you think the nanny was involved in the kidnap."

"Sure seemed like an inside job. No signs of forced entry to the house."

"Signs point to the nanny," Caity agreed. "But then again, she wound up dead, whereas Laura was left unharmed."

"Sure. But we believe Angelina had an accomplice, a boyfriend. That he got rid of her in order to eliminate any witnesses. Wanted to keep the money for himself."

"Then why leave Laura, a potential witness, alive?" It didn't add up for Spense.

"We don't think he planned to let Laura go. We think, somehow, she managed to get away while he was dealing with Angelina. There were no rope marks on Laura's body to suggest she'd been bound, and she didn't have any defensive wounds."

"So she might've gone willingly, indicating her abductor was someone she trusted. But since she wasn't tied up later, it seems more likely she was drugged," Caity said.

"Drugged," Hatcher confirmed.

Spense supposed it stood to reason that with her kidnapper still at large, and Laura the only one left alive who might identify him, her parents would take measures to secure her safety.

Hatcher went on, "Laura's parents hired Cayman to protect her, and he lived and traveled with the family for over a decade, until about three months ago, when Laura officially declared her independence. She pronounced herself an adult and insisted she didn't have to abide by her parents' rules anymore. At twenty-one, she came into a large sum from her grandparents' trust fund, and she was no longer financially dependent on her mother and father. She quit therapy, ditched her meds, and revealed she'd been accepted to Holly Hill College."

"How long has she been back in the Denver area?"

"That's one more heartbreak. She's been back in Denver just two short months. Now she's missing. The Chaucers blame themselves for 'allowing' her to claim her inheritance. They say Webber advised them to contest the trust on grounds of Laura's mental instability. But instead they followed the advice of Laura's DC therapist—a Dr. Duncan—to encourage her to become more self-sufficient. Now the Chaucers are second-guessing themselves. Without the money, Laura couldn't have left home—she's never held a job of any kind."

Spense guessed that was because she'd never been permitted to seek employment.

"Even though they had Cayman watching her, he couldn't guard her effectively without her consent," Hatcher went on.

"Didn't he make use of surveillance equipment?" Spense asked.

Caity's eyebrows shot up, and Spense knew she was troubled by the way the Chaucers had overridden their daughter's wishes. Caity would be in the DC therapist's camp. No doubt about that.

"No cameras or listening devices." Hatcher ran a hand through his hair. "Naturally we have to look hard at those closest to Laura, but every action the Chaucers have taken tells me they love their daughter. A wealthy, prominent family, one who's paid a ransom already, makes a prime target for kidnappers and other predators. And then, there's the matter of Angelina's killer still being at large."

"Could be dead or in prison by now," Spense thought aloud.

"We believe he's still in play. Marked bills used in the ransom drop still show up now and then, but there's no consistent pattern to when and where. I don't blame the parents for keeping their daughter locked down tight."

"But they didn't use surveillance," Spense said. *Inconsistent.*

"They told me Tracy couldn't stand the thought of someone watching Laura in her private moments—it seemed like yet another violation. Cayman stayed in their home in a room adjoining Laura's, but the family never allowed cameras, not even when she was a child."

Spense was developing more empathy for the entire family. It sounded like the parents struggled to balance protecting their daughter's safety with respecting her privacy and growing need for independence. And he could understand why the senator kept Cayman on Laura without her consent. He might've done the same thing in Chaucer's shoes.

"Sounds like Laura's been locked in a prison of fear most of her life—hard to blame her for wanting to break out." Caity, on the other hand, clearly didn't approve of the parental subterfuge.

Not a surprise. Caity didn't take violations of individual freedoms lightly. Because of her father's execution, which had been based in part on a coerced confession, she was a strong proponent of civil liberties—in every form.

"But Laura is still a loose end. The danger to her is real," Spense said. It was unnecessary to add that if Laura had been abducted again, Angelina's killer would be the prime suspect.

"The bastard is still in the wind, but it's even worse than that." Hatcher lowered his gaze. "We have very few clues to his identity. That's one reason I'm glad you're here. I'm counting on the two of you to develop an accurate profile of our mystery man. He could be anyone. He could be anywhere. He could be right under our noses, and we wouldn't even smell his stink."

Chapter 8

FIND YOUR STRENGTHS *and stretch them farther than you ever dreamed possible.*

Laura recalled her counselor's beaming, naïve face as she'd led the evening lesson at wilderness survival camp, and how, at the time, she'd found the idealism shining from that young woman's eyes nauseating. What did the counselor know about survival compared to Laura?

But now, she stopped to consider what *were* her strong points?

Definitely her brain and her body. She'd always excelled at school. And she'd trained hard, partly because she'd been bored and lonely with little companionship other than Cayman, who was a gym rat; but mostly because she feared she might someday have to fight for her life.

Her parents sent her to survival camp and kept a bodyguard on her.

Who wouldn't be afraid?

Too bad at the moment her body was wrecked, but at least her head was beginning to clear. She closed her eyes, and the counselor's beaming face appeared. Laura opened her eyes and drew her shoulders back. Maybe, if she could buy time to recover, she could turn this thing around. With logic telling her *he* wasn't coming back for her, she decided to trust in reason and let it, rather than fear, guide her actions. She needed water and warmth and food, in that order, to regain her mental and physical strength. She should take care of her body first, then plan her next move.

Out the window, light shone down, bouncing brightly off the scattered patches of snow and packed ice. These conditions told her two things. First, the temperature dropped below freezing at night, so even inside the cabin, she might succumb to hypothermia if she didn't bundle up. Second, she was at higher altitude—in Denver, there was still no snow on the ground. Hugging the sheet tightly around herself, she ventured onto the porch for a better look around.

The cabin was surrounded by few trees, most of them bristlecone pine and krumholtz—knee timber. There was snow, but only here and there. So, she was nearing, but not yet at, the tree line and the snow line. That meant she was at least 9,000 feet above sea level, maybe 10,000—another tidbit she'd picked up in wilderness camp. A few yards ahead the sun glinted off something shiny—metal. She shaded her eyes and squinted.

An outdoor spigot!

Fresh water!

She hoped.

She lifted her hands to heaven in gratitude. Part of getting strong was getting clean. The bodily fluids caking her skin demoralized her, weakening her spirits, and in this moment, taking back her dignity seemed almost more important than food.

She longed to feel human again.

Suddenly, her back tingled a warning, then went into a full-blown spasm. She massaged it until the ball of pain adjacent to her spine unwound. The muscles in her legs, always well-defined, appeared like small rocks, with puffy veins chiseled on top. When she tried to stretch, the tendons in the backs of her knees felt dangerously brittle, like they might snap. Lying unconscious on a cabin floor, for lord knew how long, had also made her ankles swell.

Her body could no longer be ignored.

Her bowels screamed, and she knew she'd soon be standing in literal shit if she didn't heed their urgent warning.

The bloating in her feet made her pumps a tight fit, but she managed to get them on. Then in almost one continuous motion, she stumbled off the porch steps, released her bowels and heaved up bile. Wiping her mouth with the back of her hand she realized she felt better—no—make that *much* better. Like her body had rid itself of a deadly poison. For no reason, she laughed. She might be hysterical. In shock. Or maybe she just needed the relief the laughter brought. Next, she scrubbed her face and teeth with snow from a patch that didn't look too dirty. At the pump, she drank first, before washing her hair and body. The frigid water and air seemed so clean and pure she wanted to linger under that blessed spigot forever, but her skin had taken on a blue hue. Her core temperature was dropping fast.

She had to get back inside.

She eyed the sheet, lying on the ground where she'd discarded it. No way would she wrap that vile thing around her again. She could wait another minute for her clean dress. With a high head, she hurried back to the cabin, naked save for her pumps. Her pace was as quick as her legs would allow, but still left her time to survey her surroundings.

Beyond the cabin, trails wound upward into majestic peaks. Peaks she'd grown up admiring. She had to be somewhere in the Gore mountain range. Her mind began to race with possibilities. She couldn't have climbed up into the wilderness on her own—that seemed certain. And it was unlikely her abductor would've carried her more than a short distance.

There was only one logical conclusion: Somewhere nearby was a road.

This time of year it would be closed, but that wouldn't stop her from using it any more than it had stopped the monster who'd brought her up here. He had to have driven it as far as he could, then carried her the rest of the way. Or maybe, he'd used an ATV.

In three directions, she saw trails—the question was which one of them led to the road . . . and where would that road lead? She filled her chest with mountain air, and smiled, because it didn't hurt. At least not as much as her previous breaths had. The more oxygen she took in, the more her lungs . . . and her brain revived. She scuttled inside the cabin and a feeling of déjà vu came over her—there was something excruciatingly familiar about this place. Something locked behind an impenetrable door in her secret mind. That's what Laura called the part of her brain that refused to give up information. Dr. Duncan, the therapist she'd started seeing when the family moved to DC, said the blank spots in her memory were the result of compartmentalization—a psychological defense mechanism that was, in fact, healthy because it allowed Laura to function normally despite the awful things she'd experienced in the past. Dr. Duncan said not to push it. That Laura was strong, and in time, she'd remember everything. Dr. Webber believed she never would.

Please let Dr. Duncan be right.

Maybe if she explored the area around the cabin, she'd recognize a landmark, or a sign on the trail.

But first, she had to get warm.

She shook out her hands, closed her eyes, then opened them again. With sharp vision, no longer tunneled from fear, she prowled systematically around the cabin, though there was little to take stock of. Perhaps cabin was too generous a term. This was really more of a hut.

All one room.

A charred, stone fireplace.

No indoor plumbing.

A bunk bed.

Table and chair . . . and, this was weird . . . a throw rug. What was a rug doing in a bare bones place like this?

Bending forward, she peeked beneath the table and saw little bottles scattered across the frayed rug. After collecting them, she placed them on the table for inspection. There were four amber pill bottles. All of them empty. All of them prescribed to *Laura Chaucer*. She recognized the names of the medicines—antidepressants and sleeping pills she hadn't taken in years.

The same ones that, in the past, had caused her hallucinations.

The same ones prescribed by, and then discontinued by, Dr. Webber.

Her hands began to shake. If she'd taken all these pills, or if they'd been fed to her, then she should be dead.

That had to have been a lethal dose.

It didn't add up until her gaze travelled to the dried puke on the floor. As she'd lain unconscious, she'd purged her stomach contents, and in all likelihood that had saved her life. And now that her body was free of the poison, she was growing stronger by the minute.

But . . . she could easily have choked on her vomit.

She shuddered.

He'd given her a lethal dose of pills and left her in the wilderness to die.

But why not finish her off with the knife?

Had he wanted it to seem like she'd done this to herself?

A sob welled in her chest.

It *did* seem like she'd done it to herself.

Maybe she had.

Maybe she was the monster.

No!

She lifted her hand and then, quite deliberately, slapped herself hard on the cheek. Feeling sorry for herself was useless . . . and letting him get in her head was dangerous.

You didn't do this.

And you didn't die.

You survived.

Now get over it!

Turning her attention back to the rug, she jerked it away and drew in a quick breath. The rug that didn't make sense suddenly did.

It'd been used to cover a trap door!

She dragged the table out of the way and heaved the trap door open, releasing a flood of dust into the room. A ladder, on which she counted seven rungs, led down to a small cellar. More of a storage closet really. She crept down, her heart climbing higher in her throat with each step. The space was small and dim. Once her eyes accommodated to the low light, she paced off the area. Six feet wide. Another six feet long. Shoved against one end of the cellar, stood a trunk.

Just the right size to hide a body.

The thought made her skin crawl, and she retreated to the opposite wall.

Don't be a ninny.

Of course there *could* be a corpse concealed inside, but far more likely, this trunk would contain supplies. And the benefit of finding supplies was well worth the risk, no matter how terrifying, of discovering a dead body.

With tiny, reluctant steps, she approached the trunk, then on a deep inhale reached out and touched the lid. Squeezing her eyes closed, she tugged it up. The hinges creaked. The space, already musty, now reeked of mothballs.

On three.

One . . . two . . . she opened her eyes.

And her jaw fell open.

She crouched down, and like a dog frantically burrowing under a fence to make his break for freedom, dug into the trunk, sending the contents flying over her shoulder.

Snow pants. A hooded jacket. Blankets. More clothes.

She came across waterproof matches, and her heart thudded in her chest. Once the trunk was finally empty, she rocked back on her knees and began sorting through all the loot: pots and pans, packets of freeze-dried food, a camel pack, and more bottles she could use to store water. She checked the expiration on the food packets. They were several years past, but she didn't care. She needed nourishment.

What more could she possibly ask for?

And then, tears began to stream down her face. Behind the trunk, she spied a pair of hiking boots—a bounty worth more than gold. She could hardly contain her gratitude. She pulled her knees to her chest, basking in the realization that she had everything she needed to prepare herself for the dangerous journey home. And home was where she longed to go. To a mother and father whose only crime was loving her too much, trying too hard keep her safe from the evil in the world.

And there was evil.

All around her.

It'd always been with her.

The strangest idea occurred to her, then.

That she was safer here.

Alone in the woods.

But that was crazy.

She had to get home.

Home meant safety.

She dragged on an undershirt, long johns and a flannel top; buttoned a knit cap beneath her chin, and loaded up the small backpack with all the supplies that would fit. Pulling on socks and boots, she shook her head at how, only a few minutes ago, she'd been intending to hike out of the wilderness in a dress and pumps.

Threading her arms into a Gore-Tex jacket, she noted one side-pocket was heavy. Inside she found a notebook and a topographic map. As she studied the map, the mystery of her good fortune turned to comprehension.

A red X marked the spot—Frank's Cabin.

She'd been left for dead all right. But her foolish monster had abandoned her in a forest service cabin—one of a string of huts intended to provide comfort for hikers and skiers on cross-country treks. In season, the popular huts were busy enough to require reservations. But this time of year, when it was too wet to hike, but not yet snowy enough to snowshoe or ski—the huts, like the roads, were closed to the public. No ranger would be stopping by to check on her—that was certain.

But her spirits climbed as she ascended the ladder out of the cellar and back into the room she now knew was "Frank's Cabin." Anchored to the bunk bed a logbook and pencil dangled from a dirty string.

She opened the book.

Inside, someone had written in heavy marker: *Take what you need. Leave what you can for others, even if it's just a note of encouragement or thanks.* The words brought a lump to her throat, and her heart swelled. At first, she'd been unable to believe her luck at finding the food and clothing, but now, she understood.

It wasn't luck.

It wasn't coincidence.

That trunk full of treasure was the direct result of the good in people.

The hikers who'd used this cabin had provided her with something far more valuable than boots and food. They'd supplied the one thing that could keep her going. The one thing that gave her a shot at outwitting a monster and making it down off this mountain alive.

They'd given her hope.

Reverently, she read the names in the book, tracing each one with her finger, and saying thank you aloud to each person represented. Had it been Louise Bertrand who'd left the hiking boots? Perhaps Steven Peters had ditched the worn backpack. Pablo with no last name, she decided, had tired of his freeze-dried fare and left it for the next guest. With her heart as warm as a belly full of brandy, she penciled her own name in the book:

Laura Chaucer.

Then she added: *Thank you fellow travelers for your generosity. I don't know if I deserve a second chance at life, but from today forward, I will strive to become worthy of the one I've been given.* Then she scratched out the word *second* and penciled in *third.* Twice now, she'd beaten her monster. Twice she'd lived when she should've died.

Dr. Webber and Dr. Duncan agreed on one thing: Survivor's guilt had plagued her since childhood.

Why me? Why am I alive when Angelina's dead?

Sometimes, when she looked in the mirror she thought she saw those questions tattooed on her forehead.

There had to be a reason.

She just didn't know what it was yet.

Fatigued, she contemplated heading out now, but quickly decided to rest here for the night, and start out fresh in the daylight. She twisted her long, black hair into a knot on the nape of her neck. Before turning in, she should try to make a fire. Boil water for a freeze-dried dinner. She returned to the pump, where she filled the water bottles and her camel pack.

After gathering wood, just enough to start a small fire, she returned to the hut and began building a wood tee-pee in the fireplace. Bending down, she got light-headed and reached up to steady herself. Her fingers landed on a piece of paper atop the mantle.

Careful not to straighten too fast, she stood up. Stared at the sealed envelope she'd pulled off the mantle.

What new treasure lay within? Perhaps a note of inspiration from a fellow traveler. Yes, she now considered herself a kindred spirit with those who'd come to the hut as part of a beautiful, intentional journey. And why shouldn't she be like them—like people who made their own plans? People who made their own choices?

She weighed the envelope, and then ripped it open. At once, her knees went watery, and she had to lean against the fireplace to keep her legs under her. Inside was a note.

Written in her own hand.

And tied with pink ribbon, were two locks of long black hair.

Chapter 9

THE TASK-FORCE KITCHEN had been designated for double duty as an interrogation room. Originally part of an executive suite, the area contained a sink, microwave, hot plate, fridge, and coffeemaker. Extra seating and tables had obviously been brought in from an outside source, lending the room the same peas-and-carrots color scheme as the others. Caitlin waited with Spense while Hatcher cleared the kitchen of hungry detectives and called Grady in for his interview.

Elbows planted on her knees, Caitlin listened intently to Hatcher's introductory remarks. He stated the time and date. Pointed out the recording devices in the room. Told Grady he was not under arrest and that any statements he made were voluntary.

He was free to go at any time. And finally: "Please state your name and your relationship to Laura Chaucer."

"I'm Dr. Grady Webber, Laura's former psychiatrist. But my relationship with the unfortunate girl extends well beyond that. I've known her since she was a babe in arms."

"How's that?" Hatcher asked.

"Whit and I go all the way back to the debate team at CU Boulder. Pledged the same fraternity, too. Of course our frat-boy days are long gone." He laughed.

Typical Grady, Caitlin thought, amused by his own cleverness no matter how small.

Nobody laughed with him.

Grady cleared his throat. "After college I did med school and residency in Denver, and eventually started a psychiatric practice here. I also landed a job at the local teaching hospital. Whit married and settled with his wife, Tracy, in the bedroom community of Piney Trails, just a few miles from my place. We've remained good friends—best friends until lately—he's become so . . . important . . . these days. But I digress. As you know—I believe you, Sergeant Hatcher, interviewed me that very day—Laura was kidnapped at the age of eight. That's when and why Whit asked me to step up in a professional capacity. Thank God Laura was unharmed physically by her abductor, but I'm afraid the ordeal caused severe psychological damage."

"Post-traumatic stress?" Hatcher asked.

"Sure. But it was more than the usual nightmares, unpredictable outbursts, and what-have-you. Her grasp on reality was tenuous at best. Whit was desperate to get her help, and I was happy to be of service. I've been Laura's psychiatrist since the day she was found covered in her nanny's blood."

"You mean until she fired you," Spense corrected.

"She didn't fire me." Grady's chin jutted forward. "When Whit was elected to the senate his entire family moved to DC. Though Inga and I often traveled with the Chaucers during my vacations, I could hardly leave my practice and my post at the hospital and relocate full time for one patient. Not even for one as important as Laura. She transferred to another psychiatrist in DC, a Dr. Duncan. That's all. No one has *ever* fired me."

I fired you from my life. Caitlin didn't say what she was thinking. Grady Webber was a tough man to get rid of. Maybe he'd used Laura to keep his relationship with the powerful Whit Chaucer going. Maybe that's why he'd kept her in therapy for more than a decade. To Caitlin's way of thinking, long before ten years had passed, Grady should've either made enough progress to end or greatly reduce the frequency of therapy sessions, or else he should have referred Laura elsewhere. "But she didn't come back to you even after she returned to the area. So basically . . ."

"Phrase it however you like, Caitlin. If you want to make it seem as though Laura chased me out the door with a broom, go ahead. It's not true, but my ego isn't fragile."

Really? A secure man didn't need to put on the kind of airs Grady did.

"Let's move on." Spense waved his hand around.

"When she arrived in Denver, Laura simply didn't wish to continue therapy *period*. Nothing to do with being dissatisfied with my care. Dr. Duncan had encouraged her to take a break and see how things went."

Like any therapist worth his salt who wasn't trying to milk his patient for all she was worth, Caitlin thought. "How do you know that? Did you communicate with Dr. Duncan?"

"Whit told me. He was worried." Webber sighed heavily. "Rightly so, it seems. Whit thought Laura needed me, and he wanted me to reach out to her. I didn't. I wish to heavens I had, but I could hardly be expected to predict something like this would happen since I'm no longer privy to her daily thoughts. Now, I can't help but wonder what if . . ."

"What if what?" Spense asked, as though irritated by Grady's habit of leaving sentences unfinished. "Just say what you mean."

"What if I had reached out to her like Whit asked me to do? Could I have prevented this? I thought it would be better to let the child come to me on her own."

"She's not a child. She's twenty-one," Caitlin said.

"And I've known her since infancy. So pardon my thinking of her childhood with fondness."

"I doubt she thinks of it fondly," Spense said, deadpan.

"And she didn't seek you out on her own, so she probably didn't think you'd be of any use," Hatcher added.

Bad cop, bad cop?

"No, but then again, she was only in town a short while before . . . before . . ."

Caitlin leaned in and looked him in the eye. "Before she disappeared, *again*. After all the years you treated her, you ought to know her inside out. But that doesn't explain how more of your therapy could've prevented her disappearance. Or do you know more than you're saying about what happened to her? Do you know where she is?"

Grady's eyes snapped. His face flushed. "Do you?"

"You told Spense and me that doctor-patient confidentiality didn't apply in Laura's case because she might be a danger to herself or others. You said you were willing to talk to us. And to the police. Maybe the limo ride over wasn't a good time to get into it, but what's stopping you now?"

"Could I get some coffee?" Grady looked around the room as if a waiter might appear.

Detective Hatcher scraped back his chair. "Anyone else want a cup?"

Spense and Caitlin declined.

Hatcher went to a sideboard that contained shelves stacked with cookies and bottled beverages. There was a small fridge below, typical of ones provided in hotel rooms. He scrounged around and produced a cellophane-wrapped sandwich, then brewed a cup of single serve coffee. No one spoke during this time. Spense amused himself with his Rubik's cube while Caitlin held a staring contest with her former mentor.

Eventually, Hatcher set the coffee, a bottle of water, and a ham sandwich in front of Grady. "Just thought I'd get a jump on any requests, so we can keep going without interruption. Did I miss anything? I could get you a cookie."

"I had one already—while I was sitting around waiting for you three to call me," Grady said, back up, feathers ruffled. "Let's get on with it."

"Yes, let's," Caitlin agreed. "You were just about to tell us what you think happened to Laura. Apparently, you don't think she's been kidnapped."

"I never said that."

"You implied it." Maybe he did believe Laura had been abducted, but was looking for a way to give them information without risking his medical license. As long as he gave lip service to the idea that Laura might hurt herself, he could reveal her confidences and stay within the letter of the law. There were other ways around doctor-patient confidentiality, but the *Duty to Warn* statutes were probably the easiest.

"I said she might be a danger to self or *others*." Grady stuck with the wording that would keep him in the clear. But Caitlin hadn't expected him to emphasize the *others* side of things.

Hatcher's eyes widened like a ghost had just popped up and hollered *boo*. "You think Laura Chaucer might be homicidal?"

"I didn't say so."

"Actually, you did," Spense said.

"I said she *might* be a danger to others." Grady squirmed in his chair. "Or she might be *in* danger from others. You're the detectives." He gave Caitlin a look that made it clear she wasn't a detective either, and he resented her inclusion in the task force. "And as investigators, I think you should know that Laura suffered more than a simple case of post-traumatic stress disorder. She was clinically depressed, and she was afflicted with paranoia, delusions, and occasional hallucinations." He paused for effect. "She was plagued by the notion that *she* might have killed Angelina."

"Surely you relieved her of that idea during her ten-plus years on your couch," Caitlin said.

"I don't employ a couch in my sessions. I'm a systems therapist not a psychoanalyst. You know that."

"And you know what I mean. It's not reasonable to suggest that a little girl strangled her nanny and stabbed her over one hundred times, after what? Convincing Angelina to hitch a ride with her into the mountains? From a logistical standpoint, it's virtually impossible for an eight-year-old to have done it. I'd think you'd have made it your primary goal to hammer the facts home to Laura and lift that burden off her shoulders. Because as long as she believes she might've killed her nanny, she can never fully recover from the trauma inflicted upon her. She isn't responsible for Angelina's death, and you should've helped her to grasp that."

"You don't know everything, Caitlin. Laura argued with Angelina. She got very, *very* angry and shouted something like *I could kill you*. Next thing she knows, she wakes up in the mountains, covered in blood, near Angelina's body and can't remember anything about what happened. It wasn't as easy to convince that child she didn't do it as you might think—and in fact I had no luck in that department. The best I ever accomplished was to persuade her to give herself the benefit of a reasonable doubt."

"I don't understand it," Hatcher said. "Why would she think such a thing? I know that even today the bloggers have some crazy-ass theories about what really happened, but Laura's parents would have shielded her from gossip at the time. Where would the child get that idea?"

Caitlin twisted in her chair to face Hatcher. "Children are prone to magical thinking. They feel responsible for everything from their parents' divorces to deaths in the family. Maybe a child tells his mother *I wish you were dead*, then a month later she's diagnosed with cancer. He thinks that somehow his wish brought on the disease."

Hatcher scratched his head.

"Step on a crack, break your mother's back," Spense said.

"Oh!" Hatcher nodded. "I still jump over the cracks."

Caitlin turned to Grady. "I can see how a combination of magical thinking and survivor's guilt could have caused a young Laura to believe she'd murdered Angelina. But as she grew older, and with your counseling and proper medication, when confronted with the facts, she should've understood, at least on an intellectual level, that belief was false—unless she's suffering from a thought disorder—a full-blown psychosis."

"She's not. Though she has teetered in that direction from time to time."

"So you're saying she might be dangerous or maybe it's the other way around—she might be *in* danger instead. And she's not crazy—but she is a little. It's a wonder, with you as her guide, she's not a bastion of clear thinking." Caitlin jumped to her feet, took a deep breath and forced herself to sit back down. It made her nuts to think someone charged with helping Laura might've confused her more instead.

"I guess as she got older, those bloggers with their wild speculations didn't help the poor kid any." Hatcher drum-rolled his knuckles on the table, randomly. "But tell me this, Dr. Webber, what does Laura say about all the evidence pointing to Angelina being in on the kidnap scheme?"

"Laura adamantly refuses to believe any of it. According to her, Angelina loved her, and she loved Angelina, even though she sometimes acted the part of an ungrateful brat. According to her, Angelina would've never harmed her. Not for money. Not for a boyfriend. Not for all the salt in the sea."

"All the salt in the sea. She said that?" Hatcher tilted his head to the side.

"My interpretation. Figure of speech." Grady didn't hide the disdain in his voice.

"Never heard that one." Hatcher shrugged.

"Like *all the tea in China*," Grady explained.

"But tea is worth good money. Salt, not so much . . . and you can't drink it."

"It's less cliché."

"Me, I like a good cliché. At least I know what the hell it means."

"Concrete thinking. Always a plus in any conversation." Grady assumed his go-to expression—the superior smirk.

Spense tossed his cube in the air and sent Caitlin an *oh-brother* look.

She smiled back at Spense, glad the inane exchange seemed to have finally run its course. She hadn't been paying much attention anyway. She'd been thinking about Angelina and Laura. Laura might be confused about what happened that night, but that didn't mean everything she said should be dismissed out-of-hand. It hadn't been proven, at least not by any overwhelming evidence, that Angelina was an accomplice. "It's possible the nanny was kidnapped, too, like the police originally suspected. Maybe she was simply in the wrong place at the wrong time."

"Laura and Angelina were asleep in separate bedrooms in the family home." Hatcher turned all business on a dime. Caitlin smiled at the thought. Good cliché. Everyone knows what it means.

"You can't be sure of that," Spense said. "It's possible Laura cried out, and the nanny went in to check on her, thus interrupting the kidnapper. Or maybe the kidnapper didn't know how to take care of a child, so he dragged the nanny along to keep Laura calm. Since Angelina wasn't ransomable, he didn't mind killing her when it suited him."

"Don't think so," Hatcher said. "Not a good enough reason to risk abducting an adult, who'd be a lot harder to manage. Besides, the kidnapper didn't have to worry about keeping Laura quiet. He drugged her with GHB—the date rape drug."

"Everyone here knows what GHB is," Grady said.

"What about Angelina? Did they find GHB in her system, too?" Caitlin asked.

"We didn't test for it." Hatcher got busy shuffling papers.

Spense narrowed his eyes. "But an autopsy was done. Tox screen would've been part of that."

"Yes. But GHB isn't included in a routine serum screen. We could've specifically requested it, but we didn't. We knew pretty quickly that Angelina's cause of death was asphyxiation due to strangulation." Hatcher's shoulders hunched defensively. "Besides, we knew the ransom note was consistent with Angelina's handwriting. We believed she was the one who drugged Laura. Still do."

"Handwriting analysis isn't an exact science," Spense said.

"Someone could've deliberately copied both Angelina's handwriting and her phrasing if they wanted to make her look guilty," Caitlin put in.

"But what would they have to gain from that?" Hatcher asked.

"Misdirection?" Spense turned his palms up.

"Look, we can walk this path later if you like, but we're wasting Dr. Webber's time." Hatcher seemed eager to shut down the conversation. Probably because it highlighted oversights on the part of the original investigators. He redirected back to Grady. "If Laura never accepted the idea that Angelina was in on the kidnapping, how does that impact her current state of mind? No figure of speeches, please. Just plain English."

"It's the penthouse suite in Laura's high-rise tower of guilt." Grady ignored Hatcher's admonition.

Thankfully, Hatcher didn't take the bait other than to arch a graying eyebrow.

"It means, best-case scenario, she's indirectly responsible for Angelina's death. In Laura's head, either she murdered Angelina or Angelina was collateral damage because she was caring for Laura. Either way, she believed it was all her fault. That is, until recently." Grady shifted his glance to Caitlin.

The look in his eyes seemed imploring. Like he wanted something from her. Approval? Acceptance? She couldn't quite get a handle on it.

"You'll be glad to know, Caitlin, that of late, at least according to Whit, Laura's changed her tune. She's ceased saying she thinks she killed Angelina. She's begun saying someone else must've done it."

"After she started seeing this new therapist. Dr. Duncan?"

"Yes. What's your point?"

"You tell me."

"My point is Laura is gaining—or *was* gaining more independence. I'd think you'd be happy to hear that report."

"Are you?"

"Frankly, I'm not sure she was ready to stop taking psychotropic medications."

"Yet after she stopped them, she began to think more rationally. Maybe the meds did her more harm than good." Maybe Grady had done her more harm than good.

"She moved out of her parents' house, returned to the Denver area and enrolled in college. Whit worried, but hoped she was finally ready to put the past behind her. I was hoping so, too. But now she's gone missing. A girl who once tried to cut her own throat."

A prior suicide attempt. Grady had dropped it in like an after-thought. "And you think she's attempted suicide again?" Caitlin asked.

"I'm not on the task force. That's for you to determine."

Spense leaned forward. "That's what you said the last time we called you out on talking in circles. You're waffling more than a politician. Maybe you've spent too much time with the senator and his cronies."

"I've got Laura's records for you—from my sessions with her." He slid an envelope across to Hatcher, ignoring Spense. "And there is one more thing. I—I hesitate to bring it up, because the Chaucers are like family."

"Family who keeps you on the payroll," Spense said.

"I just think you should know . . . Laura has a history of violence. She once tried to strangle her mother, Tracy, and on a separate occasion she was found standing over her parents' bed with a knife."

"Before or after the kidnapping?"

"Before," Grady said gravely. "Surely you can understand my concerns." He hesitated. Looked toward the door. He was still hold-ing something back. Or at least he wanted it to appear that way.

"What else aren't you telling us?" Spense asked.

"I—I don't know that it would help you find her. It may have significance, but I'm struggling because I—I don't know how it figures into all of this. But . . . ." He heaved a sigh. "I feel obligated to tell you."

"If you withhold anything, and something happens to that girl, I'm going to make sure you're brought up on charges," Hatcher said.

"Don't threaten me."

Despite his protest, Grady looked relieved. And Caitlin thought she knew why. He could now claim they had dragged whatever it was out of him under duress. If this was something he was supposed to keep quiet about, his friend, Whit, would know the police had given him no choice.

Grady waited another beat before spitting it out. "There's another reason Laura thought she might have killed Angelina. The day after Laura was rescued she found a lock of dark brown hair, tied with a pink ribbon. It was hidden inside a sock in her top drawer. Laura believed the hair was Angelina's."

Hatcher slammed his fist on the table. A few drops of Grady's coffee, which hadn't been touched, sloshed over the top of the cup and beaded onto the cellophane wrapped sandwich. "You've known this for thirteen years. You withheld physical evidence in a criminal investigation. I should slap the cuffs on you right this minute."

"Doctor-patient confidentiality—"

"Doesn't extend to withholding physical evidence in a criminal investigation."

"I don't have any physical evidence in my possession. I never did. So your point doesn't apply."

"What happened to the lock of hair?" Spense asked, for once the coolest head in the room.

Caitlin considered marking down the date.

"I have no idea." Grady's voice contained a slight tremor. The threat of arrest had shaken his usual implacability. "For all I know, there might not have been any lock of hair. For all I know, Laura dreamt it up. Maybe it was a false memory, created by that magical thinking we discussed earlier. Laura claimed it was in a sock that later disappeared." He offered a halfhearted smile. "Maybe it went where all missing socks go. Maybe it wasn't Angelina's hair at all. Or maybe Angelina gave it to Laura as a memento and Laura forgot."

There seemed to be no shortage of *for all I knows* and *maybes*.

"He's right." Hatcher's hunched shoulders lowered. "That lock of hair might not mean a damn thing."

Spense leaned back in his chair and put his hands behind his head. "Or it might be the key that unlocks this entire case."

Chapter 10

Afternoon
Frank's Cabin
Eagles Nest Wilderness
Colorado

THE NOTE SLIPPED from Laura's hand, drifting slowly to the floor on a breeze from the cracked window. Her other hand clasped open and shut around the ribboned bundles of hair. Each time she looked down, she held her breath, waiting for them to disappear, willing them to be a dream, a hallucination, a wisp of her fevered imagination.

But each time, they remained, the soft strands of hair brushing innocently against her hand, like lovingly clipped souvenirs for a baby's memory book.

You can't *feel* imagination.

She brought the locks of hair close to her nose.

You can't *smell* a person's lingering scent in your dreams.

No. Just like every other thing about her current situation, these locks of hair were real.

Real hair that had once belonged to real human beings.

Angelina appeared before her in her mind's eye. All true memories of her nanny's face had faded away long ago. Now, when Laura pictured her, it was always the image from a photograph she kept secreted away in a shoe box: Angelina smiling down at her, pushing her on a swing in a green park on a sunny day. Angelina's long dark hair lifting in the wind.

Laura's eyes stung as though she might cry, but no tears fell.

She was too empty inside.

Her tears had been stolen from her along with her childhood, her innocence, her*self*.

Sometimes it seemed the woman who stared back at her in the mirror was more like a ghost than a flesh and bone human being. That she was nothing more than haze—night mist that drew life from the lake and rose predestined to die with the morning sun.

She gouged one of the wounds on her neck, hungry for the pain, because pain meant life, substance. That she hadn't vanished yet.

Laura, you're losing what's left of your mind.

Losing it, or being driven out of it?

For a long time, she studied the objects in her hand.

This could be doll's hair couldn't it? Sure it could. There was no proof it was Angelina's or anyone else's. For that matter, it could be her own hair.

He must have put it here along with the note.

Written in your own hand?

Either she'd done something terrible . . . she slapped herself again and her cheek answered with a satisfying ache . . . or someone was setting her up to make it look like she had.

If she was the evil one, she didn't deserve mercy.

But she remembered *nothing* about this note, these locks of hair.

And how could she have done the terrible things the note said?

Not just to Angelina, but to the others?

It was impossible!

The others.

Were they real? Or had she merely concocted an insane theory to make herself believe she hadn't killed anyone? Because if her theories were true, it meant she was innocent of any crime. It also might mean she was doomed. A monster that evil and that clever would never let her live. Once he found out she was alive, he'd come for her.

She had to find him before he found her.

Then another thought came to her that made her choke.

She should've realized it before, but she'd *wanted* so badly to believe she was safe, even if only for a short while. But now the unassailable truth confronted her. Whoever had done this might very well come back here. What if he'd had to leave in a rush and planned to return to dispose of her corpse? Or to set the scene to suit his purposes? Or to kill again?

There was no guarantee at all that he wouldn't return.

She should go, and quickly. But . . .

She stared down at her palm for the hundredth time. She didn't know what to do with the locks of hair—they were important evidence in a crime.

But they might get her locked up. The hair and the note made her look guilty.

She had matches.

She could burn everything.

But what if the hair could be tested for DNA and helped a family learn what had happened to a loved one?

From her purse, she took a handkerchief with little blue flowers embroidered in the corners. Carefully, she wrapped the locks of hair. Then she zipped them into an inside pocket of the backpack she'd prepared.

Time to go home.

Her parents would know what to do.

Or perhaps she ought to go straight to the police and tell them everything. That she'd been kidnapped. That she'd found these locks of hair. Show them the cuts on her throat that implied her innocence. Bring them back here to the cabin. But . . . would they believe her?

No one ever has before.

She definitely couldn't show anyone the note. That was one thing she was clear about. The note was a lie that would only make it harder for the police to find the truth. Before she left the cabin, she had to burn that lie in the fireplace. She shuddered to think about what the note said and about the second lock of hair.

Believe in your own goodness.

She put on her jacket, slid the backpack on, then closed her eyes.

Reason dictated her path. She should go home, talk to her parents and to the authorities. But her gut clenched at the thought. How could she convince them with mere words? She needed evidence to back up her theories.

Proof of the others.

A thud sounded outside, and her eyes flew open. The sound

of footsteps, crunch, crunch, crunching over the ground broke through her dizzy indecision. They were heavy menacing footfalls growing closer and closer.

His footfalls?

Her purse still sat on the plank table. She grabbed it and bolted out the back door.

Chapter 11

Thursday, October 24
1:45 P.M.
Task force headquarters
Highlands Hotel
Denver, Colorado

WITH THE INTERVIEW concluded, Grady left, giving a terse good-bye and offering yet again to join the task force should they come to their senses and recognize the value he could add. Caitlin was glad to see him go for more reasons than one. She had her eye on the powder room and was just about to excuse herself when a short, heavyset man barreled through the door Grady had just exited. The squat detective's legs were scissoring hard enough that Caitlin could hear the slap of his polyester pants whipping against each other. What this man lacked in height he made up for in speed and alacrity.

Spense arched an eyebrow.

Hatcher replied to his unspoken question, "Cliff's one of my best men."

"Jordo!" The pitch of Cliff's voice was much higher than Caitlin had expected from such a burly source. He was worked up about something. That much seemed sure. "Jordo, we got something."

Her first thought, her first hope, really, was that someone had spotted Laura out and about. But since they hadn't yet notified the press, a Laura sighting seemed unlikely. The public didn't know she was missing.

"Get the usual suspects together for a press conference. Let's say ten a.m. tomorrow," Hatcher replied, apparently thinking along the same lines as Caitlin.

It was time to ask for the public's help. And holding the press conference in the morning would give Hatcher time to craft a statement. She and Spense would be expected to come up with a preliminary profile by then, too.

A tall order.

Hard to profile the perpetrator when it wasn't yet clear what crime, if any, had been committed.

"Consider it done. But Jordo, I just talked to Rhonda." The detective bent and put both hands on his knees then quickly straightened up again.

"Rhonda's desk sergeant at District 2," Hatcher clarified for her benefit and for Spense's.

"Per Rhonda, a call came in to Dillon and Dillon relayed to Piney Trails. Piney Trails relayed to District 2." He was panting now. "Hiker. Up in the mountains. Near—get this—Frank's Cabin."

"Frank's Cabin?" Hatcher's hands flew up to his wiry hair.

"You heard me right."

Caitlin wasn't sure but if she had to guess . . .

"Thirteen years ago Angelina's body was found in the mountains near a cabin. That would be Frank's Cabin?" Spense asked.

Hatcher was on his feet. "Same."

The stocky detective let out a long wheeze.

"Take a breath, Cliff. Then get on with it." Hatcher pinned him with a commanding look.

"Road from Dillon to the Angel Rock trailhead is officially closed, but this dude, he hiked up anyway. Photographer looking for what he called Magic Mike. Magic light . . . magic hour? I don't remember what kind of magic."

"That part's not important," Hatcher answered.

Cliff took a puff off a red inhaler he'd pulled from his pocket. "Right. He planned to stay the night at Frank's Cabin, but when he got there, he heard noise. Saw a flash out the back door. Somebody small, he thinks a female. Running—maybe limping a little. He considered giving chase, but didn't see a reason, until he got inside, and by then it was too late."

To Caitlin's way of thinking, Cliff should've *started* his story with that reason inside the cabin. But he was flustered enough already, so she tried to be patient while he got on with it.

"Blood all over the place."

Finally, the punch line.

"And a green dress."

"When did the call come in?" Spense asked. He and Caitlin had both gotten to their feet as well. Everyone huddled in a rapt circle around Cliff.

"Now. It came in just now. Rhonda, she said she knew right away we'd want to hear about it. Guy called from his cell as soon as he got signal. He's on his way out, but he's gotta finish hiking down. You want he should wait in Dillon or come here?"

"Take Frampton and meet the photographer in Dillon. Get his statement. Then check in. Our honored guests, here, will come with me, up to the cabin. And, Cliff, get a park ranger and a couple of techs, maybe some uniforms, to meet us at the road. Hopefully it's passable and we won't have to hike up it ourselves. That all you got?"

"Blood, a green dress, and a witness ain't enough?" Cliff asked. "You're just like the wife—never satisfied. What more do you want, conjugal rights?"

"Long as I get to be on top," Hatcher shot back. "And you're right, I won't be satisfied with anything short of finding Laura Chaucer alive and getting her home to her family. And this time, I intend to nail the bastard responsible." He jerked a gaze around the circle. "Anyone needs to powder his nose better hurry. We're going on a field trip and the bus leaves in five."

Chapter 12

Thursday, October 24
1:48 P.M.
Task force headquarters
Highlands Hotel
Denver, Colorado

CAITLIN FINISHED DRYING her hands and glanced in the mirror. Touching her cracked lips with her index finger, she remembered the Chapstick in her purse and wished she'd brought it with her into the bathroom. Her hair was a mess. She dragged her fingers through the tangled waves and tucked them behind her ears.

A door creaked.

She let out an involuntary gasp as she whipped around to confront the man whose image suddenly loomed in the mirror behind her.

"You startled me," she said to Grady. "Last I heard, knocking before entering a restroom was standard operating procedure."

He gave her a superior look. "I knew it was you in here. I

watched you down a full liter of water during my interview. The way you kept looking toward the bathroom, I surmised you'd be headed here within minutes of concluding the questioning. However, it took you long enough. Cliff's news must've been compelling indeed."

She doubted Grady and Cliff had been introduced. If he knew the detective's name, most likely he'd been eavesdropping on their conversation after leaving the interview room. This took bad manners to a whole new level—almost a criminal one. "Why ask when you were obviously listening through the door while lying in wait to accost me in the bathroom?"

"Accost is a strong word. And hardly fair since I waited until I heard the toilet flush and the water running. I knew you'd be decent when I walked in."

He was behaving as though this was normal, appropriate, even polite behavior. A hot burst of anger flared inside her, setting her cheeks on fire. "Get out!"

He grabbed her by the wrists and pulled her toward him. "C'mon, Caitlin. I just want to talk to you. I didn't know a better way to get you alone. And let this be a lesson to you. Always lock the door."

He had the nerve, with his fingers locked around her wrists and digging painfully into her flesh, to assert that he was looking out for her—teaching her a lesson. A spider crawling up her back would've creeped her out less. And she *had* locked the door she entered by. But this was a massive, multi-room suite and the bath could be entered from either side. She'd made the mistake of assuming the door on the opposite side was already locked. A mistake she wouldn't make twice. Grady had gone back around and then entered via the other door.

"Any one of these sketchy detectives, all of whom have less consideration for your dignity than I do, could've walked in on you."

"The only *sketchy* one around here is you. So take your hands off me." She jerked her wrists free and pushed him away.

"Relax, Caitlin. You misunderstand my intent."

Doubtful. She took a step back. He took a bigger one forward. She considering grinding her heel into his instep, but she knew he'd draw satisfaction from it. It would prove he'd gotten to her. It would make her appear frightened. And she wasn't frightened. She was pissed. Grady might be twice her size, but she didn't need to fear him . . . at least not in this moment. Just outside the door, an entire room full of detectives—not to mention Spense—stood at the ready. Grady was too smart to take things further while they were in a setting where he was certain to be found out.

She waited a moment for her breathing to return to normal, then said, "You admitted you followed me into the bathroom. That's way out of line, and you know it. Don't ever do that to me again. In the future, if you want to speak to me alone, you'll need to ask my permission. I may or may not give it, as is my right." Then she smiled, as graciously as she could manage to do while picturing herself gouging his eyes out. "However, it seems you've caught me in a generous mood." She swept her palm out invitingly. "If you want to chat in a bathroom, then by all means, let's." For good measure she straightened her shoulders and moved in close. Now *she* was the invader of personal space. "What's up, Grady?"

"That's what I'd like to know."

"Not following." She checked out her fingernails to signal her indifference.

"From the moment we said hello in the limo, you've been acting distant."

"I've been polite."

"You've been formal, even cold. I can't imagine what I could possibly have done to deserve such treatment from a very dear old friend."

One of them needed a reality check, and it wasn't her. "Then let me explain it to you. A: We're not dear old friends or any other kind of friends. B: You shouldn't have said a damn word about our past relationship in front of other people."

"You're the one who insisted on making it known."

"Not at all. I simply insisted on not pretending we'd never met. Your subterfuge is what called attention to it. Made it seem like a big deal. Even though we only dated briefly, and so long ago."

"But it was a big deal. I was your first. And it wasn't so long ago."

"Not my first. But, I was young and—"

"Beautiful."

"I was going to say impressionable. And you were someone I looked up to—my teacher and mentor. You took advantage of my naiveté and because of my father, you knew I'd be vulnerable to an older, wiser man."

"Really, Caitlin, you make me sound like a terrible letch. A dirty old man. When in truth, I'm little more than a decade your senior. And if you've got a daddy complex, that's hardly my fault."

She'd never punched a man in the face, but a first time just might be on the horizon.

"I didn't force myself on you. As I recall, you were quite enamored of me."

"In the beginning, yes. But when I tried to end things, you refused to accept it. You stalked me through the halls of the hospital."

"I *worked* at the hospital. You were my resident. I was your attending. It was my job to keep close tabs on you. And I fully embraced the breakup. I, too, was happy to part ways . . . eventually." He raised his right hand. "Caitlin, I swear to you that it was Inga, not you, who was the love of my life. Inga's loss is what keeps me up nights. It's her face I see in my dreams when I do finally fall asleep. This may come as a crushing blow to your inflated ego, but I haven't given you a second thought in *that way* since the day I met my sweet Inga. So, rest easy, darling. I have absolutely no intention of trying to rekindle a dead flame."

A pang of pity assailed her—for *Inga*. "Is that what you followed me in here to say?"

"Yes. Your behavior's been strange, and I just wanted to make sure you didn't have the idea I still . . ."

Caitlin hadn't really had time to process the news of Inga's death. Though they hadn't been close, she'd always liked her. She remembered Inga compassionately reaching out to touch a patient's hand during rounds. She remembered the lively way Inga debated the merits of Freud versus Skinner with her fellow residents. She remembered Inga humming as she worked on her progress notes. She remembered Inga *alive*. The pressure of unshed tears rose behind Caitlin's eyes, and her shoulders softened as the anger she felt for Grady slowly drained from her heart.

He'd lost his wife.

"I'm truly sorry for your loss." She met his eyes, her own moist. "I thought the world of Inga. And I want you to know, that even though you could've chosen a better way of getting my ear, I *am* glad we had this talk. I'd like to put the past behind us. I'd like to move forward without animosity—as colleagues." She took a breath. She felt compelled to add, "Colleagues and nothing more. We're going to have to stay in touch regarding this case, so I'd like to keep a good working relationship."

"Colleagues only. We're on the same page. What a relief." He extended his hand, and she gladly shook it. "You go ahead," he said, as though she were a maiden with her reputation in danger. "I'll wait here for a minute, and then I'll leave the same way I came in."

She felt relieved, too, but not for long. As she exited the room, she caught Grady's reflection in the mirror, and the hairs on the back of her neck prickled. Grady didn't notice her watching him watching her . . . because his lascivious gaze was glued to her bottom.

Chapter 13

Late afternoon
Near Frank's Cabin
Eagles Nest Wilderness
Colorado

ANOTHER DEAD END.

Like the others she'd taken before it, this turned out not to be a trail at all.

Laura's muscles strained eagerly, propelling her body into a ready crouch as she peered down over the edge of a precipice. How perverse that just a couple of hours after the burning will to live sent her running out of Frank's Cabin, she found herself battling a powerful urge to jump off a cliff.

Instead of hurtling from the ledge, she scooped up a stone and tossed it over. Her gaze jealously followed its arc for as long as she could make out its path. It tumbled down, down, down. That lucky rock easily found its way off the mountain. A task that was proving difficult for her. When she'd gone tearing out of the cabin, sheer adrenaline had fueled her flight, blocking out all awareness of physical discomfort. It wasn't until later that she'd noticed the shooting pains in her side and the watery ache in her legs. The places where her ill-fitting borrowed boots abraded her feet.

She didn't think she'd been followed, but that didn't mean she was safe. Whether those were her monster's footsteps she'd heard outside the cabin or someone else's, *he* would be looking for her.

Hunting her.

If not now, then soon—the very moment he learned her dead body wasn't lying on that cabin floor.

She indulged in one last glance at the gaping chasm below, then walked to a less tempting distance from the ledge. The trudge up the mountain had exhausted her almost as quickly as the sun had begun to sink in the sky. And no matter how hard she'd studied her topo map, she simply hadn't been able to find her way. A half-dozen false trails had led her farther and farther up the mountain.

She was badly lost.

According to the map, Frank's Cabin was only a few miles from Dillon, but once the sun went down, she'd be surrounded by the darkest kind of night—the kind without city lights. She couldn't risk trying to make it to town tonight—and when she did get there, to whom would she turn?

Shading her eyes with her hand, she surveyed the area. That group of boulders over there would make a good enough spot to camp. She could spread a blanket at the base, and the weathered rocks would shield her not only from view, but from the wind and cold. It would be a long night, but she had warm clothing and supplies, and there was no way she'd ever find the road in the dark.

Huddling in the shelter of the boulders, she settled in. Despite her fatigue, she felt mentally stronger. The air was clean, and the shadow of evil that hung over the cabin was nowhere to be found. It was another world out here, a beautiful, wondrous place where lodge pole pines and quaking aspen gave way to ground-hugging grasses, knee timber, and eventually alpine meadows. A world so unlike the prison of a home she'd grown up in.

Always under the watchful eye of Cayman and her parents.

Medicated.

Protected not only from the outside world, but from the dangers of her own mind.

She stared at a lonely red flower, amazed it had somehow survived the cold and wind and altitude, then she lifted her face to catch the warmth of the sun's last rays. Life was a gift and though hers, like the little red flower's, had been a struggle, in this moment she knew for certain she would never willingly relinquish it.

Her stomach growled, and that made her happy. Her appetite had returned—yet another miracle. All that fresh air and exercise, she supposed. She didn't dare chance a fire, so she poured cold water from one of her canteens into a bag of freeze-dried beef stroganoff. The meat was chewy, and the noodles turned to powder on her tongue, but the flavor was good—downright tasty even—and the meal satisfied her clamoring stomach. Deciding she wouldn't wait for night to sleep, she zipped her coat tight and wrapped the blanket around her shoulders.

The more rest she got, the more her strength—and hopefully her ability to read a map—would be restored. She folded a shirt for a pillow and half lay, half sat with her back propped against a low, smooth rock. She closed her eyes, but her mind refused to slumber. Her thoughts kept returning to the locks of hair in her backpack.

And to that horrible note.

She'd bolted so suddenly she hadn't had time to burn it.

She had no idea what had become of it, or what might happen to her if it were found.

Chapter 14

Thursday, October 24
4:30 P.M.
Near Frank's Cabin
Eagles Nest Wilderness area
Colorado

PANDORA MCBAIN FROM the Dillon Ranger District met Spense, Caity, and Hatcher at the foot of the county road leading to the Angel Rock trailhead, which in turn led to Frank's Cabin—part of the Eagles Nest Wilderness's hut system. The road was closed yearly between winter season and summer season. In other words, now. However, though wet, the road was still passable to four-wheel-drive vehicles.

Also present, having arrived separately, were eight other men and women: an eclectic group made up of crime-scene techs, detectives, and a local cop. Some had extensive training in wilderness search and rescue.

Most did not.

Ranger Pandy, as she'd introduced herself, headed up the junior park ranger program and the Seniors Gone Wild volunteer program. She'd also been personally responsible for the location and rescue of more lost hikers than any other official in Colorado history.

Spense estimated the redheaded ranger's stature to be a few inches shy of five feet. By her take-charge manner, he estimated her wallop to be a couple of sticks shy of a keg of dynamite. "Who here doesn't know jack about wilderness search and rescue?" she barked to the assembly.

Several hands rose.

"Okay then, unless Detective Hatcher needs you at the cabin . . ." She paused, waiting for him to speak now.

He held his peace.

"You folks are officially assigned to containment."

The uniform from Dillon shot his hand up again. "What does that mean exactly?"

"It means you and the tall dude in the Broncos shirt have the incredibly important task of parking your butts halfway up this road and waiting for our subject to come to you. There's a spooky old house about three quarters of the way up, so keep a ways below that marker. The rest of the rookies will set up track traps once we figure out where to put them."

"We aren't going to search at all?"

"You're going to contain. It's not glamorous, but in a situation like this, containment reduces the area we have to search. And that increases our POD—probability of detection."

"Track traps?" another novice asked.

"So you really don't know jack." But there was no impatience in Pandy's voice. She was simply a very straightforward individual, and Spense liked straightforward individuals. Especially when they were dedicated and smart. "We're gonna dump sand over key spots on the trails and what-have-you. If our subject crosses that way, we'll know it."

"What if they attempt to conceal their footprints?"

"Then we'll see evidence of that, too. Now if you'll hold your questions, I'd appreciate it. Everyone else, unless you're needed to process the crime scene, you'll pair up for a *hasty search*. If you haven't done one of these before, it's just like it sounds. *Hasty*. No grid. No coordinates. It'll be dark soon, so we gotta move quick. We'll fan out and stay in touch by radio. Move fast. Jog—that's right, I said jog—the trails and check the most likely spots. Anywhere you think a victim might be. Look for clues. Stuff that's out of place. Our PLS—point last seen—is Frank's Cabin. We believe the subject to be female. Likely weak or injured. Even if she can only cover one mile an hour, we have no idea which direction she headed. A one mile 360-degree radius is still a lot of area to search, and we won't get it done before the sun goes down, but let's give it our all just the same. Somebody's life depends on it."

"I heard this girl might just be a runaway," one of the searchers said.

"Not likely. According to our witness, there's a significant amount of blood at the cabin. That means we're not gonna find our subject holed up doing coke with her boyfriend in an Idaho Springs motel room. So what say we quit shooting the shit and haul our tails up to Frank's place?"

Chapter 15

Thursday, October 24
5:15 P.M.
Frank's Cabin
Eagles Nest Wilderness
Colorado

"THERE'S BLOOD ALL right. Everyone keep back and let the techs do their thing." Standing on the porch of Frank's Cabin with paper booties on his feet, Hatcher put up a stop sign with one hand and motioned his CSIs inside with the other. The wind was blowing hard and carried with it the tang of spilt blood mixed with something less familiar. The final result was an odor noxious enough to trigger Spense's gag reflex, and he had a well-seasoned, cast-iron stomach.

The rookies had been designated to either track traps or containment, leaving Spense, Caity, Ranger Pandy, and Hatcher to conduct the *hasty search*. Except Hatcher would probably need to stay back and manage the troops.

"I'll join you in a minute—but I wanna get a preliminary read from the techs first," Hatcher said, confirming Spense's assumption.

And then there were three.

Spense cast his gaze over at Caity and Pandy. Ideally, the searchers would pair up—hard to manage when all you had was a trio.

"Subject's not inside," Hatcher continued. "But according to Cayman, Laura was wearing a green dress at dinner with Ron Saas on Monday night. As advertised, there's a green dress on the cabin floor."

"Bloodied?" Spense asked.

"Not at first glance, but I didn't touch anything. We'll find out when we get a good look-see."

"Based on the amount of visible blood inside, you think she's alive?" Despite his itch to check out the cabin himself, Spense knew it was best to stick to his assigned duties. They were short on both daylight and personnel. He took time to ask only because Laura's condition, assuming that's who belonged to the green dress on the cabin floor, would inform their search. If she'd been badly wounded, she wouldn't make it far, and there might be a blood trail to guide them. If she was dead, they'd be looking for a concealed body or shallow grave. As they jogged the trails, they'd be homing in on a whole different set of indicators.

Hatcher wiped his forehead with the back of his hand.

It was as cold outside as Angelina Antonelli's unsolved murder, but the detective was sweating. Clearly, this case meant more to him than most—redemption perhaps.

"I've seen a lot worse where we still got ourselves a survivor. But something bad happened in there—no question about that.

There's plenty of gore to go around, and we got feces and vomit, too."

That explained the other smells.

Hatcher covered his mouth and nose with a handkerchief. "Trust me, you're better off on search duty."

"As a shortcut, let's assume it was Laura who fled out the back. We still don't know that it's *her* blood in there." Spense could hear the note of hope in Caity's voice.

And she had a point. Given the green dress, odds were good Laura had been in the cabin, but that didn't mean that any or all of the blood was hers. "The hiker who called it in did say the female subject took off quickly. A mortally wounded victim wouldn't have been able to flee at all."

Hatcher's expression remained grim. "Maybe it was the perpetrator who ran. Or one of those off-the-grid types, someone who might've wanted to use the cabin for shelter, but found a crime scene instead."

"Or someone who found Laura and did her harm." Best to consider all angles. "It's off season. Road's closed. They'd be expecting the cabin to be vacant. And even though the dress is a good indicator Laura was here, it doesn't tell us when or how she got here. If it wasn't her fleeing, we have to consider the possibility we may be looking for her body," Spense said gravely.

Caity's face fell. "You've got mountain folk up here?" she asked Pandy.

"I'm afraid so, on occasion. Most of them loners—sort of paranoid only not crazy—I know there's a term for that . . ."

"Schizoid," Caity said.

"Right. Schizoid personalities. The type who don't like to hang out with other people. But, we haven't had any reports of mountain men . . . or women recently." Pandy swung her slender frame in a full circle as if expecting one of the hermits to appear. She kept her hand on the weapon at her side.

"Is your rifle loaded?" Caity asked.

Spense, too, had been wondering what kind of firepower the ranger was carrying.

"Tranquilizer darts. Just in case we come across a critter we don't want to harm," Pandy answered.

Too bad she wasn't carrying live ammo. No telling what situation they might encounter, and Spense had been hoping he could pair Caity off with Pandy. They needed to divide and conquer to cover the most ground, and he didn't want to send either one of them off alone.

Ranger Pandy pulled her jacket aside, revealing a holstered pistol. "Here's the good stuff."

Spense released his breath, relieved to know Pandy was armed and ready after all. The tension in his shoulders eased up, too. Caity had her Glock, and he knew she knew how to use it, at least from short distances. The women could safely team up, leaving him free to focus his attention on the search. He wouldn't have to worry about Caity—*much*.

No matter how small the risk, fear for her safety inevitably coated moments like these with a razor's edge. It was one of the un-perks of his and Caity's on-the-job romance.

"Let's fan out," Pandy said. "Not much daylight left, but we can make a good start. Once the light runs out, we'll meet back at the cabin. I'll go east. Cassidy and Spenser, you go west."

He respected the ranger's authority, but that wasn't the best plan. "Caity will stick with you. We're on the buddy system."

Pandy tiptoed up to a good four-foot ten, at least. She got in his face, or as close as someone her height could manage. "She's *your* buddy. She goes with you."

"I can move faster alone."

"We can all move faster alone." Caity stepped between him and Pandy. "Let's forget the pairs. We can cover more ground that way."

"Absolutely not." It was Hatcher. "The women should team up. Don't want them out there alone."

Spense tried not to show it, but he was damn glad Hatcher had backed him up. It wasn't that the women were less able, it was just that if anyone out here had to travel without a safety buddy it was going to be him. He would've felt the same if it were a male ranger. Or if Caity were a man, which thank God in heaven she wasn't.

Pandy spat on the ground. "I get it. I'm small. I look like a little kid. But I'm not a child. I can handle myself in the mountains without an escort—and I've got the record to back it up. I *am* the escort around these parts."

"This isn't a standard lost hiker search, Pandy. There could be an armed madman—or madwoman out there," Spense said.

"I assure you, I know how to handle myself around predators of all varieties."

Caity stretched her hands to arm's length, bridging the distance between Pandy and him. "We're wasting time. I don't give a fig about your ego, Pandy." She shot him a look. "Or yours either, Spense. Pandy, I've got your back, and I'd appreciate it if you'd get mine."

Pandy nodded. "Deal."

Hatcher dusted his palms as though washing his hands of them, turned his back and went inside.

"Let's do this," Pandy called over her shoulder, already jogging east.

Chapter 16

Thursday, October 24
5:20 P.M.
Frank's Cabin
Eagles Nest Wilderness
Colorado

CAITLIN TOOK OFF behind Pandy, a few yards to the side to increase coverage, making sure to keep Pandy's bright orange hair in sight.

Despite the fact Caitlin hadn't had any formal search and rescue training, she'd been put in some pretty tough situations on the job—like playing hide-and-seek with killers while searching for a lost teen in a blazing corn maze. Plus, she'd always been an outdoor girl and thus could easily spot something amiss on a mountain trail.

Her confidence level was high.

She could've gone without a buddy, but if Spense felt better knowing she was paired with Pandy, she wasn't going to fight him.

Though she had her Glock, and could use it in a pinch, she wasn't a trained marksman, and she'd been in enough close scrapes to know her own limitations. More importantly, she wanted Spense to focus on finding Laura. If he was distracted by worry over her, she'd be a liability rather than an asset, and she was determined not to let that happen.

But mere moments later, she lost sight of Pandy.

She picked up her pace.

For someone with such short legs, that ranger could haul.

A flash of red hair appeared up ahead.

Good.

It wasn't easy to keep up with Pandy. Every breath Caitlin took was like a blast of frozen buckshot to her lungs.

Keep going.

Most of the snow that'd fallen overnight had melted in the afternoon sun. Only scattered patches remained. In places, she saw soft, moist dirt, but it quickly merged with scree and dense vegetative ground cover. Her gaze alternated between the horizon and the trail as her brain processed each broken branch, every snapped twig, looking for a pattern. A sign someone had come this way before her.

Still no footprints.

But under these conditions a herd of elephants could've tromped through and left no tracks. The sand traps were definitely needed. She tripped over some knee timber, breaking the fall with her hands, but hit her hip hard against a rock. Her palms burned where they scraped the ground. Her chest ached, and her lungs were frostbitten, but she couldn't stop to rest. Not without losing Pandy again.

Caitlin concentrated hard, dividing her thoughts between watching and wondering: watching for signs; wondering which way Laura would head if she was lost, or where she would hide if she didn't want to be found. If she was disoriented, she might be wandering in circles or doubling back randomly.

Caitlin lifted her knees higher to cover ground faster. Tried not to focus on the low odds a hasty search like this one would produce results. It wasn't until her teeth started to hurt, and her tongue went painfully dry that she realized her mouth was hanging open. She was panting like a winded pup.

The altitude!

Of course!

They were above 9,000 feet. Pandy might be little, but she hiked up here on a routine basis. She was acclimated to the thin air. No wonder she could move faster. Caitlin's gaze darted to all sides and her frustration mounted. She could no longer see the back of a red head bobbing in the distance. How far behind the ranger was she?

"Pandy!"

Only a bird called back.

"Pandy, I need you to slow down!"

Still no response. She tried to accelerate, and though her muscles answered the call, her heart and lungs simply couldn't.

She'd hit her max.

She needed oxygen.

She kept jogging anyway, but she knew she was flagging, falling farther and farther behind. The sun dipped below the mountains, and though there was still light, its red-gold hue made it hard to catch the detail she was after.

She flipped on her flashlight.

And froze.

There, in a dirty patch of snow, she saw two dents: prints from the heel and toe of a boot?

Her heart jumped to her throat.

"Pandy!" Her voice floated on the wind, bouncing off the boulders that seemed to rise up from nowhere. "Over here! I found something!"

Chapter 17

Thursday, October 24
5:45 P.M.
Eagles Nest Wilderness
Colorado

LAURA WOKE TO the sound of shouting. Her head jerked, and her ears rang from the crack of her skull hitting a rock. She raised her hand and felt her pulse throbbing in her temples.

She jumped up.

Quickly crouched back down.

Stay out of sight!

There it was again—a woman's voice. Urgent. Determined. Getting closer.

They're looking for you!

Laura bit her hand to keep from answering back. Her body drew tight as a slingshot ready to fire. Her heart and mind tugged in opposite directions until she thought she really might snap. Her heart told her to run straight into the arms of that shouting woman. Her heart *wanted* to be rescued. Her heart longed to be carried home to the safety of her parents and tucked lovingly into the comfort of her own bed.

But her mind screamed at her to get away. Home wasn't safe. It never had been.

She'd been kidnapped from her own bed once before, then returned to her family by rescuers, only to be made a prisoner in a house where she could never feel secure again.

And this time it would be worse.

Then she'd been presumed innocent: a young victim to be guarded and protected.

Now she'd be presumed guilty. It wouldn't be *her* safety the guards would concern themselves with. Not this time. Not with these locks of hair in her possession. Not with that note, if they'd found it.

And if she'd truly done what the letter claimed, she'd be locked away for the rest of her days.

Silent sobs choked her as sure as hands tightening around her throat. She opened her mouth and gasped in breath after breath until the spasms passed.

Lies! Nothing but lies!

But lies written in her own hand . . . and all-too-real locks of hair stuffed in her backpack.

Her memory entirely black since Monday night.

How could she defend herself against the falsehoods if she didn't have the truth on hand? If she went back now, she'd be thrown in prison, or even worse, locked away someplace for the criminally insane. Then she'd never be free of doctors who only made her worse and pills that made her crazy instead of sane.

She sneaked a glance between the boulders and saw no one.

There was still time to make a run for it. Looking down, she watched her hands working busily, loading her pack, smoothing the ground to remove any trace she'd ever been here. Apparently her brain had overridden her heart without even notifying her. And rightly so, she thought, as she stealthily made her way across the rocky terrain, moving farther and farther from the voice.

She put one foot in front of the other.

Slowly, staying very, very quiet.

She was getting away!

The heavy burden crushing her soul lightened.

Her heart raced with excitement, then slowed again.

Even if she did manage to evade the searchers today, the knee-buckling truth was she didn't know what she had or hadn't done.

She stuck her chin up.

She wouldn't be locked up and drugged, not again. *No one* deserved to have to live like that. If she'd truly done what the letter said, maybe she should reconsider and end it all. Spare her parents the humiliation of a trial, the pain of visiting her in prison or in a mental institution. She didn't want to watch them try to pretend she wasn't a monster as their world crumbled around them.

She fell to her knees and lifted her hands in supplication.

Please don't let it be true.

Then she heard a voice, but this one wasn't carried to her on the wind. This was a voice in her head. A voice made of memory instead of sound. Dr. Duncan's reassuring words, telling her she wasn't crazy: *Your confusion is a combination of post-traumatic stress, survivor's guilt, and too many tranquilizers. Let's give you a trial off medication, give your head a chance to clear. I want you to believe in yourself, to learn to trust your own eyes and ears. You haven't done anything wrong. I know you, Laura. You're a good person.*

Dr. Duncan was smart. And he believed in Laura. Even Dr. Webber said he didn't think she'd killed Angelina—though he invariably reminded her he couldn't be absolutely certain. Dr. Webber gave her the benefit of reasonable doubt. And she could cling to reasonable doubt in this circumstance. Her monster could've forced her to write that note when he brought her to the cabin and planted the locks of hair.

Reasonable doubt.

It wasn't much, but it would have to do for now.

Scanning the area around her, she realized she was still alone. She rose to her feet and brushed the dirt and ice from her knees. She would *not* take her own life—she'd promised Dr. Duncan, and more importantly, just hours ago, she'd promised herself. Whatever the truth was, sooner or later she was going to have to face it, because there was a monster in her life.

It was real, and it had to be stopped, no matter who or what it turned out to be.

Suddenly, from behind, she heard the sound of footfalls coming straight for her.

Both dread and hope shot through her.

Two emotions. One result: paralysis.

She had no idea what to do next. She felt better than before her nap, yes, but not like she could outrun an able-bodied person. Finally, blessed instinct kicked in, and she sank behind a rock. Hiding, holding her breath, waiting for the footsteps to catch up to her. She barely had time to find a good spyhole when a slender young woman appeared.

Panting.

Laura covered her mouth with her hand, trying to muffle the sound of her own heavy breathing. The woman with wild, dark tresses stood with her hands on her knees not more than a few feet away. Her face was red from exertion, and her blue eyes glowed with energy. Those eyes reminded Laura of Angelina, and of herself, before her own eyes had turned from ocean blue to the dull slate-gray of impending doom. She hadn't known that hopelessness could physically change a person, but it had indeed changed her.

Maybe because the woman resembled Angelina, Laura felt drawn to her by an undeniable, tangible, pull. It was as if the air up here had magnetized her. It took all Laura's will not to leap out from her hiding place and surrender.

Instead, she decided to follow her.

Chapter 18

Thursday, October 24
6:00 P.M.
Eagles Nest Wilderness
Colorado

WITH A BROAD motion, Caitlin swept the light back and forth in front of her, carefully following the trail of crushed vegetation that appeared beyond the boot print she'd found. Because the grasses had not yet rebounded, she guessed the trail was fresh. She was definitely onto something and needed to go slow. The time to hurry had passed.

A scrape coming from behind a large boulder made her stop short, and her ears prick, but then a squirrel scampered over the top of the rock. A shriek of wind, then all was quiet once more. Straightening, she turned full circle, straining her eyes to catch a glimpse of Pandy or Spense. But there was none. Hadn't either of them heard her calling out?

She clicked the button on her radio, but it didn't crackle to life. She turned it upside down and saw that the thin plastic battery cover had come loose, and the compartment was empty. The battery must've dropped out when she hit her hip on that rock, but it was too late now to go back and hunt for it. At the moment, she had more important quarry to track.

Worst-case scenario, that boot print belonged to Pandy, and Caitlin needed to find her anyway. It seemed every forward step consumed an eternity of time, as she swung her light to and fro. The crushed vegetation led toward a scree-covered slope, and she knew when the grasses ended so would her lead. Then her flashlight hit a spot of mud and more prints.

Her hand rose to her throat.

These prints were from a four-legged creature.

She touched her belt to reassure herself her pepper spray was still there and had not gone the way of her battery. Then she squatted down for a closer look.

M shaped.

Three pads.

Not a bear print—the bears would already be hibernating. This print was large . . . and catlike.

Her heart picked up speed.

A mountain lion.

But, if she was right, there was no need to panic. Mountain lions didn't usually trouble humans—at least not fully grown ones. They preferred to prey on smaller creatures, though she was certain if provoked, they would attack. She made a clucking sound with her tongue, and found a stick to tap the rocks to give plenty of warning. She didn't want to surprise a mamma lion and her cubs, and she had to hope that if Laura was out here, she'd welcome a rescue party.

The more noise Caitlin made, the better.

She reached the talus-covered slope, and sure enough the trail disappeared. With nothing but instinct to guide her, she decided to skirt the slope, rather than climb it. As she marched ahead, continuing to give as much warning as possible, she heard a melodic sound coming from the east.

She aimed her flashlight in that direction.

Its beam found a grove of dwarfed bristlecone pines. She headed toward them, her boots thudding loudly on the ground. And then she heard the soft noise again.

Her breath whooshed from her chest.

A human voice.

It wasn't the wind whistling through the trees as she'd imagined before.

"I'm here!" The feminine voice unscrambled itself into words as Caitlin drew nearer.

Pandy.

Or perhaps . . . "Laura!" Caitlin cupped her hands around her mouth. "Laura, help is on the way! Stay right where you are. I'm coming to you."

A thunder of branches answered back.

"Don't run! I'm here to help!" she yelled, tearing across the rough terrain toward the little grove of trees. From nowhere, a root jumped up and caught her ankle. She sprang forward, reached out to stop her fall, but it was too late. Her head thunked against the hard ground, narrowly missing a pointy rock. Her cheek pressed against the earth, and the earth rumbled beneath it.

A loud roar set her body vibrating, rattling her teeth.

A bone-chilling scream sounded, just as she lifted her chin and saw a blur of muscle covered in sleek, tawny fur flying through the air.

Oh dear God!

The dark cavernous jaws of the mountain lion gaped open. It sprang again, knocking the slight, redheaded figure to the ground. The sound of thundering branches had come from the charge of a wild beast, not from a woman running away.

"Pandy!" she cried out.

About a dozen yards from where Caitlin had fallen, the petite ranger now lay stretched out, unconscious, like a Raggedy Ann tossed away by a child.

As it circled the fallen ranger, the lion's roar changed to a low growl.

Caitlin's pulse boomed in her ears, and her breathing all but ceased.

Time slowed as she struggled to process the situation.

Child-sized Pandy was completely vulnerable, a choice target for the beast. But what had angered the mountain lion? The cougars weren't docile creatures by any means, but they didn't hunt humans. Something must've provoked it to attack.

Had Pandy surprised the animal?

A thousand thoughts flashed through her aching head.

If she jumped to her feet, she might startle the lion. It hadn't made contact with Pandy after knocking her down. It continued to circle her, ominously enough, but a sudden movement might spur it on to deadly action.

Still, she couldn't just lie there with Pandy in jeopardy. Her entire body went numb, as her thoughts continued to race. How did one handle a mountain lion? Not by fleeing. That much she knew for sure. It was either freeze, or make yourself big and bad to frighten it away.

Two completely opposite tactics, and she couldn't recall which one was supposed to work.

She had her pistol, but from this distance, the chance of infuriating the cougar was far greater than the chance of hitting it.

Her heartbeat counted down the seconds until she would be forced to make a decision, knowing the wrong one might cost both Pandy and her their lives.

Chapter 19

Thursday, October 24
6:00 P.M.
Eagles Nest Wilderness
Colorado

THE OPEN TERRAIN, save for a few scattered boulders and dwarfed pines, made it difficult to follow the dark-haired woman undetected, but Laura did her best. Luckily, the woman moved with great care, so it was easier to keep up. Each step she took seemed to be in slow motion, and she kept her gaze ahead, rarely looking back at ground already covered. Twice, Laura was able to read the woman's body language and anticipate her turning in time to conceal herself.

What she didn't anticipate was the other voice, then the dark-haired woman bolting for a grove of pines...the scream.

Laura willed her legs to spring into action, but they responded with a whimper. She limped to the trees and found a hiding place where she could get a decent view. In the clearing, a cougar circled a young girl who lay prone on the ground.

Laura's breath caught in her throat.

Curling her hands into makeshift binoculars, she brought them to her eyes. The narrowed visual fields allowed her to focus on the downed figure.

Not a child at all.

This was a small redheaded woman, helpless against the stalking beast.

Do something, Laura!

She didn't want to die, but better her than an innocent. If it were the only way, she'd walk straight over and punch the lion in the gut. She'd never be able to take the animal down, but if it turned on her, that just might give the woman on the ground time to escape.

Laura was willing to do whatever it took to give her a chance.

As a child, her mother taught Laura to pray.

If ever there was a time to consider her soul, it was now.

She closed her eyes.

One tear slid down her cheek, followed by another.

Prepare to die.

She pictured herself leaping onto the lion, rolling around on the ground.

Ready.

Set.

And then . . . her heart stopped as suddenly as a bird that had soared blindly into the sheer rock walls of a mountain.

She opened her eyes.

The monster was far more dangerous than any mountain lion.

If Laura died before she had a chance to expose it, the monster would go on living, and that meant more victims—more young women would die.

Yes. She had to save the woman from the cougar, but she owed it to the other victims to stay alive.

As she filled her lungs with untainted mountain air, her resolve grew steely.

She made a decision: She had to find some way to distract the lion that would give the woman time to escape, and Laura the best chance to stay alive. In her weakened condition, if she attacked the lion directly, it would mean certain death.

Her eyes darted in all directions and eventually landed on the scree-covered ground.

Her thoughts sharpened, and her heart quickened.

If she hurled one of those small rocks to the opposite edge of the clearing, it should startle the lion, and hopefully it would turn away, stalk toward the new threat—away from both Laura and the woman on the ground. If the woman was conscious, she'd have a good chance of escaping on her own, but if she wasn't, Laura would enter the clearing and drag her to safety.

All she needed was a little bit of luck, and her plan would work.

Only trouble was Laura had never been lucky.

CAITLIN CONSIDERED HER plan of careful observation and masterful inactivity a success—thus far. Her lungs were working so hard she might as well have been doing push-ups instead of lying quietly on the ground, but the lion seemed to be calming down. Its growling had grown softer. Now and then, it paused to look at something other than Pandy.

Ten more seconds passed.

Pandy remained untouched by the beast, and Caitlin remained

unnoticed at the periphery of the grove. Any minute now, the wind might shift and carry her scent to the lion, but just as likely, it would grow tired of its game, decide Pandy was no threat, turn and stalk away.

Caitlin focused on melding her mind with the lion's.

Walk away, Mamma.

The lion halted midstride, lifting one paw.

That's it, girl. Go home to your babies. No one here wants to hurt you.

Bam!

A rock landed near the lion's head, sending a landslide of scree raining down.

The lion let out a great roar, shaking debris off its fur like a wet kitten—only this was no kitten. It crouched, eyes locked on its target—Pandy.

Caitlin's do-nothing strategy went up in smoke.

She catapulted to her feet, threw her arms above her head, and made herself as big as possible. Using all the energy left in her lungs, she pushed out a mighty roar.

The lion pivoted.

Their eyes locked.

Her heart beat not at all, and then much too fast.

"Run, Pandy! Run!" she screamed.

The lion crouched, ready to vault at Caitlin.

No time to run.

Every muscle in her body contracted in anticipation as the beast became a blur of color and motion.

Boom!

The lion's paws hit her square in the chest.

All the air rushed from her lungs, and her feet dropped out

from under her. Her body, now on autopilot, squeezed into a protective ball. One hand tightened into a fist. She drew it back, then landed a blow to the lion's skull. The impact reverberated down her arm like the kick of a gun. Blood dripped into her eyes, obstructing her vision. Her heart revved in her chest, fueling her muscles with oxygen.

Then all thought fled, as she fought for her next breath with every ounce of her being.

THE WIND CARRIED a faint cry to Spense.

Caity's voice.

No other sound got his attention that fast. Not a siren, not a gunshot, not anything. In a split second, his world tunneled down to her. Other beats and tones existed, but held little importance. The noise of his feet pounding against the ground as he ran full tilt mattered only because it told him how fast he could get to her.

It was as though his mind had tuned itself to a radio station that only played one song.

His vision, too, recalibrated. The soft evening sky became a vibrant crimson. Ground cover greener, snow patches a blinding white. Objects swept past like a landscape viewed from a speeding train. He couldn't feel his legs moving, but saw that his position on the earth was changing.

He had no idea how long it took him to reach the grove of trees, but when he did, he saw everything unfolding in front of him at once. Images viewed on a split screen.

Pandy up on her knees, first rocking on them, then crawling toward him.

Caity!

She was a blur of motion. Wrestling a tan, powerful beast.

Mountain lion.

Caity's name exploded from his lips.

Then he detached completely.

He went to that place where muscle memory took over—the result of his special training. He played the scenario the same way a pianist plays a concerto; fluidly, automatically—without fear.

His hand found his Glock.

Too dangerous.

Caity rolled with the lion, her legs wrapping his body, her hands lifting to block her face.

He followed Pandy's gaze to a thick tangle of ground cover. Something long and brown stood out among the twisted vines.

His blood surged.

Hurdling knee timber and rocks, he reached the rifle.

Ripped it from the grip of tangled vines, hefted it to his shoulder.

The weight was lighter than expected, a confirmation the gun was loaded with tranquilizer darts, not live ammo.

On a long steady breath, he sighted the lion, waited for his shot . . .

Took it.

The gun kicked against his shoulder.

The lion let out an angry yowl. With its paws it hugged Caity's body to its own.

Caity's arms pushed up.

Somehow, she got air beneath her shoulders.

Now!

Spense took aim, and fired again.

The lion made a mewling sound.

Caity's boot landed in its paunch. Spense ran toward them, preparing to leap atop. But before he reached the pair, Caity knocked the lion away and rolled out from under it.

The lion staggered back, eased onto its side, and passed out cold.

Spense lifted Caity into his arms and carried her to the edge of the clearing.

Two things he need to know right now.

First, was Caity okay?

The tight grip of her arms around his neck, her words of love whispered in between the soft kisses she planted on his cheek told him she wasn't seriously hurt.

Second, what had gotten into that mountain lion?

An attack like this was highly unusual.

Pandy was too smart to have provoked it. And as far as he could see there were no cubs around. Which left the sixty-four-thousand-dollar question.

What in the hell was this animal trying to protect?

Chapter 20

LAURA'S LUCK WAS holding—as usual it was no good. Because she was normally in great shape, she'd overestimated how far she could hurl that rock. But due to her weakened condition, it had landed shy of its mark, putting everyone in more danger.

She crept closer to get a better look and listen. In a flush of relief, blood rushed to her head. The little one had her radio to her ear. The dark-haired woman was on her feet, mouthing words Laura couldn't quite make out to the tall man who'd fired the rifle. Even the lion seemed to be okay, lolling on its side, its belly rising and falling with big steady breaths.

They were all alive.

Maybe she wasn't so unlucky after all.

And maybe life wasn't only about luck. Maybe it was about

choices, too. Laura wasn't in the habit of choosing. In her world, her parents and her doctors had always decided for her. Like Dr. Duncan said, she just needed a bit of practice.

Her plan hadn't turned out the way she'd expected, but one bad decision wasn't a reason to go back to letting someone else make them for her. And there was something else that was beginning to dawn like the sun, slowly inching up over the mountaintops. She'd been willing to risk her life for a complete stranger.

She held her head higher. Noticing her cheeks were wet, she batted away the moisture. Too bad she hadn't come across a mountain lion thirteen years ago, because in a single beat, her own heart was revealed to her.

Laura Chaucer, *who did not want to die*, had been willing to give her life for another—and in truth, she still was.

Locks of hair and notes in her own hand meant nothing compared to that.

It was a truth more solid than any she'd ever known.

The decisions she'd made, just moments ago, were not those of a monster.

She didn't have the heart of a killer.

Her hands began to tingle with excitement.

Dr. Duncan had been right all along—she wished she could tell him.

She wanted to shout it for the entire world to hear.

There would be no more self-doubt—not about this.

Her theories about the monster might be wrong. She might even be as crazy as her parents believed she was, but she wasn't capable of true evil. She could never have killed anyone and she made a silent vow, right then that she would never let anyone make her question *that.*

The voices carried to her on the wind again—they sounded high-pitched, urgent.

She shook her hands out and concentrated on what was taking place just a short distance away. Leaning forward, she strained to hear the conversation over the static of the radio, but couldn't make out what the little group in the clearing was talking about.

Time to make her next decision.

She needed to know what was going on, and it was worth the risk of being found out to get closer.

Be patient.

An opportunity came quicker than she'd expected. The lion made a noise, and all three turned to check on it. Laura darted forward, then concealed herself behind a clump of trees and held her breath, listening.

"I promise I'm okay, Spense, you should check on Ranger Pandy."

The redhead, whom Laura now knew to be a park ranger named Pandy, waved off the man called Spense. "No need. Barely got a scratch on me. Knocked the wind out of me, but after, I was just playing possum, waiting for it to get tired of circling me." Pandy went to the lion and stroked its coat.

Unlike Laura, the ranger was fearless. Laura's heartbeat accelerated at the realization she might soon be left alone with the lion.

"I've got more rangers on the way. We're going to need to watch the cougar for a few days, make sure it has no ill-effects from the tranquilizers and . . ." Pandy arched an eyebrow at the dark-haired woman, ". . . for Caitlin's sake. If it shows no sign of rabies after seventy-two hours, Caitlin won't need shots."

Spense nodded and held up Caitlin's arm. "But she does need stitches."

"I've got a medical kit in my pack," Caitlin said. "Can you do the honors if I talk you through it?"

"I'm on it." Spense shed his jacket and rolled up his sleeves.

Caitlin took a seat on the ground, her legs stretched out in front while Spense dug through one of the packs. Laura's stomach tended toward the squeamish side, but she couldn't bring herself to look away as Spense cleaned and stitched Caitlin's wounds. Laura's throat tightened when he rested his hand on Caitlin's, and at the tender way she looked at him when he wasn't watching. From the extra glances and smiles they shared it seemed they cared about each other a lot—maybe they were even in love.

A sigh rose to her lips, but she didn't let it escape for fear of being heard. Love was something she'd had little experience with. She hadn't been allowed to date, and she'd never had a boyfriend. But up until now, she'd never really minded. While other girls her age were dreaming of boys, she was busy just trying to make it through another day—really living was something she'd never even considered.

Spense touched Caitlin's cheek, and for the millionth time, she smiled up at him.

These were good people.

Laura wanted to trust them. She understood they were searching for her, and it was hard not to shout out, "Here I am!"

Maybe Spense would tend her wounds like he'd tended Caitlin's.

Right. Just before he cuffed her and led her away in shame.

Spense pulled his jacket on, then climbed to a stand. "I don't get it." He was speaking to Ranger Pandy. "These guys don't usually go after humans. I know they attack children on occasion."

"Guess I really do look like a kid," Pandy said without a trace of defensiveness. "But yeah, I don't understand what made her go wild like that."

"She's a female?" Caitlin asked.

Pandy nodded. "Looks like it."

"Maybe she was protecting her cubs." Caitlin frowned. "But I haven't seen any trace of them . . ." Her voice trailed off. She twisted her hands, as if worried. "You don't think she might've been protecting . . ."

"A kill." Spense shouldered his pack. "Pandy, you okay to stay here with her?"

The ranger nodded.

"I'm coming with you, this time," Caitlin said.

"No argument here. Which way did she come from, Pandy?"

The ranger pointed, and Spense and Caity took off in that direction. Laura's heart dropped to her stomach. They were headed toward *her*. Crouching, she squeezed her eyes shut. If she opened them, she might be tempted to surrender as they passed by.

Laura waited until she could no longer hear their voices, then eased out from behind the trees. Spense's boots had left muddy tracks over the rocks, easy enough to follow, and by the time the trail disappeared, she'd caught sight of them up ahead.

"Spense!" Caitlin cried out.

Laura hurried forward, barely bothering to conceal herself.

"I'll radio for help." He spread his feet wide and pulled a flag from inside his pack. Planted it in the ground.

Laura crept closer. The leaves rustling beneath her feet sounded so loud to her ears it seemed she had a microphone in her boots. But neither Caitlin nor Spense turned. When she got within about ten yards of them, she saw some brush that would provide cover.

She dared go no further.

Spense had his phone out, snapping photos of something near the flag on the ground.

Quietly, Laura positioned herself for a better view. Beneath a pile of leaves and loose debris she saw an arm.

Then a bare leg.

Her hands started to shake.

She blinked hard in disbelief, staring at the leaves until a hank of long black hair came into focus.

No!

Her back arched in a sudden spasm. After the first shock wave passed, she threw her body forward, clasping her hands behind her head, and pulling her face down to her knees to muffle her sobs. She couldn't bear to open her eyes, couldn't bear to see the terrible truth.

She gagged, and then wretched up the remnants of her freeze-dried meal.

The gore would've made anyone ill, but that wasn't the only thing that sickened her.

All that blood at the cabin—it couldn't have been Laura's. And now she knew the thing she'd feared but hadn't wanted to believe was really true. *This* was the woman whose blood soaked the floors.

And Laura knew exactly who she was.

Her *friend*.

Chapter 21

Thursday, October 24
6:40 P.M.
Eagles Nest Wilderness
Colorado

LAURA WAS ALIVE for a reason, and that reason was to stop the monster. When she'd seen her friend's body, tossed out into the elements like a piece of meat for the animals, her will had hardened into steel.

Not one more innocent woman would die because Laura failed to act.

This evil had been on the prowl, claiming victims, for years, and no one else had even noticed, much less investigated. Not her family, not her doctors, not law enforcement.

And it wasn't as though she'd kept quiet about it.

Several times, over the years, she'd mentioned the idea to Dr. Webber. But he hadn't taken her seriously at all. His response was always the same: *get some rest, take another pill*—in other words, *you're crazy.*

A refrain she'd heard her entire life.

Well, that was one tune she had to get out of her head, because if she kept on listening to it *he'd* be free to go on killing.

No more.

On Monday night, she'd shared the idea that there were other victims—besides Angelina—with Ronald Saas, the newspaperman. But she hadn't any real proof, or any names, or any dates. He hadn't been convinced. He'd said there was no evidence.

Now, she had not just one, but *two* locks of hair in her possession. And she had an idea about how to get more evidence, too.

She tightened her fists.

She had to stop the monster.

But the first step in completing her mission was getting down off this mountain without getting caught. She had to get back to civilization where she could think and make plans and hunt her prey. The idea of stalking the man who'd killed her friend sent a thrill up her spine, and that gave her pause. It didn't seem normal to enjoy the idea as much as she did.

Shake it off. You're not crazy.

The bad news was it was all too easy to go back to that old refrain—she'd have to be vigilant to stop her mind from slipping back into old habits. The good news was that finding the way down would now be simple. She had the others to guide her. They would lead her straight to the road. All she had to do was stay out of sight and hide in the lengthening shadows as darkness fell over the mountain.

The prospect of hiking down the road in the dark was daunting, but she was prepared to do it. She knew how to move noiselessly—she'd been doing it all day. The other lucky thing was they no longer appeared to be searching for her. The cops probably assumed it was her lying dead on the ground. In the flurry of activity that followed the discovery of the body, Laura herself seemed to have been forgotten.

She managed to track a man in uniform past the cabin, all the way back to the road and his truck, before she thought herself at risk of being found out. There was little cover for her here—but by now it was full-on dark. His pickup was her chance to get out the easy way, and she was determined to take it before law enforcement swarmed the area.

The truck bed was covered by a rain tarp. When the man turned his back, she lifted the tarp at the corner and crawled beneath it. As she settled herself amongst the buckets and shovels and bags of sand, the truck's engine roared to life.

Her heart revved along with the engine.

She was going to make it down off this mountain alive.

What she had to do now was get back to Denver, then catch the monster before he struck again.

Chapter 22

Friday, October 25
7:00 A.M.
Medical examiner's office
Denver, Colorado

EVEN BEFORE SPENSE opened the door to the autopsy suite, the anticipation of the smell sickened Caitlin. It wasn't the mingled scents of blood and guts and vinyl body bags she dreaded. It was that *je ne sais quoi*, that intangible sense of one's own mortality that hung in the air, the *plus one* that accompanied death to every party. But without places like this, justice might never be done. And justice was what she craved. It was one of the main reasons she got up in the morning.

Until she'd met Spense, it had been the only reason.

Bracing her shoulders, she swept through the door beside Spense and Hatcher, as though the men were escorting her to a Broadway play instead of the macabre theater that awaited inside.

"Dammit, we're early." Hatcher pointed at Dr. Hadley Gaines.

The skeletal medical examiner hunched over the head of a cold steel table, his white lab coat flapping around the knees of his scrubs. Air from the vent above blew what remained of his thin black hair off his forehead. His brow wrinkled in concentration as he used a syringe to extract vitreous fluid from one of the victim's eyeballs. He then handed the sample off to an assistant and straightened, bumping his head on a hanging meat scale in the process. "Early bird gets his killer."

"Pardon me if I don't want to stand around and watch you pop the top off this thing and weigh its brains. I just wanna know—is it her or not?"

Hatcher's question raised Caitlin's hackles, perhaps, a bit unfairly, because in truth a corpse was no longer a person, so the term *it* technically applied. But this body the detective referred to so carelessly had belonged, only a short time ago, to a living breathing young woman. Though the dehumanization of the dead made it easier for some to do their jobs, witnessing that dehumanization never failed to make her heart shrink in her chest.

"Then come back later," Gaines said indifferently. "Go have yourself a donut or something."

"We might as well stay." Caitlin certainly had no appetite for breakfast or even coffee, and they just might glean something extra if they hung around.

"I'm in," Spense said.

Hatcher grimaced. "Fine."

"Suit yourselves." Gaines began the Y incision, preparing to break into the body cavity. Only this thief would be stealing the victim's organs, and more importantly, her secrets. Without further prompting, he began narrating his crime.

One thing Caitlin had learned: medical examiners loved to spin a good story.

"Unfortunately, the elements and the scavengers got to her before we did. As you can see, the face is unrecognizable. From the extent of body decomp, I'd estimate she's been out there somewhere between three and seven days."

"That as close as you can say?" Hatcher sounded irritated.

"For now, yes."

That meant it might be Laura's body . . . or not. She'd barely been missing three days.

"In the good news department, we've got Chaucer's dental records coming, and I can tell you the age of our Jane Doe is late teens to very early twenties. Preliminary inspection of the pelvis suggests she's nulliparous."

"Nulli what?" Hatcher asked.

"This young woman has never borne children." Gaines picked up the shears and went to work opening the rib cage, then began slapping organs one by one onto the meat scale while the assistant wrote their weights on a dry erase board. "The examination of the skin revealed lividity in the back, suggesting the victim died in a supine position."

"We found her lying prone," Spense said. "You think the body was moved?"

"Yes, but who knows if it was man or beast who flipped her over."

"What about sexual assault—did you find evidence of that?" Hatcher asked.

"Hard to say for sure. Again, the animals did a number on her. Most of her inner thighs have been chewed off. The vaginal area is smooth, suggesting sexual activity, but in a woman her age that's to be expected. The hands and fingernails show no obvious defensive wounds. We've scraped the nails of course."

"She might've been drugged," Spense said. "That would account for the lack of defensive wounds."

"Like everything else, toxicology is pending."

"You've included GHB, I hope." Caitlin didn't necessarily enjoy telling the man how to do his job, but the test had to be ordered specifically, it wasn't routine.

"That and other date rape drugs." Gaines dropped his shears and rolled the now empty body cavity onto one side, revealing a small purple dolphin on the left hip. "Did Laura Chaucer have any tattoos?"

"Not according to her family." Hatcher who'd been backed against the wall moved in for a closer look at the ink.

"Maybe the folks aren't aware," Gaines continued.

"Laura's parents controlled her tightly, so it's possible she hid it from them." Caitlin made a mental note to check with the bodyguard. "Maybe Cayman's seen something they haven't. Or maybe she confided in her psychiatrist."

"Multiple stab wounds make this an obvious homicide." Gaines swept a gloved hand above the length of the body. "But they weren't the cause of death."

"Then what was?" Hatcher asked.

"Impatient, aren't we? But to answer to your question, I checked for retinal hemorrhages before you arrived. Cause of death appears to be asphyxiation."

"So she was strangled."

"There are many ways death by asphyxiation can occur. For all that tells us she could've been gassed in a garage with carbon monoxide."

"But you don't believe that." Hatcher paced from top to bottom of the room with his hands crossed behind his back.

"No. But I need more than just belief. I need evidence." Gaines sighed. "And here we have it." He motioned them over to observe as he delicately dissected the neck, revealing a broken piece of bone—the hyoid. "Without question, the young woman on my table was strangled to death."

Chapter 23

"Jordo . . ." Cliff poked his head into the interview room. "What do you want me to do about the reporters?"

The press conference.

Spense had forgotten all about it, and apparently so had Hatcher.

"What time did we say?"

"Ten."

Hatcher checked his watch. "Ain't happening. Call 'em up and tell them it's a slow news day, sorry for the false alarm."

"Sir." Cliff cleared his throat. "They've been harassing Rhonda already. If I don't hand out some inside information, they'll probably make up some tall tale about you cheating on Louise."

"Louise knows no one else will have me."

"That may be," Spense said. "But Cliff's got a point. We've got to give them something to hold them at bay or no telling how creative they'll get. We need to control the media on this one. Use it to our advantage."

"Let's see, then. We'll just say the senator is missing a daughter—again—and she might or might not be the corpse laid out in the morgue. Considering her parents don't yet know what we found up in the Eagles Nest Wilderness, seems like poor form to me."

"What have they been told?" If it'd been up to Caity, Spense knew she'd have personally called on the family hours ago.

"That we have news. That we need them here ASAP. They're staying at Laura's apartment in case she returns. I offered to go out last night, but Mrs. Chaucer was sleeping, and it was the senator who set the meeting time of 8:00 A.M. With this amount of destruction to the body, we don't expect the family to be able to make an ID. I didn't see a reason to push the meeting earlier since we don't know for sure the young woman we found is Laura."

Spense checked his watch. "Past eight now."

"Guess they're late."

"For an update on their missing daughter?" Spense didn't like it. "They should be beating down the door to find out what's going on."

"I think *Mrs. Chaucer is sleeping* is code for drunk out of her gourd," Hatcher said. "I think the senator's trying to save her face."

"Let's hope the Chaucers get here soon," Caity said. "There were too many people up on that mountain to keep this under wraps for long. By tomorrow, someone will have leaked the story. What if instead of telling the press to come back tomorrow, we reschedule for later this afternoon. That'll give Spense and me time to at least start on a profile, time to get the parents in, and hopefully time for Gaines to make a positive ID."

"I like the way she thinks," Cliff said.

"I don't see a downside to that. Tell the vultures we'll meet up with them this afternoon—at a time to be determined later."

"I don't know if that's going to hold them, Jordo."

"Best I can do."

Cliff backed out of the room, looking only moderately appeased.

"While we're waiting, we might as well talk about the original kidnap. If our Jane Doe turns out to be Laura, and even if she doesn't, there's little doubt it figures into our current case. The body was found near Frank's Cabin, same MO. And close to the anniversary of the first kidnapping. Officially, that case is cold. But what about unofficially?" Spense asked.

"Unofficially that case is still cold."

Caity leaned forward, resting her elbows on the table. "Sure, but you must have a theory about what really happened. There must be persons of interests not yet ruled out."

Hatcher stood up and went to the door, checked to see if the Chaucers might be within earshot. Apparently, they weren't. Hatcher clicked the lock. "Just want to be sure we don't get a surprise interruption." He sat down and put his hands behind his head. "There are about as many theories as I've got fingers and toes, but the three main ones are as follows: The Vendetta. The Opportunist. The Greedy Bastard."

"You named the theories?" Caity asked.

"Makes it more fun," he said.

In this, Spense felt a certain kinship to Hatcher. Solving

puzzles was fun, and it helped to make the job bearable. Solve a puzzle. Save a life. Not a bad gig. "Three theories will likely lead to three profiles. Maybe we should pick one. We're going to have to make some assumptions or we'll never get anywhere. As long as we remember the profile has to come second to the evidence—"

"Don't worry." Hatcher swigged from a bottled water. "I'll have no trouble reminding you that whatever you come up with is full of crap until proven otherwise."

"Let's start with The Vendetta." Caity went to the whiteboard. She liked playing scribe, and Spense liked watching her. This morning she looked particularly curvy in the skinny jeans and red sweater she'd thrown on. He was secretly glad she hadn't had time to unpack and press her work clothes.

"That's the theory most favored by Senator Chaucer, himself. He's absolutely convinced that whoever kidnapped Laura . . ."

"And murdered Angelina," Caity put in.

"Goes without saying." Hatcher shrugged.

"Let's say it anyway, since *two* young women are now dead and whether or not Angelina was an accomplice has yet to be proven. She could've been collateral damage, and even if she was in on the scheme, she didn't deserve the death penalty."

"This public service announcement has been brought to you by bleeding heart liberals everywhere." Hatcher waved his hand in the air. "Now can we return to our regular programming?"

"Of course." Caity laid a calming hand on Spense's shoulder before he came out of his chair. It was one thing for *him* to call her a bleeding-heart liberal . . . "Just looking for truth in broadcasting," she told Hatcher without rancor.

"The Vendetta theory proposes that someone with a grudge against Whit Chaucer or against Mrs. Chaucer . . ." Hatcher paused, giving Caity time to write as he talked. "Kidnapped Laura as an act of retribution, seeking revenge on the family."

"Interesting that the senator favors that theory," Caity said.

"How so?"

"Because it makes it his fault. In a way, he's taking blame for what happened to his daughter. It also gives him the comfort of a cause and effect metaphor."

"What the hell's she talking about?" Hatcher asked Spense.

Spense said nothing, allowing Caity to speak for herself.

"I'm talking about the fact that the idea of a random universe scares people. Most of us want to believe that our actions control our fate, even though sometimes that's not the case. It may be comforting for the senator to believe something he did caused his daughter to be kidnapped. If his behavior led to Laura's kidnapping and Angelina's murder, it's a good thing in a way, because his behavior is something he can modify."

"But he can't change the past."

"No, but it gives him the power to control his future."

"I guess."

"It's also a reflection of narcissism. The world revolves around him. Laura was taken because of him. It's not about her—it's about *him*."

"A narcissistic politician. Go figure," Spense said. "But do our theorists think it was a personal vendetta or something related to the business realm? A personal vendetta suggests our UNSUB would be someone with close ties to the family. A friend, a relative, or someone on their staff such as a housekeeper."

"Seems like I remember Mrs. Chaucer telling a reporter she suspected a cook." Caity looked to Hatcher for confirmation.

"Yes, the cook had prepared two separate meals for the

Chaucers—fish sticks for Laura and chicken for her parents. Whit is allergic to fish, and apparently the chicken was prepared on the same cutting board. Following dinner he wound up in the emergency room. Cook had recently asked for a raise and been turned down. Tracy Chaucer was convinced the fish sticks incident was deliberate. She fired the cook the next morning. Cook had a key to the house and was quite familiar with the family's comings and goings. She had motive, means, and opportunity."

"And a violent streak?" Spense asked.

"Not that we know of. No criminal record. Cooperated fully with the inquiry. Nobody but Mrs. Chaucer liked her for it—crime was too vicious for a nice middle-age lady with no history of nothing."

"Except nearly killing Whit Chaucer," Caity said.

"Accident. Besides, her sister alibied her for the night of the kidnapping. If she had done it, and she had the ransom money, why stick around Denver and keep working as the hired help? But she's still in the area if you want to talk to her."

They wrote the cook's information down, but in Spense's mind she was low on the suspect list. "Okay, who else? Close friend? What about the Chaucers' inner circle?"

"You want me to alibi every socialite in Denver?"

"I'm talking about really close friends," Spense said. "What about Grady Webber?"

"Him, we talked to. He also had a key to the home, sometimes checked on things for the family while they were out of town—unless he was tagging along. He got along swimmingly with the entire family. Not so much as a ripple over a bad round of golf between Whit and him. And Tracy Chaucer is Webber's biggest fan. A bachelor at the time, Dr. Webber claimed to be home sleeping that night—alone. So he had means and opportunity but zilch for motive."

"What about on the business side?"

"Now there's a long list, and that's where Chaucer puts his money. Lots of people don't like you when you're rich and powerful—at least that's what the senator tells me, because how else would a guy like me know? And some of his company policies were thought to be unfriendly to the environment."

Caity frowned. "That would encompass a lot of people. Anyone overlooked for a promotion. Anyone in the Sierra Club."

"And he had financial dealings abroad, too. Based on the business enemy theory, we were buried in suspects. We combed through long lists of names, but couldn't connect anyone to the kidnapping. And that was still better than where the Greedy Bastard theory took us.

"In that scenario, someone without a personal vendetta, who was simply looking for financial gain, targeted the Chaucers for money. It's a reasonable supposition, but without the personal connection, we didn't know where to start. It could've been absolutely anyone who'd read about Whit Chaucer in the papers, and he'd been written up a lot in the months preceding the kidnapping."

"Not absolutely anyone," Spense offered. "There are plenty of Greedy Bastards around, but someone looking to cash out by targeting a wealthy businessman would have to be a thrill seeker, someone unafraid of risks and consequences. We're talking about a con man, or woman, with personal access to the family. Might be an overlap between the Greedy Bastard category and the Vendetta category—that could narrow it down."

"Maybe. Where were you thirteen years ago?"

"We're here now."

"Let's not forget The Opportunist," Caity said. "I'm guessing you're thinking a vagrant or criminal. Someone who did yard work, or passed by the area and just what, happened to see a window open or an unlocked door, crawled through and grabbed Laura and Angelina?"

"Bingo. But it's my least favored theory. We chased down a few sex offenders in the area and some parolees but came up empty."

Caity nodded. "I agree. If Angelina was involved, that wouldn't fly either. Hard to believe some homeless guy colluded with her to kidnap Laura. So that leaves us . . ."

"Thirteen years later with no viable suspects, and Laura gone missing again—only this time, it looks like she might not be coming home alive."

Chapter 24

Friday, October 25
8:00 A.M.
Holly Hill College
Denver, Colorado

LAURA'S LUCK WAS finally starting to change. The pickup she'd stowed away in last night had carried her all the way to Denver and parked in a lot just yards from a budget motel. The desk clerk hadn't looked at her twice or asked for identification when she'd signed in as Ruby Rogers, paying cash for the room. Tonight, she'd move to a youth hostel. Even forty bucks was too steep a price to pay when she had to make five hundred dollars stretch indefinitely. But she wasn't going to dwell on the negative.

She'd been given another chance at life, and as horrible as her mission might be, having one gave her a sense of purpose. She was bruised and sore and tired, but she didn't recall ever awakening to a sweeter morning.

At a dive near the motel, she'd splurged on waffles and sausage and coffee. No one bothered her, or looked at her funny. A greasy paper lay on the counter, and she'd checked it and found nothing about her disappearance or about the dead body in the wilderness. She didn't know if she had hours or days until it all hit the front page, but for now, it seemed she was free to come and go without attracting notice—as long as she was careful. As an extra precaution she'd bought a blond wig. Though she wasn't wearing it now, she was quite looking forward to seeing a whole new Laura staring back at her in the mirror.

She climbed out of the cab, pulled the collar of her jacket over her neck and zipped it all the way to cover the marks on her throat. Then she tied her hoodie under her chin and ducked her head before entering the student union at Holly Hill College. A directory on the wall told her the college newspaper office was in room 101, just down the hall. Ronald Saas was the student advisor, and she knew he kept office hours on Friday mornings.

She didn't know for sure that she could trust him, but he'd been polite when she'd met with him for dinner on Monday. He hadn't told her she was crazy, only that he found her theories *unlikely*. She'd been surprised by the way he'd reacted. He didn't seem disturbed by anything she'd said—but then again, he was a professional. He'd neither encouraged her, nor discouraged her. In fact he'd said very little other than that she didn't have any real evidence. But that was exactly what she *might* have in her backpack. She could only hope it would be enough.

She couldn't risk going to the cops or to her parents, who very likely would lock her up in either a jail or a hospital respectively. At least Saas couldn't slap her in cuffs right then and there, even if he did rat her out to the authorities later. She'd talk to the man first, feel him out, and then decide whether or not to entrust him with the locks of hair. The one thing she definitely could not do was destroy the evidence that might put a killer behind bars for good.

She took a deep breath, opened the glass doors to the college newspaper office and approached the receptionist. "Ruby Rogers for Ronald Saas."

The receptionist typed something into a computer then shook her head. "I don't see you on this morning's calendar."

"I have an eight o'clock with Mr. Saas. I'm doing a piece on the backcountry ski club."

"Sorry, but I don't have anyone down for eight o'clock. I've got a nine o'clock as his first appointment."

"Oh, that's mine. Guess I got the time wrong," Laura tried. "It's under my buddy's name. We're sharing a byline."

The woman arched an eyebrow. "Not unless your buddy's the dean of behavioral sciences."

Laura dug her heels into the carpet. "Okay, look, I don't have an appointment. But since he's free until nine, maybe you could give me a break. It's urgent that I see Mr. Saas."

"You should've been honest in the first place." The receptionist tapped her pen on her teeth, contemplating, then let out a long breath. "What was your name, again? And no more shenanigans if you want me to get you in."

To stop herself from running around the desk and hugging the receptionist, Laura stuck her hands behind her back. "If you'll just tell him his Monday night dinner companion is here, I'm certain he'll see me."

"Take a seat, and I'll see what I can do."

How she'd won the receptionist over, she had no idea. Maybe she noticed the dark circles under Laura's eyes and felt sorry for her. Or maybe, unlike some other people Laura knew, the receptionist wasn't on a power trip and didn't mind helping another person out, even if she wasn't going to get a darn thing out of it for herself.

Laura tried to sit quietly, but couldn't manage it. She flipped one page of a *People Magazine* then climbed to her feet, twisting her hands as she watched the blinds in the office labeled *Ronald Saas, Community Advisor* slowly inch up. When they reached the halfway point, the receptionist gave her the thumbs-up.

A man stood with his back to the window.

He turned.

The blinds raised higher.

Through the glass their eyes locked.

His were brown.

He was short . . . and balding.

She stared at him, uncomprehending. Pressing her hand to her throat, she tried in vain to swallow. The man she dined with on Monday night had blue eyes and a full head of curly blond hair. Adrenaline flooded her system, sending her into a near panic. But panic was a luxury that only the weak would indulge. And she wasn't weak.

Not anymore.

She slammed her fist into her chest, as if to restart a useless heart, then turned and bolted for the door.

Chapter 25

"LET'S MOVE TO the war room." Caitlin touched Spense's shoulder. It was time to get started on that profile and most of what they needed was there: autopsy reports, case photographs, witness interviews, and more. The amount of paperwork associated with Laura's cold case made Caitlin's head spin. It seemed if you stacked the boxes, they'd fill a skyscraper. Sorting out the relevant facts was overwhelming—a bit too overwhelming, to her way of thinking.

Hatcher checked his phone. "Meet you guys later. The commander's on the horn."

Spense trailed her to the war room, and they settled down in the back, surrounded by mountains of old case files. Twenty minutes later, she still hadn't located Angelina Antonelli's autopsy report. She kicked one of the more substantial cartons. "If I go postal on you, try not to take it personally."

Spense reached down, grabbed her ankle and laughed, then he waved an accordion file marked *Antonelli* triumphantly beneath her nose. "This smell like what you're looking for?"

"Yes!" She ripped it from his grasp.

"Keep in mind for later, you owe me big."

"Yeah, yeah." She flipped through the materials in the file, her chest deflating. "This can't possibly be all of it."

"Only one box with Angelina's name on it, and that's the only file I found inside that's actually related to her. There are probably some additional items, mixed in with all this other stuff, but this looks like the only folder dedicated to Laura's nanny." He gave her an exaggerated wink. "I was hoping you'd be more grateful."

She'd asked Spense repeatedly not to flirt with her on the job, but he never seemed to learn—and apparently neither did she. She found herself grinning back at him. The devil in his eyes was simply too hard to resist. She gave herself exactly ten seconds to enjoy the warm, sexy tingles now populating her solar plexus, then forced her mind back to the task at hand. "Be serious, Spense. This doesn't seem right to me."

"What doesn't seem right?"

"All these boxes filled to the brim about Laura, and this one tiny little accordion file with a handful of photos and an autopsy report for Angelina. Even the autopsy was half-assed." She pointed to a lab report. "Just look at this tox screen. Super basic. No special substances requested."

"Hatcher already explained that."

She wanted to strangle someone herself right about now—the

cold case ME who didn't order the proper tests. "Right. Angelina was in on it. No need to bother checking to see if she'd been drugged. They never considered her a victim at all, and yet, she's the one who wound up dead."

Spense's expression turned thoughtful. "Wonder how her family feels about that. It must've been hard on them to lose her, and then have her murder go virtually ignored. I'm surprised they didn't push back."

Caitlin passed one of the handful of papers in Angelina's file across to him.

"Aha. Only child. Both parents deceased," Spense said.

"Angelina had no one to look out for her."

"Until now." Spense first checked over his shoulder, then tucked his finger beneath her chin, lifting her gaze to his. "I have a feeling you're going to do a pretty good job of that from here on out."

She looked away, her breath accelerating from just that small touch from Spense. "We both will."

"Agreed." He dropped his hand and sat back in his chair. "But Caity, don't get too attached to Angelina. We gotta stay objective. Look at all sides."

"That's exactly what I'm talking about. I don't think anyone looked at this case from her side at all. I don't think it was handled objectively."

"People did get a little carried away by the Chaucer family being so prominent in the community."

"Exactly. Between the talk shows and the obsessed bloggers, there were a million crazy theories. But you and I both know most crimes are simple and motivated by common human themes. Usually one of the big three . . ."

"Money. Sex. Power."

She wagged her foot, thinking. "Let's make it the big four. I wouldn't count out revenge. But look at all the resources that went into chasing down false leads, like Chaucer's business partner who'd never even left Tokyo for goodness' sake."

"Agreed. With all the wild ideas being thrown around, the cops got distracted from the basics. A young woman was murdered, and no one really cared, because Whit Chaucer's daughter was kidnapped. And even though Angelina was never tried or convicted for her involvement in that kidnapping, she was presumed guilty," Spense said.

"What evidence is there that she was really an accomplice?"

"According to the experts, the handwriting in the ransom note—and its phrasing resembled hers."

If Caitlin's mother hadn't raised her better, she would've spit. Handwriting analysis was soft science at best. "Even *if* a good attorney manages to get his handwriting expert on the stand, most judges won't allow that expert to present a conclusion as to the author's identity. They can only state whether certain characteristics do or don't resemble supplied samples. It's nuts that one thinly supported hypothesis—Angelina *might* have written the ransom note—changed the course of the entire investigation."

"You make some mean points." Spense stood and stretched, then resumed his seat and began to study Angelina's autopsy photos. "So you think Angelina was an innocent victim."

"I think the cops should've considered the possibility."

He brought one of the photographs closer to his face. Laid it down. Slid a magnifying viewer over it. "Stab wounds on the torso and genitalia. Like our Jane Doe in the wilderness. Wonder if they were postmortem, too."

"According to Angelina's autopsy report, they were inflicted after death. Despite the number of wounds, there was very little blood. And Angelina's hyoid bone was broken—cause of death: asphyxiation due to strangulation. Sound familiar?"

"Yeah. And very personal. Overkill." Spense steepled his fingers and rested them beneath his chin. "That could support the accomplice theory. What if Angelina turned on her partner? Let's say she wanted the money all to herself."

"Or she had second thoughts and wanted to let Laura go."

"Either way. Then her partner kills her in a fit of rage."

"Maybe." But it didn't feel right. It didn't explain their Jane Doe being found in the same area where Angelina had been found, practically on the anniversary of her murder. "What if Angelina's death was a sexual homicide? Strangulation. Stabbing. That definitely fits with a predator. No semen, but our UNSUB could've used a condom," she said.

"Or the stabbing, itself, is what turns him on. He doesn't need to complete the act to get sexual gratification. In any case, he left no trace DNA. We have a very clever UNSUB on our hands."

"More like diabolical." Caitlin leaned forward, certain she was onto something. She could feel it in her bones. "We know our UNSUB had access to GHB because it was found in Laura's system. If Angelina was also drugged, she could've been raped, and we wouldn't see clear evidence of it, since she was, presumably a sexually active female."

"Like today's Jane Doe, Angelina showed no defensive wounds. Both women were strangled and stabbed but didn't fight back. Our first ME screwed up."

She slammed the file down. "Dammit. He should've run a more complete toxicology screen on Angelina. What if it was Laura, not Angelina, who was the collateral damage? What if *Angelina* was abducted for the purpose of sexual gratification, but somehow, *Laura* got in the way . . ."

"So the UNSUB grabbed her, too?"

"Laura has always maintained that Angelina would never have hurt her. That she couldn't have been part of a kidnapping scheme. If Laura was right, then the UNSUB forged the note to make it look as though Angelina were in on it." No one seemed to have listened to Laura, and that made Caitlin want to pull out her boxing gloves.

"Would've had to have been someone with access to Angelina's journal. And clever enough to predict that the police would latch on to her as suspect. It's simple, but one miscue can throw an entire investigation off course."

"Victimology isn't just key to profiling, it's key to crime solving. If the police were focusing on the wrong victim, that would explain their inability to come up with a viable suspect."

Spense turned his palms up. "What bothers me about *Angelina as victim* is the ransom."

"We've covered that—"

Spense shook his head. "Not the ransom *note*. The ransom itself—it was paid, remember? And Laura was released unharmed. That doesn't fit with Angelina being the primary target."

No, it didn't. "I don't think we have all the pieces to this puzzle, yet. But we do have something." Caitlin laid out Angelina's autopsy photos on the table. Then one by one, she scrolled through the photos of their Jane Doe that she'd snapped on her phone before the body was moved.

Spense downed the remainder of his coffee and crumpled the paper cup in his hand. "Same MO. Same location. Same victim age and physical type."

"Our UNSUB just might be a highly intelligent individual driven by sexual compulsion: a sadist clever enough to come up with the idea of leaving a ransom note to make his crime look like a kidnap instead of a murder-rape. Then he makes use of the ransom paid, because why the hell not? He releases Laura alive, and that takes the heat off. She's been drugged, so she can't identify him. It all fits with a kidnapping, so the police never realize who and what he really is."

"I've never heard of a sexual sadist like that." Spense pulled his cube out, solved it, returned it to his pocket. She knew he was taking her hypothesis as seriously as she was or he wouldn't be working his cube. "Maybe he's more like what Hatcher called The Opportunist."

She didn't have a Rubik's cube, nor could she solve it if she did. She had to make do with doodling circles with her finger on the table instead. A few beats passed in silence, and then, she could practically hear something snap into place in her head. "What if we're both right. What if we're dealing not with a *sexual sadist* per se, but rather with a sexual opportunist?"

"Is *sexual opportunist* an actual diagnostic category, because I've never heard of it." Even as he challenged her with his words, he was nodding an affirmation. He couldn't dismiss the facts as coincidence any more than she could.

Imitating one of Spense's favorite mannerisms, Caitlin turned her palms up. "If it isn't, it sure as hell ought to be."

"And if we're right, that Angelina's death was sexually motivated, I can tell you one thing for sure." His voice lowered ominously. "Somewhere out there, there are other victims."

Caitlin met his gaze. "And if we don't catch this monster soon, there are going to be even more."

Chapter 26

LAURA RUBBED HER chest. There was a sore spot where her heart was trying to drill a hole through her rib cage. She'd run all the way from campus. Now, like a kid who'd gotten the wind kicked out of her by a schoolyard bully, she collapsed into a heap on the ground. She was breathless, and she was scared to pick herself up, because she had no idea what would hit her next.

On instinct she'd come straight here—to her apartment building—the first and only place that had ever been hers alone.

It was walking distance from Holly Hill College.

It was familiar.

It's freakin' dangerous.

On Monday night, she'd been kidnapped from this very building.

Easing herself into a full upright stance, she realized she could breathe a lot better this way. As oxygen returned to her brain, she could think a lot better, too.

Best not go inside. Her monster might be waiting. Best to stay here in the bushes like a hunted rabbit until she could figure out what to do.

Youth hostel.

That's right. She'd had a plan when she'd woken up this morning. She could still find a youth hostel and stay there overnight, though spilling her guts to Ronald Saas was no longer an option. Apparently she'd never met the man, and she certainly couldn't trust him with the locks of hair she had in her pack. The dinner had been a setup, and the real Saas might very well have been in on it, too. Her stomach clenched. This was a major setback, since she'd been hoping to find an ally—someone who could help her investigate and get to the truth.

Unbidden, the face of the woman with the blazing, energetic eyes—Caitlin—flashed across her mind.

Maybe she can help me.

In any case, she'd have to think about that later. For now, she had other things to figure out. Like who was the guy who'd bought her a prime rib dinner on Monday night.

The answer didn't take a nuclear scientist to figure out, and it made her chest hurt again: her monster . . . or if not, then her monster's minion.

In order to lock it safely into her memory, she closed her eyes, forcing herself to catalogue the details of her dinner companion's appearance. He was tall, at least six feet, and older than she'd expected. He was dressed in a decent but ill-fitting dark gray suit and white dress shirt. His complexion was weathered, his nails tobacco-stained. He had unruly blond hair. His watery blue eyes had surprised her. They were hard—like they'd seen a lot of things most people hadn't. At the time, she'd told herself the man had been wizened from his life as a newsman. But now, as she thought about his eyes, she decided she should've known something was off.

That window to the soul thing was really true.

Too bad she hadn't tried harder to glimpse inside his.

She opened her eyes and shifted her stance to get the sun out of her face, and that's when she saw him. Not her monster.

Cayman.

Her pulse bounded harder, and she instinctively took a step toward the man who'd protected her for so many years. But she quickly thought better of it and shrank back into the bushes to observe.

She should've been more observant all along—about everything and *everyone* around her. She shouldn't have opened up at Monday's dinner about her theories to a man she'd never met. And it shouldn't have taken her so many years to open her eyes to the evil that seemed to follow everywhere she went. She wouldn't make the mistake of trusting blindly again.

Not even Cayman.

Cayman approached the Campus Ridge apartment building with long purposeful strides and then disappeared inside.

Now would be a good time to run—if she wanted to go on being a rabbit.

She bit her bottom lip, hard.

She was done with that.

She was on a mission, now.

It felt good to choose, and she was choosing not to be the rabbit.

Now she was the hunter, and she liked it.

So what next?

Hunting required patience. So she waited, and for lack of anything better to do, she counted. When she got to four hundred, Cayman came back outside with Ben, the nerdy grad student who managed the off-campus apartment building. Cayman and Ben walked right past her, halting on the lawn just a few yards away from her hunter's blind.

"Like I told you Tuesday, I haven't seen Laura in a while," Ben said.

Even though there was nothing in the papers, she knew people were looking for her. After all, she'd been gone for days. The police had been at the cabin. She was sure they'd found the dress, and probably, by now, they knew it was hers. And if they'd found the note . . . her throat closed, and her legs turned to jelly. She mentally gave herself a hard slap.

Don't think about that now.

She dragged her mind back to the issue at hand.

Okay. What were they saying? Cayman had been looking for her since *Tuesday.* But everything was fine until Monday night. The timeline didn't quite fit. How did Cayman know that she was missing so quickly? It would've taken time for people to notice that she hadn't been around. It wasn't as though she had a job and a boss, or a large group of friends who would miss her.

Ben stood close to Cayman, like he was comfortable. Like he knew him.

There were a lot of good explanations. Maybe one of her teachers worried when she didn't show up for class and called her parents, and her parents sent Cayman down to find out what was up . . . only . . . this wasn't grade school. In college, skipping class was no big deal. No one called your mommy and daddy.

There could've been a ransom note.

Like last time. But—why would Ben seem so relaxed if he thought she'd been kidnapped? So how, exactly, did Cayman know she was missing so fast?

Her mind kept circling around one explanation. It wasn't the only possibility, but she just couldn't shake the idea, that maybe, just maybe, Cayman had been in Denver all along. There was that time she'd thought she'd seen him at the student union. She'd looked down to grab her books, and when she'd looked up again he was gone. She'd convinced herself she'd imagined him, there, lurking behind a newspaper. Because that was what she did. She was always telling herself she was imagining things. After all, that's what she'd been trained to believe.

Then another idea got in her throat and choked her like a fish bone. Cayman had spent the past decade as her protector. If he had been here all along, because her parents had kept him on the payroll behind her back, which definitely seemed like something they would pull, then why hadn't he done his job?

Cayman was smart, and he was good at being a bodyguard. Too many times, she'd tried and failed to escape his watchful eye. She simply could not believe that *if* he'd been watching her, he wouldn't have seen someone follow her home on Monday night . . . because Cayman, himself, would've been on her tail.

Tears stung her eyes at an idea she wouldn't allow to fully blossom.

Cayman was her friend.

Cayman would never hurt her.

She thought of all the times she'd confided in him about how much her father's rules chafed. That time he'd snuck a neighbor kid in to see her when she was on lockdown. The night she'd been sick, and he'd gone out at eleven p.m. for her favorite lobster bisque because she finally felt like eating.

Had it all been an act?

Could a man she'd trusted, and yes, even loved . . . could the man she'd considered an uncle be the monster that brought evil into her life?

No!

It wasn't Cayman.

It simply couldn't be.

"Here's my card. If you see her, call me first." Cayman handed something off to Ben.

"Shouldn't I call the cops first?"

"Then call me right after. I guarantee I'll get here first."

Ben went back inside, and Cayman approached a young woman walking toward the building. He showed her something. Probably Laura's photograph. She shook her head.

Cayman turned a corner, and Laura slid, as quietly as possible from behind the bushes. She pulled her hoodie far over her face. Cayman moved down the sidewalk, showing the photograph to everyone he encountered. Each time he was answered with the shake of a head.

Using her best tracking skills—thank the lord for that damn wilderness survival class—she tailed him.

More than once he turned around, as if he'd heard something behind him, but he always kept moving forward. At the bottom of the hill, he got on a beat-up blue bicycle that looked like it should belong to a college kid and pedaled away. It was easier to get around campus with a bike than with a car and that made her wonder again if he'd been following her around for a while.

She waited until he was completely out of sight before making her way to the bike rack. One bicycle remained. It was chained up. But there was a hardware store around the corner.

Five minutes later, she returned with wire cutters. She scanned the area around her and saw an old woman coming up the street with a bag of groceries. Laura tossed the cutters behind a tree and when the woman got close, Laura waved. The woman waved back and went into a nearby home.

Laura checked the area again, and this time, saw no one. She cut the chain. Got on the bike—a green ten-speed—and rode, following the dirty tire track Cayman's bike had left on the sidewalk, all the way to Elm Street.

She got off the bike and parked it behind a tree.

Then, heart pounding in her chest, she walked up and down the street until she saw it.

There, chained up on the porch of a two-story brown frame home, with a tall elm tree growing in the front yard, was a beat-up blue bike.

She found a good hunter's blind, from which she had a clear view of the front door.

Cayman would never hurt her.

Cayman was her friend.

Chapter 27

Friday, October 25
9:00 A.M.
Task force headquarters
Highlands Hotel
Denver, Colorado

HATCHER RUSHED INTO the war room, his face bright red. He shoved his spectacles to the top of his head and wiped his brow with a handkerchief. Something had gotten him worked up in a big way.

"Are the Chaucers here?" Spense asked, wondering if that alone was enough to produce such a copious amount of sweat on one man's forehead.

Hatcher mopped his entire face before responding. "Yes. And there's been a change of plans."

"Which plans?" Caity asked.

Spense, too, was confused. Hatcher had been summoned for a conference call with his commander a good forty-five minutes ago. There must've been a new development in the case, or maybe Hatcher had decided to inform the parents about the discovery of the body on his own. "Should we leave you to it?"

"Oh, hell no. The Chaucers are waiting for us in the interview room. I want you both there when I tell them we found a young woman's corpse in the Eagles Nest Wilderness—and it is *not* their daughter."

Caity's pupils bloomed. "You're sure?"

"Dental records don't match. Blood type doesn't match. The press conference is back on—in less than an hour."

Spense's neck and shoulders loosened. Someone had still lost a daughter, but at least for the time being, they didn't have to jerk all hope from the parents waiting in the next room.

"I might warn you, the Chaucers aren't alone," Hatcher said, the timbre of his voice suddenly rising. He was definitely not pleased about the sidekick.

"They brought a lawyer?" That would be a dick move on their part. With their daughter missing, naturally, the task force would have to look at the parents carefully, but lawyering up would only make it harder to get to the truth, and the truth was what a loving parent should be after. Of course, sometimes, good people get bad advice from others around them.

"Not a lawyer." Hatcher grimaced. "The senator insisted on bringing along our favorite shrink. Just in case we have bad news, he wants someone there to comfort his wife."

To Spense's way of thinking, Chaucer, himself, should be that someone. All he said, though, was, "Caity's my favorite shrink." Then he opened the door and placed his hand on the small of her back as she preceded Hatcher and him into the interview room.

Caity approached the senator's wife and extended her hand. "Mrs. Chaucer, I'm Dr. Caitlin Cassidy, and I want you to know Agent Spenser and I will do all we can to help bring Laura home. We're developing a profile—"

Mrs. Chaucer's already pasty complexion transformed to a sickly gray. She wobbled on her feet, and her husband extended a supportive hand. "Profiles are for killers. Does that mean you think our daughter is dead?" she asked.

Caity kept a poker face. "Profiles are for all kinds of things. And I'd love for you to call me Caitlin. May I call you Tracy?"

"Of course."

"Tracy, we'd prefer to speak with you and the senator alone." Caity aimed a polite smile at Webber. "For the sake of their privacy."

Good for her. Clearing Webber out was in everyone's best interest. If the Chaucers wanted to fill Webber in later, that was their business, but Spense knew his presence in the room could influence the parents' responses, and that would be no good for anyone.

Tracy Chaucer gripped Webber's hand. "Oh, you can speak freely in front of Grady. He's part of the family."

Spense kept his manner businesslike. "It's better for *Laura* if we speak to you alone. We have information for you, but we also have questions. It's helpful not to have any outside—"

Webber threw his arm around Tracy Chaucer. "I'm not an outsider. I'm Tracy's psychiatrist, and I'm here at her request." He turned to the senator. "And my friend, Whit's. I'll thank you to respect their wishes. If you're worried about leaks, don't be. I'm a vault."

But they'd had no trouble prying Laura's secrets out of him.

Which was good for the investigation, but Spense wasn't buying the vault comparison. Hard to trust a man you don't like, and Webber had rubbed him the wrong way from the get-go. "You're treating both mother and daughter. Isn't that a conflict of interests?"

"I'd think Caitlin would have educated you more than that. I'm a systems therapist. I don't believe in treating a patient in isolation from her family. I get everyone involved."

"Including the senator?" Spense asked.

"Whit doesn't have time." Rather abruptly, Tracy let go of her therapist's hand. "But I've been going all these years—for Laura's sake. I have to admit Grady's been a tremendous help to me, too. Sometimes I think he knows our family better than we know ourselves. So when he offered to come with us, today, I was truly grateful."

Spense caught the surprise on Caity's face.

Supposedly the family had requested Webber's presence, but now it seemed . . . "So then, it was actually your idea to come along, not the senator's," Spense said, addressing Webber.

"I really don't recall who suggested it first." Webber exaggeratedly turned to Hatcher as if to make the point it was the detective who would decide who could stay. "But I'm sure whatever Tracy says is right. In any case, she's been through a lot, and I'd like to be here to make sure no undue pressure or bullying tactics—"

Caity's shoulders drew back. "We have news for the family. And the purpose of any questions we ask is to help bring Laura home."

"The Chaucers aren't persons of interest in her disappearance? Don't the police always consider the family members suspect?"

With that kind of talk, Webber would have the Chaucers on the defensive in no time.

Spense rubbed his tight jaw. "Everyone, just sit down and we'll explain what's going on."

Tracy and Webber complied but Chaucer approached Hatcher. "I'm not sitting down. Not until you tell me why we're here. Last night, you were all set to come to the apartment. Now you're stalling, making a federal case out of my wife wanting her doctor present."

"Like we said," Hatcher responded with commendable calm. "For Laura's sake, we'd prefer to keep this between us, but of course if you'd like to have someone present—like an attorney—that's your right."

"I don't want an attorney!" Whit slapped his hand against his thigh. "I just want to know where my little girl is. Have you found her? Is she . . . is she dead?"

"No, we haven't found her," Spense answered immediately. The Chaucers had waited long enough for the news. Even though it was their own fault—they'd postponed the meeting until morning and then showed up late. Still, he didn't want them imagining the worst one second longer.

Whit collapsed onto the couch next to Tracy and covered his face with trembling hands.

Tears began to stream down Tracy's cheeks. "Oh, thank God. Thank God." She met Spense's eyes. "I was sure you'd found . . . something terrible. She's alive?"

Spense looked to Hatcher to take the lead. Most of this was going to be made public at the press conference, but it was up to the detective to determine which details to reveal. Some would be held back—likely, the existence of the cabin, for example—for the sake of the investigation. And until cleared, both parents were, in fact, persons of interest.

"We hope to find Laura alive. But we can't say for certain that she is. The reason we brought you in today is we found the body of a *different* young woman in the Eagles Nest Wilderness."

Chaucer's face went completely white, and his head bobbed like he might faint. "You didn't find Laura?"

Caity rushed to the senator and his wife with bottles of water she took from the mini-fridge in the room.

While Tracy encouraged her husband to sip, Hatcher repeated, "The young woman we found is *not* Laura."

Hatcher waited for Chaucer to regain his sea legs, and then continued. "Perhaps our finding a Jane Doe and Laura going missing are completely unrelated events, but then again, there may be a connection. It's imperative we locate your daughter as soon as possible."

"How can we help?" The senator reached for his knees, clasping them with both hands.

"We just have a few questions."

"We'll tell you everything we can, but Whit and I were both back in DC when she . . . when she . . ." Tracy's voice broke. "You don't think whoever killed this other woman has our Laura, do you?"

"Maybe you should call a lawyer," Webber said aside to Whit.

"Shut up, Grady," the senator ground out. "We're going to give them whatever they need."

"I think that's wise." Caity took a now empty water bottle from Chaucer and handed him another. "You both look dehydrated. Try to remember to eat and drink, even if you're not feeling hungry or thirsty."

The senator and Tracy nodded, but said nothing.

Hatcher pulled out a notebook. "I know we went through this when you first arrived from DC, but just for the record, do either of you have any idea where your daughter might be? Did she give you any indication she might leave town, take a trip with a friend, that kind of thing?"

"No. We don't know anything. We haven't talked to her since we got home from parents' weekend."

"And how did that go? Was she in good spirits? Did you argue?" Spense asked Chaucer.

"Parents' weekend went fine." Chaucer sat back, the color finally returning to his cheeks. "Laura was a bit anxious, maybe even a little blue, but not more so than usual. She talked a lot about her classes, and she said she'd made a friend who didn't care that she was a senator's daughter, and who didn't know about her past. We didn't argue about anything—to speak of. The only issue between us was that she wanted more independence from her mom and me. She reiterated that she didn't want a bodyguard." Chaucer looked down at his feet. "So, yes, I lied to her. I promised her I wouldn't force the matter, and then I kept Cayman in place here in Denver with orders to stay on her. You'll have to ask Cayman what happened after that. My wife and I took a private jet back to DC, first thing Monday. I had an important meeting on the Hill at eight a.m. If I hadn't done that—kept Cayman in place, I mean, we wouldn't have realized she was gone until much later. Maybe we still wouldn't know. So don't blame me, Tracy. It was the right thing to do."

"Maybe she found out we lied, and now she's run away." Resentment crept through in Tracy's voice.

"We'll look into that possibility," Hatcher assured her. "And we'll get Cayman back in for more questioning ASAP. But right now, Agent Spenser and Dr. Cassidy have some questions about the *other* time Laura disappeared. Thirteen years ago."

"What for?" Webber just couldn't stay out of it.

"Agent Spenser and I need to get a clear picture of everything that happened leading up to and including the day Laura disappeared from her family home thirteen years ago," Caity said.

"That doesn't tell us *why*," Webber persisted obstinately.

"I'm sorry, but we're not free to explain all of our reasons at this time." Caity kept her gaze on the Chaucers.

"So you think this is the same man," Whit said, as though resigned to it.

"That would be premature to conclude. Just trying to get the big picture," Spense said.

Tracy started to sob into her hands. "You don't think she ran away at all. You think she's been kidnapped again."

Caity slid a box of tissues across the table. "Take all the time you need."

"I'm ready now." Tracy blew her nose and looked around for a wastebasket. Eventually, she settled for folding the used tissue and laying it in her lap.

"Tell us, in your own words, what happened October 13, thirteen years ago," Spense said.

Tracy glanced over at Webber.

He gave a slight nod.

"We've been over it a thousand times with Detective Hatcher, but if you think it will help . . . Whit and Laura and I spent the day with our friends Lillian and Martin Banks. We attended services at the First Presbyterian Church and later visited their home. Lillian's cook prepared a lovely meal—rack of lamb. Laura refused to eat her meat because she had a stuffed toy lamby of her own. Grady arrived later, and we played charades. Then we had leftovers for dinner and cocktails after. We arrived home about ten o'clock that night. I went straight to my room, and Angelina put Laura to bed. Whit went to his study. There was a bit of a kerfuffle at the City Council over school funding, so Whit stayed up late reviewing the matter."

"Sounds like a long, fun party. Had you and your husband had a lot to drink?" Caity asked matter-of-factly.

"Whit's not a drinker. But I may have had a few too many." Tracy sighed. "If you must know, I'm probably self-medicating. Is that right, Grady?"

Grady again gave the slightest of nods. It wouldn't surprise Spense to see him break out a set of secret hand signals.

"I have anxiety. I take medicine for it, and it doesn't mix well with alcohol. Believe me, I've wondered what would've happened if I'd been sober. But Grady says my guilt won't change the past."

Didn't seem to be changing the present either, at least not if Hatcher was correct that Chaucer declined an interview last night because his wife was drunk.

"Then, around midnight, I woke up screaming. I've had bad dreams my entire life."

"Tell us more about that." Caity nodded encouragement.

"Is this necessary? I don't think this is going to help bring Laura back," Webber interrupted.

"Let her tell it," the senator said. "It's no secret to the cops anyway."

"My father was a drunk. I guess that's one reason a straight arrow like Whit appealed to me. I know some people think I married for his money—but I promise you I love this man." She sent her husband a watery smile. "I've never known anyone so kind as Whit. But . . . I guess what I'm avoiding telling you..." She cast her eyes back to Grady. "My father repeatedly abused me . . . he'd come in my room several nights a month. Anyway, I've had nightmares and anxiety my entire life because of that."

"Post-traumatic stress." Webber patted Tracy's hand. "No shame in that, Tracy."

She nodded absently. "Where were we?"

"About midnight you woke up screaming."

"Yes, Whit held me until I fell back asleep. The next morning, he woke me around eight. He'd gotten up to make coffee and . . . and he found a ransom note on the breakfast table."

"Did you read the note?" Spense leaned in to hear her answer. Her voice had become very soft.

"Whit read it to me. It said they had taken Laura and Angelina, too. They asked for a one-hundred-thousand-dollar ransom. They said they'd be in touch. The note also said they'd torture and kill Laura if we tried to contact the authorities."

"But you called 911," Caity said.

"Not me. That was Whit. He said we needed help if we were going to get Laura home. I was terrified, but I looked to Whit for guidance. After he called 911, he called Grady to come over. I—I was hysterical, and Grady gave me a sedative."

"So then—" Spense pinned Webber with his stare "—you were present on both the evening before and the morning after Laura Chaucer went missing."

"I don't care for the insinuation, Agent Spenser. I've been a friend of the family for years."

"And were you a friend of Laura's, too?" Spense asked.

"Hardly. Laura was an eight-year-old child."

"Oh, but she adored Grady." Tracy looked admiringly at her psychiatrist, then added, "Angelina was crazy about him, too."

CAITLIN TURNED THE volume up on the flat screen television that hung on the war room wall. Hatcher and the rest of the task force detectives had convened downstairs in the hotel ballroom, where a press conference was already in full swing, but she and Spense had remained behind. Of late, they'd had more than their share of media attention. Neither of them wanted to siphon the focus off the Chaucer family, who planned to make a direct appeal for the safe return of their daughter.

The commander introduced Hatcher, his lead investigator. Hatcher told reporters about a hiker's report of suspicious activity in the Eagles Nest Wilderness and the subsequent gruesome discovery of the body of a young woman, late teens to early twenties, with long dark hair and slender build.

A hotline number flashed behind him on the screen. "Anyone with any information about a young woman fitting this description, or any other information you may deem useful to this investigation, please call the hotline."

A cacophony of voices shouted questions at once. Hatcher pointed, and the camera zoomed in on a short, balding man. The man climbed to his feet. "Ronald Saas—*Mountain Times*. Is there a reward?"

Hatcher cleared his throat. "I'm going to get to that in a moment."

"Why not get to it now?" Saas fired back.

"Take a seat and I will." Hatcher removed his handkerchief from his pocket as if to wipe the perspiration beading on his brow, but didn't use it. "We have another missing woman. But she is *not* our Jane Doe."

A photograph of Laura, standing in front of the Holly Hill College entrance sign, appeared on the screen behind Hatcher. The hotline number was printed in bold across the bottom of the image. "Laura Chaucer, age twenty-one, a student at Holly Hill College was last seen on Monday night, October 21, entering her off-campus apartment. The family is offering a ten-thousand-dollar reward for information leading to her return."

A shuffling noise sounded from backstage. Then Whit and Tracy Chaucer appeared. An audible buzz started up in the crowd. Once it finally died down, Grady Webber walked to the podium.

"Son of a bitch," Spense muttered.

"I'm going to hand things over to Dr. Grady Webber, the family spokesperson." Hatcher made way at the mic for Grady.

"Senator and Mrs. Whitmore Chaucer are unable to speak, due to their grief. On their behalf, I'm begging you, if you have any knowledge of Laura's whereabouts call this number immediately." He looked piercingly into the camera. "If you have Laura in your custody, please return her to the loving arms of her mother and father. They miss her. Think of the pain you're causing . . . if you've taken her. And Laura . . ." He spread his arms wide. "If you're watching this, please come home. No matter what you've done, your parents love you."

Blood rushed to Caitlin's face. She jumped to her feet. "What the hell did Grady just do?"

"Blamed Laura for her own disappearance, or maybe worse."

Bile rose in her throat.

"Remember." Webber turned his remarks to the general viewing audience. "There's a ten-thousand-dollar reward for information leading to the return of Laura Chaucer."

Caitlin's hands clenched at her sides. She swallowed back a stream of expletives.

She and Spense exchanged a glance.

The hotline was ringing.

Chapter 28

CAYMAN HAD SOMETHING Laura desperately needed, and until she got hold of it, she couldn't go home. The locks of hair alone weren't enough proof. Because of that note, the locks of hair could make her look even more guilty. But if she could get into Cayman's house, maybe she could find the one thing that could prove her theory: that there were more victims.

Over the years, she'd seen pictures on the news of other women who looked like Angelina—women who'd gone missing or turned up dead. But her mind was so jumbled, she'd been so heavily medicated, she couldn't recall the pertinent details . . . like who and where and when. She needed a thread that would connect the dots, shore up her faulty memory. And she had a good idea about where to find that thread.

She scratched her arm and noticed a couple of red welts appear. Hopefully, it was just from the sun concentrating its fire on her skin and not an allergy to this fragrant, pokey hedge she was hiding behind. Twisting her wrist, she frowned. She needed a watch to keep time. Counting might work for a minute or two, but there was no telling how long she'd been sitting here cross-legged on the dirt, staring at the door of that brown frame house, waiting for Cayman to emerge. More than one thousand seconds for sure, since that's when she'd given up keeping track.

Buried in her backpack was her purse. The pack in turn was lashed to her stolen bike, also hidden behind the hedgerow. But she could figure her remaining cash in her head. She'd spent forty dollars at the motel, nine ninety-nine on breakfast, twenty-one dollars for a cab from the diner to campus, seventeen-fifty on wire cutters, and fifty-three dollars on a blond wig. That left three hundred fifty-eight dollars and fifty-one cents. The youth hostel would hopefully run her around ten dollars a night.

If she could find a watch for twenty dollars, she'd buy it. She smacked herself on the forehead. Yes, she needed a watch, but more importantly she needed a burner phone in case she needed to call in an anonymous tip to the cops . . . or to Caitlin. She liked Caitlin, and she wondered if there might be some way to reach her directly—maybe an internet search would turn something up. A trip to the electronics store and to a coffee shop with Wi-Fi was definitely in order.

The thought of her strange to-do list made her smile.

1. Break and enter Cayman's house.
2. Hit the electronics store.

3. Order a venti latte.
4. Catch a killer.

The wind shifted. The sun ducked behind a bank of clouds, taking her smile with it. She let out a long, lonely breath. It felt wrong, spying on Cayman. He'd been as much a friend to her as a bodyguard. And she'd had very few friends since Angelina died. Laura considered marching up the front steps, ringing the bell and announcing to Cayman that she was back. But then she thought about her friend's body lying mutilated in the wilderness and about Angelina's bright smile. The way her sweet nanny had always read *Harry Potter* to her before tucking her into bed with a good-night kiss.

And she thought about the monster.

No.

She wasn't going to ring the front bell. She was going to sit here on the hard ground until her butt flattened into a pancake and her muscles atrophied. However long it took for Cayman to leave— that's how long she'd keep watch.

It was a sad day—whatever the outcome, she wouldn't be rejoicing. She wasn't a killer—she knew that, finally—her soul simply wasn't black enough, but there was still the question of her sanity.

Yet even if she was nuts, even if her theory was all wrong, someone had killed Angelina. Someone had killed her friend. And Laura was determined to do everything in her power to stop that someone from striking again.

She heard the creak of a garage door opening.

Craning her neck, she saw a black sedan pull out from the house where the blue bike was still chained up on the porch.

She held her breath.

It looked like a man driving the sedan, but the side window was tinted so she couldn't be sure who.

The window buzzed down.

Cayman.

He was leaving. And from the way he peeled out of that drive, he was in a hurry to get wherever he was going.

This was her chance.

She crawled out from behind the bushes, heart in her throat, palms sweaty.

But what if he'd taken the one thing she needed with him? Then there would be no point breaking into his house.

Stop stalling.

As she sauntered casually across the road, she pursed her lips, attempting a carefree whistle, but her mouth was too dry.

Just act cool.

First, she approached the neighbor's yard that contained a treasure she'd had her eye on while lurking behind the bushes. A football, lying in the grass, waiting for its quarterback to come out and play. She felt a pang of guilt, knowing that quarterback would probably have to take the blame for her sin . . . but wasn't that the point?

Just do it.

She snagged the football and kept moving.

She reached the backyard of Cayman's house. No screens on the windows.

Good.

She hauled her right arm back and concentrated. She'd often played touch football with Cayman, and it was he who'd taught her to throw a mean pass. When the ball smashed through the bedroom window, she did a victory dance, like she'd just hit a wide receiver fifty yards downfield.

Touchdown!

Spurred on by her unqualified success—the window had shattered to bits—she made quick work of clearing away the glass stalactites and stalagmites from the windowsill with her jacketed arm. Then she removed her dusty boots and crawled through the window into Cayman's bedroom in her stocking feet.

Center stage, the football nestled in the gray shag carpet, announcing to all the world that the only foul play here had been that of a rowdy neighbor kid with bad aim.

She drew the curtains across the broken window, and they lifted in the breeze. Lucky for her the high masonry fence surrounding the backyard kept her safe from view.

What next?

If she was careful, no one would ever know she'd been here. The football explained the broken window, and Cayman might not realize what she'd stolen for ages, and even then he'd probably think he'd simply misplaced it. Determined to leave no trace behind, she hurried into the bathroom and found a clean washcloth. She didn't have gloves, but she could make do with this instead.

Back in the bedroom, she wiped down the windowsill and the adjacent wall in case she'd left a palm print. Using the cloth, she pulled open the top dresser drawer then carefully sorted through its contents: Socks. Boxers. A dirty magazine—one of the tamer kind that ran a lot of celebrity interviews.

A deep, dark fear that she didn't want to face, surfaced for the second time that day, then quickly evaporated like steam from a boiling pot.

Cayman couldn't be her monster.

Such a beast would require more twisted fare than a garden-variety girlie mag to satisfy his carnal urges. She slipped the magazine back into place and moved on.

Drawer after drawer left her disappointed. She didn't know why Cayman would hide it, but in case he had she should try the obvious places. She dragged the mattress off the bed and was left huffing and sneezing from the effort.

Nothing but dust mites under here.

And now she had to deal with the mess she'd made. With weary arms, she shoved and tugged the mattress back into place. She jerked the sheets up and smoothed them. Had the bed been neatly made, or had the covers been pulled up in a jumble? She couldn't remember. If she was lucky, neither would Cayman.

Stupid. Stupid. Stupid.

She should've checked the closet before wrestling with that mattress. Something to think about the next time she broke into someone's bedroom! With her rag in hand once again, she stepped into the walk-in. His closet was full, containing clothing for all seasons. This was no spur-of-the-moment trip. So he really had been here, watching her, all along. She batted her worry away, and rifled through all the pockets of his pants and jackets. When she came across a wad of cash, she opened and closed her fist around it three, four times, before making up her mind and stuffing the bills in her pocket. Funds were running low, and she didn't know how long she'd be on the run.

She glanced at her bare wrist, realizing she had no clue how much time had passed. At least now she could buy that watch.

Hurry!

Tiptoeing up she stretched her neck, trying to get a good view of the top shelf. The absence of dust in one spot told her something rectangular had been shoved to the rear. She dragged a hard-shell suitcase over and stood on it.

Yes!

She'd been right.

A box had been shoved to the back of the shelf.

An ordinary shoe box.

Probably containing ordinary shoes.

Extending her arm, she wiggled her fingers but couldn't quite reach her goal. With a hanger, she coaxed the box toward her. Finally, she got her fingertips under the lip and fished the thing off the shelf. She lost her balance. One foot came off the suitcase, and she bumped her head against the wall, making her brain zing with pain.

When she touched her scalp, she was relieved to note that although it was sore and a goose-egg was already beginning to from, her hand came away free of blood. She carried the box to the bed she'd just made and sat down, cradling the contraband in her lap. The box felt lightweight, not what you'd expect if it contained a pair of men's shoes.

She closed her eyes.

Please. Pease. Please.

Let it be here.

She sucked in a breath, and then opened her eyes and the box at the same moment.

Her spirits soared.

She might really be able to stop the monster after all. The status of her mission had just been upgraded from snowball's chance to highly unlikely because lying right on top of a bunch of odds and

ends was what she'd been seeking: the thread she needed to connect the dots in her memory.

Cayman's passports.

As she turned the pages, her fingers tingled with excitement.
She flipped through them, touching each stamp reverently. It was
everything she'd hoped to find.

Because Cayman's travels were her travels.

Where she'd gone, he'd gone.

Her parents kept her passports under lock and key, which made
it impossible for her to reconstruct a timeline of her life abroad.
But it was all laid out for her now. Cayman had been with her
since the day she'd been ransomed. These little booklets, trembling in her hand, showed every country she'd visited and every
date since Angelina had been murdered.

If she could cross-check the dates of her travel with reports
of missing women in the same locations, she might find the victims whose faces she recalled from the news, but whose names she
didn't know.

Exhaling a long breath, she zipped the passports into the pocket
of her jacket.

Before she put the box away, curiosity prompted her to inspect
the remaining contents. It was an odd collection of receipts, ticket
stubs, and mementos mixed with utilitarian items like toenail
clippers and super glue. At the bottom, an envelope caught her
eye. She could tell from the firm sleek feel of it that she'd found a
rarity in today's world—a physical photograph—the kind you can
hold in your hand. Sure enough, inside the envelope was a long
narrow strip of photo paper.

Outside the window, a car engine roared to life.

Her shoulders jumped, but then relaxed when she heard the car buzz down the street. It wasn't Cayman . . . yet. But she'd better get out of here fast. She'd peek at the photo, return the shoe box to the top of the closet, and then get the hell out.

She turned the photo strip face up.

It had obviously been taken in a fun booth.

Her eyes blurred with tears, and it took her a minute to process what she was seeing.

But when she did, her bones, her lungs, her skin seemed to freeze, as though she'd just stepped naked into a cryotherapy chamber.

A couple was pictured pulling a series of funny faces for the camera.

They looked very happy together. Cayman and his beautiful companion—a young woman with blue eyes and long dark hair.

Chapter 29

"TRUELLA UNDERLAND . . ." SPENSE began to read, rapid-fire, invoking his sternest tone ". . . you have the right to remain silent and refuse to answer questions. Anything you do say may be used against you in a court of law. You have the right to consult an attorney before speaking to the police and to have an attorney present during questioning now or in the future. Do you understand?"

The young woman's jaw dropped, and her facial muscles went slack.

She seemed both stunned and confused—exactly the effect Spense had been going for, not to mention it never hurts to cover your ass with Miranda rights just in case. When he'd finished reading them, he slipped the card back in his suit pocket and produced a pair of handcuffs he'd lifted from a detective's desk back in the war room.

She slumped against the open door, giving Caity the opportunity to swoop around her and enter Truella's Campus Ridge apartment.

"Agent Spenser!" Caity offered a supporting arm to Truella. "Put those away. You can't arrest this young woman simply for being a bad roommate."

Truella accepted Caity's help, pulling herself upright. But it only took an instant for the grateful look she'd sent Caity to change to something more . . . pissed off. Truella ducked out from under Caity's supporting arm. "I am *not* a bad roommate."

Spense stepped inside as well. Truella had vacated the doorway, and that was invitation enough for him. "Oh I'm not going to charge her with *that*, though clearly she's not winning any friendship medals, here." He pinned Truella with a hard glare and dangled the handcuffs inches from her face, allowing them to chime musically against each other. "Your roommate hasn't been home since parents' weekend. That's a week ago, and you haven't bothered to report her missing."

"I didn't know she was missing. I thought she was on one of her *excursions*." She pulled her shoulders back. "Anyway, you're bluffing. Just because you're FBI doesn't mean you can go around arresting anyone you feel like for no reason."

"Agent Spenser doesn't bluff. I'm sure he has *some* reason." Caity walked from the front door to the living area like she was the hostess and Truella the guest. Spense followed, and Truella, looking very confused, did, too. The room was small and opened onto a kitchen with a gas stove and beat-up dinette set.

Spense stood, arms crossed over his chest while Caity and

Truella seated themselves on a tan faux leather sofa. Off to the left, he could see a room with an unmade bed and clothes piled on the floor.

Truella followed his gaze. "That's Harriet's room. She's a slob."

Yeah. No friendship medals for this one.

"So, then, if you're not arresting Tru for failing to report Harriet as missing, what kind of charges did you have in mind?" Caity narrowed her eyes at him, while inching closer to Truella in an exaggerated show of support.

"I was thinking obstruction of justice." He widened his stance. "Only because accessory to murder seems a bit premature."

"I don't know." Caity slid Truella a questioning gaze. "I think she'll talk to us."

"Of course I will! I'm the one who called you, remember?"

"Well, Tru, you did hang up as soon as you found out the reward was only for information about Laura Chaucer," Spense said.

"No, no, no. We got disconnected. My cell lost signal. My battery died."

Spense grabbed a phone off the coffee table. "This yours? One hundred percent charged—and look at that signal."

"Now. I had to charge it up so I could call you back."

Spense uncrossed his arms and spread his palms. "Luckily, we're here, so you won't have to worry about either the battery or the signal anymore. Which was the problem, again?"

Truella blinked rapidly. "I'll tell you whatever you want to know."

Caity shook a finger at Spense. "Put those cuffs away. Tru's a good egg. I just know it."

"She waited this long to call the cops. And then, it was just because she thought she'd get a reward. She clammed up as soon as she found out she wouldn't get money for telling us about Harriet," Spense said.

"I don't need a reward. I promise I'll cooperate."

Spense offered Truella her cell. "You'd better."

Truella's hand shook as she accepted her phone from Spense. "Honest, I didn't know anything bad happened to her—not until I saw that press conference on TV. Maybe it's not really Harriet."

"I hope not." Caity's false chumminess suddenly disappeared. Spense could hear genuine empathy for Truella in her tone. He'd known Caity couldn't keep up a pretense for long, but it didn't matter. She'd played her part of the ruse well, and just long enough.

Truella leaned forward, wringing her hands, a dazed look in her eyes.

Spense had no doubt she'd tell them everything she knew about Harriet Beckerman—to save her own hide. "On the phone, you said you thought the body that was found up in the wilderness might be that of your roommate. Describe Harriet, please."

"She has long dark hair—almost black—and blue eyes."

"Keep going."

"She turned twenty last month. She's shorter than me—I'm five four. And she's thinner and prettier than me, too. She . . ." Truella's eyebrows flattened. "She's the kind of girl who doesn't mind stealing her friend's boyfriend."

Maybe that was why Truella seemed so angry with Harriet.

"Let's get back to her physical description. Does she have any distinguishing marks or features?" Caity asked.

Spense pricked his ears. The dolphin tattoo hadn't been mentioned in the press conference.

"A tattoo on one of her hips. I don't remember which one. It was some kind of fish, a whale, I think."

"Okay. You're doing great," Caity said, her voice suddenly subdued. "Harriet fit the description you heard on the news, so you called the hotline. That was the right thing to do. But, Tru, why did you wait so long? What did you mean when you said you thought Harriet was on one of her excursions?"

"Harriet has a problem—she likes to party. Booze it up big-time. I've known her two years, and she's disappeared for a few days maybe three other times before. But she always showed up eventually. You can see why I wasn't too worried."

Not worried that her friend was out there on a bender, and no one knew where. "Did you at least talk to her parents?" Spense asked.

"Harriet's dad's not around. And she barely speaks to her mom even when they are getting along."

"They're not getting along now?"

"Mrs. Beckerman put Harriet on probation. If Harriet didn't get sober, her mom said she'd pull her out of school and stick her back in rehab. And Harriet didn't want to go to rehab. I thought she'd gotten clean for real this time . . . until she went out that one Saturday and didn't come home."

"Saturday October 19?"

"Yeah."

"I think I understand," Caity said. "You didn't want to get Harriet in trouble with her mother. Even though you were mad at her, you still wanted to protect her. Like you're doing now. Only at the moment, you actually are helping, so keep it up."

"That's right." Truella's eyes grew moist. "I'm not a bad

person. I did want the reward money—I admit it. But that's not the reason I hung up. I've got more to tell than just about . . . I hung up because I was scared."

And from the pallor of her skin, Spense could tell she was still scared. He wasn't immune to her feelings, but there was too much at stake to go easy on the kid. Tragic that the one nice thing Truella tried to do for Harriet—keeping her secret from her mother—turned out to be the worst possible thing she could've done. Classic enabler. "You didn't call Harriet's mom, but did her mom try to contact you?"

"Not until this morning."

Spense waited.

"She said Harriet was supposed to check in with her by phone once a week. She said she'd gotten a few texts, but when she told Harriet to either call her or pay the piper, the texts stopped."

Didn't help much. Whoever had taken Harriet, assuming she was in fact their Jane Doe, would have her phone and could've sent the texts. Still, they might reveal something useful. He drummed his fingers together, sensing Truella was still holding out. "What about you? Did you get any texts?"

Her throat moved in a long visible swallow. "Mrs. Beckerman asked me did I know where Harriet was, and I told her the truth. I didn't. I don't. I bet I'm wrong. I bet she's just on a binge like I told you before."

"Tru, Agent Spenser asked you a question." Caity placed her hands on the young woman's shoulders and turned Truella toward her. "Did you get any texts from Harriet's phone?"

Truella looked around for an escape route. There weren't any. Spense was in front of her, Caity beside her. "Just one—on

Monday. The text said she was with a friend." Her voice trembled uncontrollably.

"Take it easy, Tru," Spense said. "I was just messing with you before. I needed you to take this seriously, and now I can see you do. Whatever it is that's got you so worried, just tell us. We're the good guys."

"We're the good guys," Caity repeated, locking eyes with Truella.

"Harriet's text said she was partying with a friend—the girl who lives in 317—Laura Chaucer."

Chapter 30

"IT'S ME." HUDDLED in a back cubicle in front of a pay-as-you-go computer, Laura tugged her blond wig to better secure it in place and whispered into her new burner phone.

"Laura, is that you?"

She heard the surprise in Dr. Webber's voice. He was the last person she ever thought she'd call, but the televisions in the electronics store, where she'd bought a phone and a watch, kept looping recorded footage of him begging her to return home. When she'd seen her mother and father standing in the background at that press conference, looking stricken and pale, she'd felt the weight of their suffering like Sisyphus's rock.

Was she doomed to disappoint them for all eternity?

She desperately wanted to make it to the top of the hill and just once be the daughter they deserved.

She could've called her father, but then when he ordered her home, she'd have to refuse. And her track record of standing up to the senator wasn't the greatest—as in when had she ever? Never, except this fall, when she'd enrolled in college away from home. She was certain he'd be quick to remind her how that had turned out.

Then there was her mother, but Tracy had always been fragile. No telling what the shock of hearing Laura's voice would do to her. So, in the end, Dr. Webber seemed like the best way to get a message to her parents.

She owed it to them to let them know she was alive . . .

And she owed it to Harriet's mom to tell the cops it was her daughter's body they'd found.

"Your parents are sick with worry. I'm sick with worry," Webber said.

"I—I'm safe."

"Safe where?" he asked, his tone suddenly coaxing.

Ah yes, good old Dr. Webber, the master manipulator.

"Just tell me where you are, dear. I'll come get you myself."

"No!" She cringed at how loudly she'd spoken. She had to be careful after that press conference. A blond wig could only hide so much.

"Laura, please let me bring you home where you belong."

"I—I can't come home. I'm sorry."

"Sorry?" he said, trying a sterner approach. "Your parents love you. They don't deserve this."

"I know that." She hesitated. She didn't trust him like her parents did, but he couldn't deliver her message if she didn't give it to him. "There's something I haven't told you yet—the reason I can't come home."

He said nothing, and she imagined herself slouching in a chair in front of his desk in that gloomy office of his. Right about now, he'd be checking his watch, impatiently waiting for her to get on with it.

"Something bad is happening again. I woke up and didn't know where I was. My throat was cut—more like scratched with a knife—but it was bleeding. And I—I . . . there were empty pill bottles."

"My God, Laura, I want you to hang up and call 911. Then call me right back."

"I can't."

"You must. You tried to hurt yourself again."

"No. It was someone else who hurt me. It was *him.*"

"Him who?" She could hear the release of a heavy breath coming through the phone.

"I told you about him once, when I found the lock of Angelina's hair."

"We've been through all this before, Laura. That was a figment of your imagination."

In other words, *you're crazy.* "No. It wasn't. It *isn't.* When I woke up, I found more locks of hair."

"You're high on pills. That's why you can't think clearly. Now, just listen to me, and I'll explain what's happening to you. You thought you found a lock of hair before, remember, and then it disappeared. It disappeared because it wasn't really there to begin with."

"I have two locks of hair tied with ribbons in my pocket, right now."

"That's a hallucination."

"No. I'm touching them. You can't touch a hallucination. You explained that to me in therapy. My hallucinations were visual, brought on by drugs. I'm not taking any drugs now."

"What about the empty medication bottles?"

"He must've fed the pills to me. But I threw them up."

"Where are you, Laura?"

"I'm calling from a pay phone in Silverthorne." She didn't know why she said that. Her parents had always told her Dr. Webber was a good friend and an excellent doctor, but she knew by the way her gut was pinging he wasn't on her side. And Dr. Duncan had told her to trust her gut. She wished she'd called Dr. Duncan instead.

"Where in Silverthorne are you? A gas station?"

Give him the message and then get off the phone. "I think my friend, Harriet Beckerman, has been murdered. I need you to tell that to the police."

"Listen to me very carefully, Laura. If you've hurt this girl, this Harriet, you really must turn yourself in. Your father will get you the finest lawyer, and I'll testify you don't know right from wrong."

"But I do know right from wrong!" Her voice had gotten too loud again. She looked around but no one seemed to have noticed.

"Then why did you kill your friend? Why did you try to kill yourself? You're not well, Laura. Just tell me where you are so I can help you."

"I never said I killed Harriet. And you're not helping me. This is the opposite of help." She could hear her own voice shaking. If only Dr. Webber would believe in her. "I would never hurt my friend. I would never hurt *anyone.*"

But his only reply was silence.

"Why won't you believe me?"

"Which thing do you want me to believe, Laura? That you would never hurt anyone or that your friend has been murdered and you have a lock of her hair in your pocket? Because frankly, I don't see how both of those things can be true. Either you're delusional or you've done something terrible and then tried to kill yourself."

"It was *him*. He killed my friend, and then he tried to kill me."

This time Dr. Webber's answer was swift and cruel. "Then why aren't you dead, Laura? Why aren't you dead?"

Chapter 31

Friday, October 25
2:00 P.M.
Task force headquarters
Highlands Hotel
Denver, Colorado

DETECTIVE JORDAN HATCHER was in Caitlin's face the moment she and Spense swung through the door into the war room. In this instance, Spense's old school *ladies first* policy had put her directly in the line of fire. Hatcher had the flophouse sweats and some of his perspiration flung onto her along with an expletive or two. He was so worked up his ears had turned the color of ketchup. "Where have you two been? All hell's been breaking loose around here."

Good to be missed?

Hatcher's agitation surprised Caitlin. She wanted to ice him down before his head exploded. Resisting the temptation to check his pulse, she said, "We were out interviewing a witness. We left a message with Cliff. I guess you didn't get it."

"Who the fuck told you that you could interview a witness without me?"

Caitlin cringed, not because of the cursing but because she anticipated Spense's response. Nobody likes being told how to do his job, and Spense was no exception. Considering just how good Spense was at what he did, she couldn't blame him if he lost his cool.

Spense's hand shot into his pocket, and she released her breath. He wasn't going to let Hatcher get his goat after all.

A beat or so passed, then Spense tossed his cube in the air and caught it. "This is a joint task force. Caity and I aren't under your command—we answer to the BAU. While you were wrapping up the press conference, a tip came in to the hotline. We followed it up, and if you weren't so busy braying like an ass I would've told you we think we know who our Jane Doe is. Her name is Harriet Beckerman. You're welcome."

"Harriet Beckerman? Holy shit."

"You can say that again." Caitlin offered the detective a conciliatory smile.

"Holy shit."

Hatcher *really* didn't get the whole figure of speech thing, but she wasn't about to go down that path with him. Caitlin glanced at the door to the interview room. It sounded like a squad of paratroopers was behind it. She could hear shoes clomping, cups clanking, chairs scraping, and voices talking over each other. "Sounds like you've had some excitement around here, too. What gives?"

Hatcher stepped closer and lowered his voice. "We're disbanding the task force."

She took a step back. How could they even think of such a thing after finding a young woman brutally murdered. "That's a bad idea." *Understatement.* "If Laura's still alive, she's in grave danger."

Hatcher angled his head toward the interview room. "Follow me if you dare—it's a madhouse in there—you'll understand everything soon enough."

Now it was Spense wearing the red ears. "You can't disband the task force at a time like this."

"Not my call. This is coming from above." Hatcher shifted back and forth on his feet. "Disband might not be the correct term. Downsize. Reorganize. Resource reallocation. Whatever you wanna call it, it sucks. I'm still on the case, and Cliff. I'm going to try to make an argument to keep you two around a while longer."

Ah, so this accounted, at least in part, for his mood. He didn't want to "downsize" any more than they did.

"But all of this—" Hatcher swept his hand around the room full of burnt orange furniture "—all the extra dough and manpower was in place to find the senator's daughter. And while Harriet Beckerman might be lying up in that morgue with her face chewed off, Laura Chaucer is very much alive . . . and no longer missing . . . technically speaking."

Caitlin's head felt like someone hit the button on the spin cycle. This was a lot to take in in such a short time. Truella Underland's story rang true. Caitlin felt sure dental records would confirm the body in the morgue was that of Harriet Beckerman, a troubled young woman who would never get the chance to turn her life around. Harriet Beckerman had lived in the same apartment complex and had been friends with Laura Chaucer . . . and now the task force was being downsized because Laura, apparently, was alive. And judging by Hatcher's reaction, he'd heard the name Harriet Beckerman before. "You found Laura?"

Hatcher opened the door between the war room and the interview room and jerked his head. "Just get inside, please. I could really use some help in there. I feel like I'm being torn apart by a pack of wolves—or mountain lions—or whatever." He sent Caitlin a feeble smile, and she knew his attempted joke was really an olive branch.

She took it. "We're all on the same team, Jordan. I'm sorry if it seemed like we left you in the lurch."

"Same team. Let's get to it," Spense said.

Hatcher was clearly beyond pissed about his resources getting pulled and had taken it out on them. But despite his rude behavior he needed Spense and her more than ever. The three entered the interview room en masse, ready to face the wild beasts—who turned out to be a rather tame-looking group, but Caitlin understood that didn't mean their fangs weren't sharp.

Whit Chaucer, his wife Tracy, and Grady Webber were all dressed in the same conservative designer garb they'd worn to the press conference. Ron Saas—she recognized him from the press conference, too—wore khaki pants, a white button-down, and a tweed sports coat. She assumed they'd been given the news that Laura was alive, and yet no one looked relieved.

Whit's angry, purple face was a stark contrast to his wife's sickly pale one. Saas's shoulders were hunched like he was ready to raise his fists and defend himself if someone else threw the first punch. Grady's face was a blank slate that she knew from experience would be written and re-written with whatever emotion he deemed opportune.

Hatcher pointed a finger at Saas. "Tell Agent Spenser and Dr. Cassidy what you told the rest of us."

Okay, not wasting time with introductions and small talk. Fine with her. Saas undoubtedly knew Spense and her from all the attention the media had showered on them anyway.

Saas crossed his arms over his chest. "Laura Chaucer scheduled an appointment with me for Monday night, but when I checked my calendar, it had been canceled. I've never had the pleasure of meeting the young lady, but I did see her this morning. She came to my office around eight, on her own steam, under no apparent duress, and demanded a meeting. She did give a false name—Ruby Rogers. My assistant wanted to help her and agreed to work her in. But then, when I was about to go out and greet her, she turned and ran out of the office."

"We've confirmed Mr. Sass's story," Hatcher said. "Cliff reviewed security footage. CCT caught Laura in several campus locations over the course of this morning—unaccompanied and unharmed."

So why did everyone look so damn miserable? Why weren't they toasting the good health of Senator Whit Chaucer's prodigal daughter? Obviously she hadn't returned to the fold.

"You should've called it in." Grady narrowed his eyes suspiciously at Saas.

"I told you already, or maybe I told the detective. I recognized her from having seen her in publicity shots with her father, but I didn't know Laura was missing until the press conference. She came to my office around eight a.m., before the announcement."

Caitlin didn't quite understand either. "You said she canceled her meeting with you earlier in the week. But you were seen at dinner with her Monday night."

"I did not meet with her. I don't know where you got your information but it's absolutely false."

"Didn't you interview him to confirm Cayman's account?" Spense asked Hatcher.

"Cayman and Senator Chaucer spent the better part of Tuesday looking for Laura, and reported her missing late that night. Wednesday, we put this task force together and got boots on the ground. Mr. Saas was scheduled to come in on Thursday for questioning—but as you know Thursday we had matters to attend up in the wilderness. We had to reschedule him for later today."

"And you didn't know why the police wanted to talk to you?" Caitlin asked Saas.

"No one told me jack, except that it was about one of the students at Holly Hill. Had Detective Hatcher bothered to inform me of the situation, naturally I would've called the instant I saw Laura. I would've had campus security detain her. Don't try to put this on me. You people blew it."

"We don't inform you vultures in the press of anything until we're ready for the entire world to know," Hatcher said gruffly, then turned to Spense and her. "Got any more questions for Mr. Saas before I kick him out?"

Caitlin nodded. "Are you in the habit of dining out with female students?"

Saas jumped to his feet. "No."

"Then why set up a dinner meeting with Laura, and why did she cancel?"

"I don't know the reason. My assistant deleted the meeting on the calendar. I don't know who called to cancel or why. I don't normally take students to dinner, but Laura is the daughter of . . ."

He didn't have to finish. Everyone knew whose daughter Laura was, and clearly Saas had wanted to give her the VIP treatment.

"She claimed she had new information about the death of Angelina Antonelli. You can't blame me for nipping at bait like that."

"So you did talk to her when you set up the dinner?"

"Yes, my assistant put her through at her request."

"But she didn't hint at the information?" Chaucer asked.

"Not a peep."

The senator got to his feet and extended his hand. Saas shook it. They both glared at Hatcher, the guy who blew it.

"Thanks for coming forward with the information Laura is alive. Her mother and I are incredibly grateful."

"Glad I could help." Saas turned to Hatcher. "Am I free to go?"

"Don't let the door hit you." Hatcher paused. "And don't leave town without telling us."

Saas made no answer as he exited the room, and Hatcher pulled the door closed behind him.

"Now that the press has left the building, would someone please tell me why everyone's so damn miserable?" Spense asked. He didn't really care who answered him. It was clear everyone else in this room still knew something he and Caity did not.

Chaucer gnawed his lower lip the same as Spense had seen him do during a debate, pondering the matter long and hard, as though world peace depended on his response. In the end he let his wife speak for them.

"Laura called Grady a couple of hours ago. She, she . . ." Tracy Chaucer's voice thinned and finally disappeared altogether.

Webber took over. "She claimed her friend, Harriet Beckerman, had been murdered and that she—Laura—had a lock of her hair. Then she concocted a wild story about being drugged and waking up with her throat slashed. But since she's running around all over campus none the worse for wear, there's no question she's lying about that part."

Chaucer turned even more purple and grabbed his old friend by the collar, yanking him to his feet. "You're the one concocting the wild story, Grady."

Webber coughed and sputtered, and put one hand up. "I'm sorry, Whit. Truly, I am. But I have to tell the truth."

Spense and Caity exchanged a glance.

Was she thinking what he was thinking? Why would Laura believe Harriet had been murdered unless she'd done it or witnessed it or . . .

"Grady, I respect your opinion, but this time, I think you've got it wrong. Laura is simply not capable of such a horrific crime." Tracy Chaucer pulled her husband by the hand to sit back down. He continued to stand, so she gave up.

"You just lost me," Spense said.

Hatcher cleared his throat. "While you and Dr. Cassidy were out, Webber rendered a professional opinion: he's fingered Laura Chaucer as a killer."

This was getting very interesting. Spense could hardly wait to hear the good doctor's theory.

"I didn't finger anybody. I just threw out the possibility. Tracy's absolutely correct. In her right mind, Laura wouldn't kill a spider if it sat down beside her. When she's lucid, she's a sweetheart of a girl with a generous spirit. I'm not suggesting anything to the contrary. But we have to face facts. If she's lost touch with reality again, we don't know what she's capable of doing. If she has a lock of Harriet Beckerman's hair, and if Harriet really has been murdered, well, I'm afraid we all know what two and two equals."

"What the hell do you mean *lost touch with reality again*? The only reason she ever lost touch with it in the first place was because you prescribed the wrong medications. She hasn't had a hallucination in years." Chaucer grabbed his chest like he was out of wind and finally, sat down next to his wife.

"Whit, please don't play the blame game with me."

"Don't play the shrink game with me. I am not a goddamn patient of yours, Grady. Save the cutesy lingo for Tracy. She appreciates your cleverness more than me."

Tracy inhaled sharply.

"Let's be clear on two things, Whit. Both you and Tracy wanted Laura . . . comfortable. You insisted I do whatever it took to keep her anxiety at bay. You're the ones who wanted her to never suffer a sleepless night. If it took some adjustments to get her meds right, that's no fault of mine."

"He's right, Whit." Tracy looked up from the floor.

"What's the other thing?" Hatcher asked.

"Hmm?"

"You said *let's be clear on two things*," Caity put in.

"Oh, yes. About Laura's hallucinations. I said they were *largely* due to the medications. But the truth is the etiology of psychosis is multi-factorial."

"English, for God's sake." Hatcher rubbed his temples.

"A break with reality is rarely due to one thing. It's the result of genetic predisposition, environment, organic issues like alterations in brain chemistry, and social stimuli."

"That's not English."

"It's nature, nurture and the bad shit that happens to you." When Webber looked at Tracy and Chaucer, Spense saw his expression turn ingratiating. "Not that you should hold yourselves in any way responsible."

"We don't," Whit retorted.

"And that's as it should be." Now Webber's tone was down-right obsequious. It wouldn't surprise Spense if the guy kissed the senator's ring.

"Hold on," Hatcher interrupted. "Regardless of Laura's sweet disposition, and who's to blame for her problems, I'd like Dr. Webber to elaborate on this break with reality theory of his."

"All right. Let's see. I believe the *bad shit that happens to you* category would include Laura's kidnapping and Angelina's murder. Now we've reached the anniversary of that traumatic event. Laura is off her meds and living away from her protected, safe, familiar environment. Her neighbor friend happens to look like her dead nanny. I believe those factors combined to create a perfect storm and cause what laymen call a nervous breakdown."

"A nervous breakdown is one thing. Killing your friend is quite another," Hatcher said.

"Well, of course I'm just hypothesizing. You're the detective." Webber made a half bow to Hatcher. "But we know Laura's never recovered from her childhood trauma. Just suppose the anniversary triggered a psychotic episode in which Laura was driven by an irresistible impulse to re-enact that awful day."

"So she lures her friend, Harriet, who looks like Angelina, up to the same wilderness area where she was taken as a child, then stabs her, strangles her, and dumps her body? Fuck you, Grady. My daughter didn't do it." Chaucer doubled his fists.

"Then why won't she come home?" Hatcher asked.

"Maybe the delusional part is true. Maybe because it's the anniversary of her kidnapping and she's off her meds, she thinks the kidnapper is after her again," Whit conceded.

"That seems possible," Tracy said, then turned to Webber. "Doesn't it?"

"I think we should warn the public Laura may be dangerous." Hatcher grimaced.

"This is preposterous," Chaucer said. "You cannot warn the public my daughter is dangerous based on unsupported bullshit. That could put *her* in danger."

"Can you live with it if we don't say anything and something else happens . . . someone else gets hurt?" Tracy's voice broke. "Are you worried about Laura or about your public image?"

"Both if it's all right with you."

"No. It most definitely is not all right with me. Just once, can't you put your family first?" Tracy went to Webber and stood beside him. "I'm not letting you run the show this time, Whit. I'm going to stay right here. I want to be included in all decisions regarding our daughter. I don't give a rat's ass—" she stuck out her jaw "—how this looks to your constituents. I want Laura home safe and lord knows I do not want someone else's daughter hurt because we didn't do the right thing."

A vein bulged in Chaucer's neck. "You're so infatuated with Grady Webber you're buying into his lies about Laura."

Her back went ramrod straight. "My feelings for Grady have nothing to do with this."

"They sure as hell do. He's got you bamboozled into believing your own daughter, *my* sweet Laura, is a murderer."

"I trust Grady. He knows Laura better than we do, and that's the God's truth. If she's done something wrong, she's not responsible."

Caity put her hand on Tracy's shoulder. "Look, you've offered a reward for Laura's safe return. That means the public may try to intervene if they spot Laura. Until we know more about her state of mind, I suggest we advise the public not to pursue Laura if they do spot her." She let out a long breath. "Senator, how about a compromise?"

"I'm listening."

"What if we say Laura has suffered a trauma and may be emotionally unstable, therefore please notify the authorities if seen, but do not attempt to make contact with her?"

"I guess that would work." Chaucer sent both Caity and him an imploring look. "Do you two believe this nonsense Grady's spouting?"

Caity didn't miss a beat. "Personally, I think Dr. Webber's theory is highly unlikely. These crimes do seem connected—but that does not mean Laura's at fault. Earlier today, Agent Spenser and I were putting a profile together that suggested a sexual opportunist may have been responsible for Angelina's death."

Tracy gasped. "Oh, my God! Are you calling Laura a sexual predator? You think she killed Angelina?"

"At the age of eight? While not impossible, it's about as likely as the trout frying up the fisherman for supper," Caity answered.

"And if we are, in fact, dealing with a sexual predator, then statistically speaking," Spense said, sending Webber a scorching look, "odds are far better that someone right here in this very room killed Angelina Antonelli and Harriet Beckerman than that Laura Chaucer did."

The air grew thin and silent. A few beats later, Caity broke it. "And by the way, we seem to be missing one of our key players. What about the bodyguard who gave the false report of Ronald Saas having dinner with Laura? Why isn't he here?"

"Cayman." Hatcher shook his head. "At the moment, we can't seem to find him."

Chapter 32

Friday, October 25
8:00 P.M.
Hostel Digs
Denver, Colorado

TWENTY-ONE DOLLARS A night was a bit more than Laura had planned on, but Hostel Digs was well worth it. She'd scored a private room, and so far the quarters next door were empty. Nevertheless, she planned to sleep in her blond wig, facing the wall just in case . . . besides, the place was a bit chilly, and the wig kept her head warm—so it all worked out.

The other good thing, and the real reason she'd shelled out the extra dough, was that Hostel Digs provided both free iPads and free Wi-Fi for guests. That meant she didn't have to risk going back to Get Wired or pay for the privilege of using the Internet. Both the device and the signal came courtesy of a host claiming to be "jazzed" to have her here.

She powered up the tablet then signed on as a guest. The tablet blinked back at her, and she found herself yawning, waiting for the signal to pick up. First order of business was to Google Caitlin and her partner. Laura had heard the park ranger call him *Agent Spenser*, so Laura assumed both he and Caitlin were FBI.

The signal indicator was still blank.

The tablet was taking a long time to connect, and her eyelids were drooping.

She yawned again, and rolled over on her side, facing the wall.

It had been a long, exhausting week.

The light from the tablet had a hypnotic effect on her brain.

She closed her eyes and felt herself fading.

Don't fight it, Laura. Just sleep . . .

Her arm jerked, and she drifted off to dreams.

Her core seemed cold, frozen solid. Shivers, originating from deep within wracked her body, and yet her palm was so moist she could barely grip the pen in her hand.

"Get on with it." That low growl in her ear was all too familiar. So why couldn't she remember him?

She *knew* the figure looming over her, but she didn't dare turn her head. She didn't dare see.

Not with a knife at her throat.

Where, where, where had she heard that voice before?

"What are you waiting for, Laura. Do exactly as you're told, or I'll end you."

That might be for the best.

He was never going to let her go—not again.

She looked around and saw the cabin walls, looked down and saw her naked body tied to a chair.

So this was why her arms had been bound only to the elbows. It wasn't an act of kindness so that she could cover herself with her hands. How absurd that she'd ever believed him capable of even a glimmer of humanity.

He'd left her hands free so that she could do his bidding—so that she could write the note.

He was making her complicit in his diabolical plan.

"Kill me, please," she managed to say. Her words sounded scratchy and weak.

"Don't worry. You're going to die. The only question is whether you want it to be a peaceful death, or a slow, agonizing one."

She swallowed, tasting tears and salt and bitter medicine. Her tongue was thick and dry. Gripping the pen tighter, she began making slow marks. Tears fell on the paper blurring the ink.

Her soul felt so very light, her body, so very heavy.

"No."

No? She'd displeased him.

She was trying, but she couldn't remember what was happening. The knife pressed into her flesh.

"Do not stop writing. How do you want to die, Laura?"

This was a question she'd asked herself many times. More than once she'd hoarded her pills with the plan to swallow them all at once. It would be so lovely to simply drift off to sleep.

"In peace," she whispered. "I want to die in peace."

"Then finish it," he said.

Despite the growing weakness in her arms, the lightness in her head, the excruciating ache in her hand, she did as she was told. Each word he whispered in her ear, she made real with ink on paper. At last, he finished. The pen slipped from her hand.

She was weak, weak, weak.

She didn't know how, but she knew this note she'd written would help him.

She should've been stronger.

If only she had another chance, she would show more courage.

I promise, next time, I'll be brave.

He grabbed the letter and read it aloud, still lurking behind her to hide his face. She pictured him with horns and red glowing eyes as he sounded out the awful words she'd written.

Her false testimony.

"Good girl." His terrible voice rumbled through her. "Now you can rest. Now you die."

Chapter 33

Friday, October 25
8:45 P.M.
Mountain View Hotel
Denver, Colorado

"So." SPENSE TOOK Caity in his arms and pulled her against him. For a moment, he just held her, his hand coasting up and down her back in time with the rhythm of her heart as it beat against his.

She sighed, and even though he wanted her badly—he always wanted her badly—he understood how tired she must be. He planted a kiss on the top of her head. Her hair smelled nice, like the balsam shampoo she'd picked up in the hotel gift shop. "It's been a long couple of days. Maybe we should hit the sack early."

"Spense . . ." When she tilted her face up, the delicate blue of her eyes seemed muted. "We need to talk."

"Okay." About Webber, he guessed. It was only yesterday, in the limo, that Webber had made it clear he had some kind of past with Caity, but it seemed an eternity had gone by since then. While Spense hadn't forgotten about Webber's remarks, he'd been so busy with mountain lions and autopsies and missing body-guards, there simply hadn't been time to dwell on Grady Webber and Caity.

Grady Webber and Caity.

It hit him now, though, and his blood rose, rushing through his body like a river with the floodgates open.

He released Caity. Working on steadying his breathing, he paced the perimeter of the room twice before returning to her side. "What's up?"

It didn't bother him that she hadn't told him about Webber before now. He and Caity hadn't been a couple long enough to exhaust all their war stories. He certainly hadn't shared all of his with her yet. Though they hadn't begun their transformation from "frenemies" into lovers until a few short months ago, it seemed to Spense they'd been together an entire lifetime. Maybe the things they'd been through together had accelerated the bonding process, or maybe, as corny as it sounded, there was truth to the notion that we all have a soul mate.

Anyway, they'd faced death together more than once, and when his life had "flashed before his eyes," it was mostly moments he'd shared with Caity. The plain truth was he didn't think much of his past before her, and he didn't want to picture a future with-out her.

So while he wasn't bothered that Caity hadn't yet told him about Grady Webber, the suspicion that Webber might've hurt her really got to him. The way her posture stiffened up around him, the wary look on her face every time Webber came near her made Spense want to wrap her in his arms and tell her he'd never let a creep like that hurt her again. He'd never let *anyone* hurt her again. "Is this about Webber?"

She nodded, and drawing a long breath, sat down on the bed.

"I hate the way that guy acts like he still has some sort of claim on you. It's nothing I can call him on, or believe me, I would have. But I don't like the way he talks to you, and I sure don't like the way he looks at you."

She grabbed his hand, gripping it tightly. "Exactly. And that's not a new problem. When I was with him . . ." She looked away.

"It's okay, hon. I'm a big boy. I know you've been with other guys."

She met his gaze. "When I was with him, he acted like he owned me. And when we broke up, he still acted that way. And now . . ."

With their hands entwined, Caity proceeded to tell him, in the most matter-of-fact way possible, all about Dr. Grady Webber. The man who was supposed to be her teacher and mentor had come on to her when she was a doctor in training. She didn't say she'd been especially vulnerable to the attentions of an older man because she was still devastated over the loss of her father, but it didn't take a genius to figure that one out. Through the entire telling, Spense kept his thoughts centered, his hand on hers, and his emotions in check.

Right up until she told him what happened yesterday at headquarters.

"He followed you into the bathroom?"

"Yes."

A bomb detonated in his chest. "That son of a bitch."

Caity's grip on his hand tightened. "Not to worry. I've already handled it."

He was on his feet, and she rose with him, still clinging to his hand.

"Spense, I said I handled it. It's over."

He pried her fingers off. At the closet, he grabbed his jacket and felt in the pocket until his keys jangled.

"Where are you going?"

He could see her breathing had accelerated.

He could see the worry in her eyes.

She should be worried.

About Webber.

She trailed him out into the hall. "I'm coming with you."

She was barefoot. It was forty degrees outside. "Ten seconds."

"What do you mean?"

"That's how long I'm giving you to get your coat and shoes."

She met his eyes. "It's also how long I'm giving you to get a grip. Start counting."

The drive over took seventeen minutes. Seventeen minutes during which Caity pleaded, cajoled, and begged him to keep a cool head. Seventeen minutes during which his blood got hotter and hotter until he could've sworn he had boiling water running through his veins. He shed his coat and cracked a window to let in cool air, but then saw Caity shivering. He rolled the window up again and turned on the heat. Perspiration dripped into his eyes, and he swatted it away with the back of his hand. "Warm enough?"

"Yes, thanks. Why are we going to Grady's place again? What are you planning to do?" Caity asked for the hundredth time.

She was going to find out sooner or later. He might as well prepare her. "Kick his ass."

"Oh good. That's just what I was hoping you'd say."

The car had now officially turned into a kiln. Some of his anger seemed to be burning off along with the top layer of his skin. "Now you're trying reverse psychology, but it's not going to stop me."

"Of course not. Because why would you forgo the fun of an ass-whooping just because I asked you to?"

"You think I'm going to enjoy . . ." He didn't finish his sentence because the truth was he relished the idea of knocking the guy flat.

"You're nearly a half foot taller than Grady. You've taken down killers in hand-to-hand combat. Grady looks in shape, I know, but he gets his muscles from a gym where they serve cucumber water. He's an academic psychiatrist. It won't be a fair fight."

"Life's not fair." But she had a point.

"You're not doing this for me."

"Like hell."

"You said it yourself. You don't like the way he talks to me. You don't like the way he looks at me. If you ask me—"

"Not asking you, babe."

"If you ask me, you've been itching for an excuse to show him who's the alpha dog around here, and now you've got one. This isn't about protecting me. This is about your big fat giant out-of-control ego." She jammed her finger on the AC. Now she was sweating.

Shit.

What he saw on her cheek wasn't a drop of perspiration.

He braked so hard his seat belt went taut over his shoulder. He slowed, looking for a place to pull over. Coincidentally, he found one right in front of Grady's place.

"Do not cry," he said through gritted teeth.

"I'm not crying."

"Caity, I swear. This has nothing to do with my ego." *Maybe just a little.* "I don't want that pissant little creep anywhere near you."

"He's a witness in our case. Which means we have to deal with him. But I've already set firm boundaries. Problem solved."

"Caity, following you into the bathroom is a big deal. He was way out of line. No telling how far he'll try to take it next time."

"There's not going to be a next time. And I'll say it again, he's a material witness. If you let your temper get the best of you, then Grady wins. He can file a complaint against you, get you kicked off the case. He could even get you arrested for assault."

"He doesn't have the balls."

"You're underestimating him. Grady's smart and manipulative. He'll make it look like you're the aggressor. You *are* the aggressor. Let's just turn around and go home." She grabbed his hand. "I can take care of myself, but if you get hurt, I get hurt. Grady has probably already figured out that's the best way to get back at me. I wouldn't be surprised if he's expecting you right now. Don't let him play you."

He put his head on the steering wheel. Tried to focus on her words. She was making a lot of sense. He'd made her promises, too, that he wouldn't let his feelings for her interfere with getting the job done. It was what they'd agreed on. That was the deal, and he was supposed to honor it.

"Okay," he said. "I'll just talk to him. But Grady Webber needs to know that if he touches a hair on your head, I'm coming after him." He blew out a breath and pocketed his keys.

He came around and got her door for her.

As they headed up the front steps to Grady's home, she smiled at him, and talking low, like a trainer soothing an unbroken horse said, "Take it easy."

She was right. Of course, she was right. "I promise. I'm just going to talk to him and set him straight." The three of them would have a nice, mature, grown-up conversation during which he'd make his position perfectly clear.

He rang the bell.

Grady Webber opened the door wearing a red-and-black silk dressing gown. He held a snifter of brandy, or perhaps whiskey, in one hand. With the other he motioned them inside. "To what do I owe the pleasure?"

He didn't look a bit surprised. Maybe, like Caity said, he'd been expecting them all along.

"We just want to talk, Grady. I hope it's not too inconvenient." Caity walked through the door, and Spense followed.

"Anytime you want to come to me, Caitlin, night or day, I'm always ready for you." Webber's tongue darted out of his mouth, and he ran it around the rim of his snifter. He fixed his gaze on Caity's breasts and then did it again.

Spense glanced down at his hand, watching it curl into a fist in slow motion. His arm drew back, then sprang forward. He heard a loud crack and saw Grady's chin snap back from his first jab, then again when he punched him square in the face.

His knuckles stung and vibrated.

Webber tottered back, and crumpled to the floor, blood gushing from his nose.

Then he looked up at Spense . . . and smiled.

BACK AT THE hotel, Caitlin rushed into the bathroom and bolted the door behind her. The irony of locking herself in against the man she loved, after having left a door wide open to a man she loathed didn't escape her.

It was an empty gesture on her part, since unlike Grady, Spense would never intrude on her privacy. But she'd wanted him to hear the click of the lock, hoping his gut would clench at the sound, the way hers had sickened when she'd heard his fist connect with Grady's chin.

She sat down on the edge of the tub and turned on the water, then absently watched as it circled down the drain.

Like Spense's career.

She dipped her hand in the water, shook the droplets from it, then turned off the faucet and stood up.

Don't be ridiculous.

Spense was far too valuable to the FBI, and far too admired by his peers for one punch to end his illustrious career. But it might get him disciplined, and most certainly would get him tossed off the case, if Grady pursued the matter. And from the way Grady had gotten to his feet, practically gloating about needing a hankie for his bleeding nose, it was clear he intended to do Spense as much harm as possible. It wouldn't surprise her a bit if Grady had something like this up his sleeve the whole time.

She kicked the base of the toilet, and then took off her shoe and rubbed her throbbing foot. She shouldn't have told Spense about the bathroom incident in the first place.

No. That wasn't right. She should've told him, and he should've acted like a reasonable adult.

"Caity." Spense rapped on the door. "You okay in there?"

"Fine."

He knocked again.

"Can I come in?"

She sighed. Now who was being childish?

"I'm coming out."

She opened the door, and there he stood, arms open, a look

of contrition on his face. She could either brush past him and be miserable the rest of the night . . . or . . . she fell against him. "Dammit, Spense. I wish you hadn't done that."

She waited for him to say he wished he hadn't too, but he didn't.

He kissed the top of her head, then her eyelids, then finally, and softly, he kissed her lips. Instinctively, she opened her mouth for him, and for one moment, forgot everything except the deliciousness of being kissed by a man who knew her every weakness. Had she not run out of breath, said kiss might've ended the discussion once and for all. Summoning all her will she came up for air and stepped out of his embrace.

His arms dangled slowly back to his sides. "I'm sorry that I upset you. But I'm not sorry I decked him. I'd do it again—"

She stopped him by pressing her fingers to his lips before he said something to make her regret the moment they'd just shared. She'd cooled off, and she had something important on her mind. "You know it was wrong, but I don't want to keep going around and around about it. It's over and done. I'd like to forget it entirely, but I don't think that's wise. Grady has ammunition against you, now—if he chooses to use it. So I'd suggest you shut up and let me get to work."

"Get to work on what?"

"The best defense is an offense. Did you copy the files of Grady's sessions with Laura?"

Spense tilted his head. "You're thinking his records might reveal some unethical practices . . ."

"We can kill two pigeons at once. Arm ourselves against an attack by Grady and figure out what the hell is happening to Laura Chaucer at the same time."

"I'm in."

"Good. Because I'm not leaving this room until I've been through every page of this thirteen-year medical record."

She sat at the table, while Spense prowled the room.

"We can split them up," he said.

She shook her head. "I need to look at these all myself. So there's really no point. No offense, but you wouldn't know what to look for."

"Then how am I going to help?"

She smiled. "You can order room service."

He ordered up a salad for himself, and a cheeseburger for her, then he hopped in the shower. When he came back the room smelled like shaving cream. He stretched out in his boxers on the bed, and she had to turn her back to avoid the distraction.

Her cheeseburger sat forgotten while she combed through the files. Spense ate his salad and thumbed through the Agatha Christie she'd been reading on the plane.

Three hours in, she laid a thick sheaf of papers down, and threw her head back. She was tired. The soft sound of snoring came from the general vicinity of the bed where Spense sprawled with his mouth open. Her eyelids drifted shut. Then suddenly, her head jerked to her chest, and the movement startled her into consciousness . . . and a sudden realization. "Oh lord. I think I'm onto something."

Spense moaned, then she felt something soft hit her in the back of her head.

A pillow.

"You woke me up." He came around and sat beside her at the work table. "This better be good."

She turned her chair toward him, her knees touching his. "Chemical restraint."

"Say again."

"Grady's been using a form of chemical restraint on Laura. It's so obvious, I don't know why it took me so long to see it."

"I think I can guess what you mean, but maybe you better spell it out."

"Chemical restraint is just exactly that. You don't have to put someone in a straitjacket to exert physical control over them—and when you use drugs to keep someone's behavior in check, there's an added benefit—you can exert control over not just their body, but their mind. There are plenty of medications designed to make a person docile."

"There ought to be a law against that."

"Believe me, there are plenty of them. But it's tricky. A lot depends on the discretion of the doctor, and how the law is interpreted."

"That's a hefty accusation. You sure he intended to use Laura's medications to control her?"

She wasn't. "No, but, whether or not it was the intent, it was definitely the result. For example, here—" She laid a medication sheet in front of him. "Grady prescribed haloperidol, lorazepam, and phenobarbital—all at the same time."

Spense dragged a hand over his face, but he no longer looked sleepy. "I thought phenobarbital was used for seizures."

"It is." She slapped down a progress note. "Says here he prescribed it for anxiety and as a sleep aid. That is a legitimate use of a barbiturate, but it causes central nervous system depression. Haloperidol is an antipsychotic but he's using it for anxiety again, *and* lorazepam *and* diazepam. Every single one of these drugs induces sleep and docility. It's a wonder Laura could hold her head up, much less understand what was happening to her."

"Webber did say the Chaucers wanted her to get a good night's rest."

"I doubt they meant they wanted her sleepwalking through life. And this is just a slice of the picture. According to these records Laura was subjected to poly-pharmacy—"

He held his hand up.

"The use of multiple meds at once, for over a decade. And Spense, some of these medications can increase the risk of suicide. All of them used together . . ." She shuddered. "Looks like Laura Chaucer's been walking around with a time bomb inside her."

"And Grady Webber has the nuclear codes."

Chapter 34

Saturday, October 26
8:00 A.M.
Task force headquarters
Highlands Hotel
Denver, Colorado

SPENSE STEPPED AROUND an upended couch in what was left of the war room. The orange monstrosity listed precariously against the wall, and he stuck out his arm to hold it in place as Caity passed by. "Didn't take long to dismantle this place," he observed to a glum Hatcher.

"All the extra furniture is going back to the rental center today. But at least the commander gave Cliff and me the suite until the end of next week—it's paid up through then."

"And the rest of the team?" Caity asked.

"Reassigned."

Their own fate, his and Caity's, suddenly became an elephant swinging from the rented chandelier.

"S'pose you're wondering why I called you in first thing."

Spense had a pretty good idea. When they'd received Hatcher's summons an hour ago, he figured Webber had already filed a complaint. "You gonna cuff me now or later?" He attempted a laugh, but if anything, it only made the doom and gloom in the room more oppressive.

"Webber's not going to press charges," Hatcher said.

A hopeful smile broke over Caity's face, but judging by Hatcher's sour expression, Spense knew the other shoe was about to drop. "So what did he want in exchange?"

"You. Off the case."

"And you agreed?"

"I said *no problemo.* Not like they haven't already cut the guts out of the task force. I didn't expect to get to keep you anyway."

"But Caity and I are on the FBI's dime. Doesn't cost your department a thing," Spense said. He understood he couldn't have any further dealings with Webber since it might taint any new evidence they got from him, but there was no reason to kick Spense to the curb altogether. He was surprised Hatcher hadn't put up more of a fight. "I can work around this thing. Stay out of Webber's way . . ."

"He wants you gone. That's part of the deal."

"What's the rest of the deal?" Caity asked quietly. Her eyes, normally such a vivid blue against the jet black of her thick lashes now seemed almost gray. Last night, they'd been a softened color, too. Those eyes of hers were like a damn mood ring.

Hatcher stared at a spot on the wall and said, "Caitlin. She's gone, too."

"Like hell." Spense slammed his fist into his palm. "Nobody's going to pay for my stupidity but me."

"Not how it works. You and Caitlin are a package deal. If one of you gets a rose, the other does, too. And if one of you gets sent home . . ."

"This isn't a dating show." Caity collapsed into one of the remaining chairs.

"Then your boyfriend shouldn't have acted like a jealous jackass."

"Jackass, I'll give you," Spense said. Though he was far from jealous of Grady Webber. Caity couldn't stand the guy. "But Webber's got to respect the boundaries Caity sets for him. I'm not going to stand by and let him get away with murder."

"Let's hope you didn't just." Caity shrugged one shoulder.

That was harsh.

And coming from Caity, the nicest kid in the world, it just about killed him. He'd hoped the way they'd cooperated last night meant she'd forgiven him. But maybe that had been more for the sake of justice than for love.

"Listen, Jordan. Keep Caity on. I'll bow out completely. Officially. Unofficially. Every-icially." He made a hands-off gesture. "I swear."

"Can't do it. Webber was crystal clear about his terms."

"Who gives a flying fuck? Go ahead and charge me with assault. I earned my lumps and I can take them. There's no reason for Caity to get the axe, too."

"It's out of my hands. Commander's officially blacklisted the both of you. The reason I called you in this morning was for one last meeting. I need you to turn over all your notes, fill me in on your working profile, etc."

"If you want our work product, then you have to keep us in the loop," Caity said.

"I've already told you, it's not up to me."

"No." She checked her nails. "I don't mean that you would go against the commander's orders. We would go off the books . . . but not off the loop. And don't try to tell me you never had anyone off book before. Besides, there's no one left around to tell tales anymore, right?"

"Just Cliff."

"You trust Cliff," she said. "It's obvious. So what've you got to lose? Spense and I operating behind the scenes could be a good thing. It gives us more freedom to bend the rules."

Spense clapped the base of his palm to his ear. Did he just hear *Caity* suggest bending the rules? Maybe he'd set a better example for her than he'd realized. But he couldn't let her make that sacrifice for him. "I don't want you to risk your reputation because I screwed up, Caity."

"You screwed up, all right."

Yep. She was still pissed.

"But I'd rather risk my career than let a predator go free."

Hatcher scratched the back of his neck, then motioned for them to sit. "You still think there's a predator out there? You're not buying Dr. Webber's theory about Laura re-enacting the murder of Angelina Antonelli?"

"The guy's a quack at best." Spense pulled up a chair next to Caity and across from Hatcher. "Last night, Caity went through a bunch of his notes and transcripts. We were hoping to find some minor professional mistakes Webber made that we could use to hold him at bay."

"Why didn't you say so? Maybe it's not too late to renegotiate."

Caity shook her heard. "We found mistakes all right, but they weren't minor. In good conscience, we can't go to Grady and make a deal with what we found. There's too much at stake. I wouldn't want to tip our hand or promise to hush his conduct up either. Once all the puzzle pieces are in place in this criminal investigation, we'll be ethically obligated to turn our findings over to the board of medical examiners."

"Why would Webber give us his files if he knows he did wrong?"

"Because he's arrogant. I'm sure he thinks, if challenged, he can explain away all the crap he pulled," Spense said.

"You gonna share that crap with me?"

"Are you keeping us in the loop?" Caity asked.

Look at her, playing hardball. Spense couldn't help but puff out his chest.

"How about you two get your asses down to Boulder, or wherever your family is, and lay low. I can't exactly keep you on speed dial, but let's just say I won't delete your number from my contacts either."

"Good enough." Caity took her time and thoroughly explained to Hatcher how Webber had been using Laura's medications as a form of chemical restraint.

"Shrinks!" Hatcher said, when Caity wrapped it all up. Then he cast a glance at his feet. "No offense, Caitlin."

"None taken. I'm well aware that although a good psychiatrist can be a godsend for someone in need, a bad one can do grave harm."

Hatcher raised his finger in the air. "You know what struck me wrong about Webber was how in that very first interview he kept dancing around the issue of whether or not he thought Laura was dangerous. One minute he was implying she killed her nanny because she had a lock of her hair in a sock, and the next he was saying the lock of hair was just a hallucination. Then he changed again and said maybe the hair in the sock was real . . ."

"But went the way of all missing socks," Caity finished Hatcher's sentence for him.

"With shrinks like that . . ."

"No wonder Laura believed she might've killed her nanny," Spense said. He scrunched his eyes up. "Caity, what's that old Ingrid Bergman movie?"

She sent Hatcher a look. "Spense gets a little distracted sometimes."

"No. No. No," Spense said. "This isn't that." He pulled out his cube and solved it in a jiff. "See?"

"Okay, sorry. But anyway, no, I don't know that old Ingrid Bergman movie. Maybe if you clue the rest of us in on how you got from a lock of hair tied with ribbon and stuffed in a sock to a classic film it might jog my memory."

"It had Claude Rains in it, too." That wasn't right. "I mean Charles Boyer."

Hatcher clasped his hands together and leaned forward. "I hear you can solve the *Times* crossword in under two minutes. I seen you work that Rubik's cube in nothing flat with your eyes closed. Some people think you're some kind of a genius. But I gotta tell you, Spense, I'm not really feeling it."

"*Gaslight!*" Caity's eyes lit up.

And he was the one who put the shine back in them. "Yep. That's the one."

"Of course." She reached her hand toward him, but quickly drew it back. "Spense, you really *are* a genius."

"Still not feeling it." Hatcher straightened in his chair.

"Go ahead, Caity, you explain it."

"Well, I'm not sure where you were going, but I'm thinking about that disappearing lock of hair."

That's exactly where he'd been going.

Caity shifted her body toward Hatcher. "In *Gaslight*, Ingrid Bergman is a psychologically vulnerable young woman who's been through a terrible trauma. She witnessed the murder of her beloved aunt. Charles Boyer plays her villainous husband who tries to make her question her own sanity."

Spense couldn't contain himself. "Paula—that's Ingrid Bergman—finds a letter signed with the killer's name—it's her husband, only now he's using a different name."

"So the husband hides the letter, and tells his wife it never existed in the first place. *Oh, my dear Paula, you imagined it. You must be losing your mind, my darling*—I'm paraphrasing."

"And then he gives her a pill and sends her to bed, or something like that." Spense spread his palms triumphantly.

"Do you see, now?" Caity asked Hatcher.

"You think somebody's Gaslighting Laura?"

"Locks of hair don't just disappear. Maybe Laura did imagine them, but maybe . . . someone in her inner circle, maybe Webber, or someone else, put them in her drawer and then took them away again to keep her off-balance and make her question her own senses. Gaslighting is a real form of psychological abuse, and it doesn't just happen in the movies. The medical term for it is introjection. When someone's traumatized, and then kept isolated, it's not uncommon for them to internalize their abuser's version of world, and of themselves. Even if that version makes absolutely no sense."

"Like the idea Laura killed Angelina," Hatcher said.

Spense jumped in. "No reasonable person could possibly believe Laura Chaucer is responsible for the murder of her nanny.

An eight-year-old child doesn't have the resources to copy her nanny's handwriting in a ransom note, convince the nanny to take her out into the wilderness, and then strangle and stab the nanny to death. But those stories of Laura standing over her sleeping mother with a knife, and the lock of hair she found in her drawer made Laura believe it was possible."

Caity grimaced. "And there have been a few unstable, obsessed bloggers over the years who've suggested Laura did it, too. As fragile as Laura's psyche is, she needed someone to anchor her to reality in the face of those wild accusations."

"Too bad no one did," Hatcher said. "Because while I don't buy Laura having anything to do with her nanny's death—Angelina was an accomplice who paid the price for associating with assholes. I do think maybe, now, Laura really has gone off the reservation.

"She's not eight years old anymore. Truella Underland told the two of you she got a text from her roommate saying that she was with Laura. And Laura called Webber to tell him Harriet had been murdered, and that she had a lock of Harriet's hair to prove it. After all Laura Chaucer has been through, and as wacked-out as everyone claims she is, I have to say I think she might well have killed her friend, Harriet Beckerman. I don't think either Angelina or Harriet were victims of a sexual opportunist. I'm sorry, but that theory is all wet."

"Jordo." Cliff entered the room. "Sorry to interrupt, Roland Pritchard from SLY entertainment news just called. He wants to speak to either Agent Spenser or Dr. Cassidy."

"Oh, dear," Caity said. "Please tell me Kourtney Kennedy's not snooping around another one of our cases."

Hatcher blew a raspberry with his lips. "SLY. Isn't that the gossip show that pays out small fortunes for dirt on celebs? And isn't Kourtney Kennedy the hot chick who broke the news about the Fallen Angel Killer a few weeks ago?"

"One and the same. What line is Pritchard on?" Spense asked.

"He didn't want to hold. He said you should turn to channel eight and watch Kourtney Kennedy's report, then give him a ring and he'll arrange to hand over the evidence."

"What evidence?" Hatcher powered on the TV. "Get him back on the damn line now!"

Chapter 35

"THIS IS KOURTNEY Kennedy bringing you breaking news from SLY entertainment."

Laura choked on the bite of cheese blintz she'd just taken and jerked her gaze to an image of long legs and red stilettos currently beaming from a television mounted in the corner of the breakfast lounge. The camera swept from the shapely legs up to some dramatic cleavage before zooming in on the face of a beautiful anchorwoman with a thousand-watt smile.

Kourtney Kennedy.

Though Laura wasn't in the habit of watching the sleazy SLY celebrity news program, she knew exactly who this woman was. Last night Laura had fallen asleep—to terrible dreams—in front of her tablet, but this morning, before venturing cautiously into the communal area for a free continental breakfast, she'd done an internet search on Cassidy and Spenser. Online, she'd learned their backgrounds and about all their recent cases. Either her father, or the police, had brought in two top mind hunters. Agent Spenser, she now knew to be a profiler for the BAU, Dr. Cassidy a consulting psychiatrist—and Kourtney Kennedy? She was the Hollywood reporter who'd scooped one of their most recent adventures: the case of the Fallen Angel Killer.

Laura gulped a sip of OJ to soothe her burning throat.

"Yesterday, via a Denver press conference, the world learned the daughter of Colorado senator Whitmore Chaucer is missing." Kourtney paused for effect. "Again."

Laura coughed violently. Droplets of juice spewed onto the napkin in her hand. She gasped, relieved to catch her breath. Her gaze darted around the room for the nearest exit.

It was blocked by a couple of granola types, making kissy faces near the croissants. But at least the PDA was distracting the server replenishing the buffet table.

Her breath loosened in her chest.

Be cool, Laura.

"It was thirteen years ago, almost to the day, that Ms. Chaucer was kidnapped from her home in Piney Trails, Colorado. A ransom was paid, and Laura, just eight years old at the time, was recovered alive."

A picture of Angelina popped onto the screen.

"This young woman, Angelina Antonelli, was not so lucky. Police theorized the nanny was an accomplice to Laura Chaucer's kidnapping, and was subsequently murdered by her cohort in crime. But was she really? The case remains famously unsolved. And as everybody knows, we here at SLY never met an unsolved case we didn't like."

There was a smattering of canned applause.

The more Laura's heart raced, the more her thoughts did, too. The press conference had been held yesterday, and Angelina was definitely not *breaking news*.

Something else must be up.

"Like this reporter, I know you, my friends, are deeply curious, given the mysterious past of one of our nation's most notable families. SLY has managed to obtain, from an anonymous source, a logbook containing an entry signed *Laura Chaucer*, as well as a shocking note, purportedly written by Laura herself."

Laura's vision clouded.

She grabbed onto the buffet table for support.

The note!

"We received this important evidence mere hours ago, and our managing editor, the esteemed Roland Pritchard, has already contacted the FBI and the Denver Major Crimes unit. Naturally, we'll be turning both items over to the authorities as soon as arrangements can be made. But the public has the right to know the contents of this disturbing letter."

Laura's heart had galloped itself out, and now was limping along at a slow clip-clop in her chest. She chugged the rest of her juice, hoping the extra fluid might keep her from fainting. It sloshed around in her stomach, making her want to retch.

Kourtney's red lips opened and closed like a talking doll.

Laura couldn't look away as the terrible words came out of the reporter's garish mouth:

Dear Mommy and Daddy,

I've done it again. I know you don't want to believe that your child, whom you have lavished with so much love, could be a murderer. But finally, I need you to believe the truth.

This is the real me.

It was I who killed Angelina Antonelli. I can't explain why or how. I have no memory of the event itself. My mind goes blank, as if I'm in a deep, deep sleep.

But now I'm awake, and I know I've done wrong. The evidence is right here in my hand. All these years, I've kept a lock of Angelina's hair.

And now, I've killed my beautiful friend, Harriet Beckerman. I'm holding her hair in my hand as well. I tied it with a ribbon, just like Angelina's.

I'll enclose both in this envelope as proof I'm telling the truth.

Harriet befriended me when I moved to Denver. She was haunted by her own demons and reached out to help me.

I can't believe this is how I repaid her.

I'm sorry, sorry, sorry.

I'm like the little girl in that movie The Bad Seed. *No matter how hard I try, I cannot control my impulses. There's only one way for me to stop.*

Please forgive me for leaving you like this, but I must end this nightmare once and for all. It's the only way I can be sure I'll never hurt anyone again. I'm such a coward. I tried once more, and failed once more, to die by cutting my own throat. But, I have pills, and I promise to finish the job.

Do not blame yourselves. You've done everything a mother and father could do.

I love you.

This is good-bye.

        Laura

Chapter 36

LAST NIGHT, AFTER being "officially" ordered off the Chaucer case and "unofficially" told to lay low nearby, Spense and Caity traveled to Boulder to be with *the moms*. Though it frustrated him, mostly because he knew he was to blame for getting Caity blackballed by the Major Crimes commander, Spense couldn't help thinking the situation wasn't all bad. He had some very important family business to attend, which was why he'd flown his mom, Agatha, out to be with Caity's mom, Arlene. This visit gave him the perfect chance to drop his bomb without having to abandon his mother before she could process the news.

And with four back-to-back cases in a row, he knew Caity could use a breather.

He knocked, waited a beat, then pushed open the door to Caity's room. He'd been to Arlene and Caity Cassidy's Boulder home before, but he'd never seen her bedroom. "Not a knick-knack kind of a girl, are you?"

Caity sat on a bench in front of the vanity mirror in the nearly naked space. She ran her fingers through her melted chocolate hair, swiped on some Chapstick and turned to him—stopping his heart dead. "I'm hardly ever here."

He knew that, of course. Caity traveled a lot with her psychiatric consulting business, and up until recently things had been tense between her mother and her. He suspected she shared a house with her mostly out of a sense of duty, and that this was more rest stop than home. Still, he'd expected something more than four vanilla walls, an off-white bedspread, and a photograph of her father displayed on the vanity.

Spense made a mental note to get her a colorful throw pillow and a scented candle. Maybe his mom could help pick them out.

"Arlene said to tell you she wants us both home for dinner."

"Why doesn't she tell me herself?"

"She just went out—some kind of friend in need."

Caity nodded. "Right. She mentioned it last night. Her neighbor, Bailey, doesn't drive. This is the day Mom chauffeurs her around to do errands and such."

She got up and took his hand.

Thank God the woman was no good at holding grudges.

"I think I'll run some errands of my own. Might be a good time for you to have your talk with Agatha."

He'd been thinking the same. He kissed the top of her head, then sat down on the vanity bench and kicked out his legs. "Agreed. What do you make of Kourtney Kennedy getting up in our business again?"

She let out a breath. "Don't be too hard on her, Spense. It's Kourtney's job to break stories. She's ambitious, but she's not mean-spirited. And I'm not sure reading that letter on the air was harmful. Now the public's got an idea that Laura might be dangerous, and Major Crimes doesn't have to take heat from the senator for putting it out there."

"But Kourtney *bought* evidence."

"You mean her news organization did, and they turned it over to the cops right away. We might never have gotten hold of that note and logbook otherwise. And, even though Kourtney didn't divulge *who* her source was, at least she told you *what* he was."

Even that, he'd had to drag out of Kourtney with threats. Her anonymous source was a mountain man. One of the loner types Ranger Pandy said lived off the grid. He'd gone to Frank's Cabin looking for shelter and found a bloody mess instead. From what Kourtney told Spense on the phone, it sounded as if the anonymous mountain man had arrived sometime after their hiker, but before the cops. He'd found a logbook in the cabin and a note that had blown under the porch. When he'd seen the Chaucer's press conference on a barroom television, he realized what he had was worth money, and he figured he could get more from the tabloids than the measly ten grand reward the Chaucers were offering.

He'd been right.

SLY News paid him double and made him a solemn promise to keep his name out of it.

"Maybe it won't wreak too much havoc. But I remember Kourtney making a big show of turning over a new leaf. She said she'd learned her lesson after interfering with the Fallen Angel Killer case."

Caity let out a low laugh. "You believed her?"

"Point taken." He pulled Caity in for a hug. "Wish me luck with Mom."

"Chocolate chip or oatmeal?" Agatha asked Spense.

"Oatmeal." He liked chocolate chip better, but oats were good for his cholesterol.

"Good choice. I wouldn't want to see you . . ." His mother's voice trailed off and he finished her sentence in his head, *go the way your father did.*

He wouldn't either. In more ways than one.

Arlene Cassidy's kitchen was the opposite of her daughter's bedroom. Painted a sunny yellow, the walls were covered with framed inspirational quotes, oversized metal spoons, wooden geese, and coloring book art from the neighborhood kids.

His mother, Agatha, pulled a chair up next to him at the kitchen table, and set a plate of homemade oatmeal cookies on the lace tablecloth.

He broke one in half, dipped it in his tumbler of milk, and took a bite that made his heart smile. His boyhood was filled with memories like these. He was very lucky in the mom department. He cleared his throat. He used to think he was lucky in the dad department, too. But after the information he'd uncovered about his father, while working his last case, that had changed.

"Not to be a Debbie downer—but a family history of early death due to heart attack puts you at risk."

He turned his palms up. "You're the one who made cookies. And I can't control my family history."

"But you can control your diet and exercise."

"Thank you, Dr. Mom. I'm a good boy, I promise. You have

no idea how much sh— . . . ribbing I take for my veggie burgers. According to the Bureau, real special agents eat meat. It's in the manifesto."

She laughed. "Thank you, son."

"For what?"

"Just for being you. Since your father died, you've been looking out for me in every way a mother could hope. And I think these good habits of yours are more for my sake than your own."

She had that right. He didn't want his mother to suffer another loss. Which was why, at the moment, his vocal cords had suddenly gone on strike.

"You said you had something important to talk about."

He sipped his milk. There, that was a bit better.

"Atticus?"

He thumped his chest with his fist and coughed to get his throat working again.

She started to refill his tumbler of milk.

He should just rip off the bandage. There really was no good way to break the news. "It's about Dad."

Her hand froze midpour. Milk overflowed onto Arlene Cassidy's fancy lace tablecloth. "Heavens to Betsy!" His mother set down the carton and tried sopping up the mess with the lone napkin available. "Look what I've done. I've got to get this tablecloth in the wash right away. I'd hate for Arlene to come home and—"

He reached out and laid his hand over hers. "It's okay. I'll buy her another one. We need to talk about Jack."

She drew her hand away and straightened in her chair. "Atticus, please don't refer to your father by his first name. It's disrespectful."

"I'm sorry." He was sorry his changed attitude toward his

father hurt his mother, even in this small way. But he wasn't sorry for disrespecting Jack. He didn't think of Jack as *Dad* anymore, so why call him that?

He could say *Father.* That would work.

Father was easy enough and accurate. Jack Spenser had sired him and raised him until he fell over from a heart attack. But even so, to Spense, he'd never be *Dad* again. "I love you, Mom."

Her chin was up, she was looking him square in the eyes, and she was so quiet, he wasn't sure she was breathing.

Which was strange.

Because he hadn't so much as hinted about a problem, yet clearly she was anticipating the worst.

Her shoulders rose and fell.

Good. She was breathing after all.

"You don't have to tell me anything, Atticus. There's very little about your father I don't already know."

"I'm afraid there is."

She wadded up the soaked napkin in her hand and tossed it with amazing accuracy into the wastebasket. "I don't think so, my love."

He rubbed his temples with his fingers. Her eyes held such love, so much compassion. The look on her face was like the one he remembered from Jack's funeral. The one that seemed to say that no matter how bad things got, she'd always be there to make it better for him.

"Don't worry, honey. Whatever it is, it's going to be all right."

There was no possible way she could guess how wrong she was. Time to stop drawing this out. It wasn't going to get any easier. "My father was unfaithful to you."

She didn't look away. Her expression didn't change. She didn't even blink.

"Not just in a small way. He . . ." It was Spense who had to look down. He hated what he had to tell her. He took a long breath and glanced up again. If she was strong enough to have this conversation without flinching, then so was he. "It went on for years—most of my childhood."

"Yes, I think it probably did." She picked up a cookie then put it back on the plate.

He felt as though he was listening to her speak from under water.

"Thank you for telling me. I didn't know, for a fact, that he cheated. But since the day of his funeral, I suspected."

"Why didn't you say something? Maybe you didn't want to tell me when I was young, but after all these years . . ."

"Like I said, I wasn't sure. And with your father dead and gone, I didn't see the point in tainting his memory for either one of us." She sighed heavily. "After the funeral, while you were on the floor of your father's study, desperately trying to put his Rubik's cube back the way it should be, I was going through bank statements, clothing, shoe boxes. I found photographs . . . . of a beautiful blond woman. I found an embroidered handkerchief that wasn't mine, scented with a strange perfume. Ticket stubs from movies your father and I had never been to. I didn't have proof, but in my heart, I felt it. All those business trips to Dallas over the years. Is that where she lived?"

"Yes."

"How did you find out?"

"I met her in Texas. On our last case." There was so much more to tell her, but she looked tired. "Let's go into the living room and hang out on the sofa. I'll pour you something stronger than milk, and I'll tell you everything."

"It's not even 9 a.m.!"

"If I can have cookies for breakfast, you can have sherry."

A half hour later, his stoic mother drained the last drop of pink liquid from her goblet, and blew her nose on the last tissue from the Kleenex box. Spense was mad as hell at Jack Spenser, but she was taking it better than expected. She'd cried a lot, yes, but she hadn't sobbed. And she hadn't uttered a single angry word. He didn't understand it, but Jack was her husband, and she had a right to react however she wanted. If she wanted to forgive the cheating bastard, Spense wasn't going to try to stop her.

"Atticus." She looked up at him with red-rimmed, watery eyes. "I need you to believe that your father loved you, because I swear to you, he truly did. You were his whole world."

That was bullshit, but let her believe whatever she needed. "Sure."

"I adored him, with all my heart. I wouldn't trade my life with your father for another, more perfect version of him, even if I could. I loved and *still* love a flawed man. But you, my dear, are as close to perfect as any son could be. You inherited all of your father's good traits and not a single one of the bad."

"I don't know about that, but I'm damn sure not a cheater."

She grabbed his hand. "Look at me, please."

It was hard. He couldn't forgive and forget so easily as his mother. But then again, it had all come as a complete shock to him, whereas she'd suspected for a long time that his father had been living a double life.

"Promise me you won't turn cynical about marriage. Promise me you won't let your father's mistakes stop you from enjoying a full, joyful life with the woman you love." She pulled his chin up so he could no longer avoid her eyes. "I'm talking about Caitlin, son. Don't you dare let her get away."

Chapter 37

Sunday, October 27
10:30 A.M.
Pearl Street
Boulder, Colorado

CAITLIN WHIRLED AND checked out her reflection in the dress-shop mirror. She didn't usually go on shopping expeditions in the middle of a case, but then again she hadn't planned on being blackballed, nor had she planned on her mother giving away her favorite fall coat along with most of her winter work clothes to the church. It seemed there was a single mom around Caitlin's age and build who needed warm clothes, and as her mom had pointed out, Caitlin hadn't bought anything new in years. This was her mother's way of nudging her into updating her look, and doing good at the same time. It was a win-win, according to Arlene Cassidy. Only Caitlin was now stuck prowling the Pearl Street Mall instead of perusing murder files.

She greatly preferred the latter.

But it was all good—Spense needed privacy to talk to his mother. News like that wouldn't be easy to either tell or hear. Hopefully, they were getting through it okay.

She wished there was something she could do to brighten their rough day.

Then she remembered an independent bookshop, just around the corner that carried crosswords, ciphers, and even San Gaku. On the way home, she'd stop and pick up some puzzles for Spense and a copy of the new Harper Lee for Agatha.

But first, she had to fulfill her promise to her mother. She waggled her eyebrows at the reflection staring back at her in the mirror. This dress ought to do the trick—a pretty blue silk she could wear to dinner with Spense. The skirt was snug in the butt and shorter than her usual fare, but she was fairly certain that was what her mother had meant when she'd used the term *update*.

Caitlin stepped out of the dressing room in her bare feet and slowly rotated in front of the triple glass to get a better look at the back.

"Is it too much?" she asked the young woman who'd been helping her—Darcy.

"It's uber sexy." Darcy put her finger on her chin. "But you still look classy—I think you can definitely pull it off. Is it for someone special?"

Caitlin flushed and hesitated. But it wasn't like Darcy would spill her secrets. "Yes. At least I hope so. We've known each other for years—but most of that time, I'm afraid we were butting heads."

"Frenemies to lovers. That's hot."

"Our romantic relationship is still pretty new."

"And exciting, I bet. Then this is just the ticket. You look stunning in it. The royal blue really complements your eyes, and that fabric really complements your figure."

Caitlin was warming up to this whole shopping thing. Maybe she should do it more often. "Okay. I'll take it."

She returned to the dressing area and slipped out of the sleek silk and into her jeans. Back at the checkout counter, Darcy hung the dress and pulled a plastic protector over it. Then she opened a box, folded a sheer lace bra and a blue thong in tissue paper and closed the lid.

"Those aren't mine," Caitlin said.

"Yes they are." Darcy winked at her.

She shook her head, confused. She hadn't even looked at lingerie, much less set it aside for purchase.

"Just the dress, please." Caitlin pulled out her wallet.

Darcy beamed at her. "Your boyfriend wanted to surprise you. And put your wallet away, because he's already paid for everything—the dress too."

A small thrill shot through her.

That was an incredibly romantic gesture—and quite a surprise.

Then her heartbeat accelerated, but not from the thrill—it was too much of a surprise.

Buying her lingerie wasn't Spense's style. He'd probably see it as more of a gift to himself, and he was too thoughtful for that. Excitement and confusion suddenly gave way to cold certainty.

Spense was at home with Agatha, delivering difficult news.

No way did he sneak over to Pearl Street for an impromptu rendezvous with Caitlin—not on a day like today.

She heard the sound of shoes squeaking across the floor. Then she sensed a presence behind her. Pulling her shoulders back, she turned to face the man who'd developed the extremely nasty habit of sneaking up on her at unexpected moments. "What the hell are you doing here, Grady?"

He stepped out of the corner and removed his sunglasses, revealing his black eye. "A simple thank-you will do nicely."

"I'll thank you to stay away from me from here on out." Caitlin turned back to Darcy. She was about to refuse all of the items and walk away, but then she thought about the woman's commission. "I'll take the dress. Sorry for the trouble, but I need you to re-ring it on my card." Caitlin already wanted to kick Grady in the shins. Now the devastated look on the woman's face made her want to aim higher. "It's okay," she told Darcy. "You haven't done anything wrong. Please do not worry about this. It was a perfectly understandable mistake." And it was also the last time she'd confide in a saleswoman whom she'd known ten seconds.

So much for shopping being fun.

"H-he said he was your boyfriend."

Grady shook his finger at Darcy. "I said no such thing."

"You certainly did. Or . . . at least you . . ."

"He implied it," Caitlin said. "I understand completely." She grabbed her credit card and the dress and hurried toward the door.

Grady swooped in front of her, bowed and opened the door in an overly polite gesture. "I'm only trying to be a gentleman."

"Then you suck at it." Caitlin wasn't going to let him reframe this to make himself seem like the innocent victim, which appeared to be his MO these days—come to think of it, that had always been his MO. "Did you follow me to Boulder?"

"I didn't even follow you into the shop."

"So this is all a big coincidence."

"Naturally. I have other business in Boulder. Don't be so full of yourself, Caitlin. I've explained to you already that I haven't given you a second thought since the day I met Inga. In fact, I'm here to see her sister, Asta. I was walking by and just happened to look in the window when you came out in that sexy little blue number. I decided to be the bigger person, and come in to say hello. After all, it wasn't you who blacked my eye." He peeked over at Darcy and pointed to his injury with a faux frown. "Besides, I feel terrible about you getting kicked off the case."

"You're the one who's responsible for that."

"No. That would be your boyfriend."

"This is ridiculous. I don't know why we're having this conversation. You've got some nerve trying to buy me lingerie."

"Again, I'm just trying to be nice. You were so upset with me the other day for the unfortunate incident in the bathroom."

Darcy edged closer. Obviously interested in the tidbits she was overhearing.

"So I thought I'd make it up to you by getting you something nice."

Darcy planted her hands on her hips. "You, sir, are no gentleman. And this is about the biggest load of crap I've ever heard. You walked in this shop one minute after she did and hid in the lingerie area. You led me to believe you were her boyfriend."

"It's not my fault if you misinterpreted my words."

"I didn't misinterpret anything. I remember what you said." Darcy didn't back down.

"What did he say exactly?" Caitlin asked, stepping shoulder to shoulder with Darcy who was proving herself more than worthy of her commission, and a perfectly good person to confide in after all.

"I said I should check with you about your bra size, and he said there was no need because he was intimately acquainted with your breasts."

"36D." Grady held up his cupped palms. "I remember them well."

Chapter 38

Sunday, October 27
5:30 P.M.
Boulder, Colorado

From: You Don't Know Me8
To: Dr. Caitlin Cassidy
Subject: Ty Cayman

Dr. Cassidy,

I'm very sorry about what happened to your father. I know you're not the type to pre-judge. I believe you are a seeker of truth. Please check out the following attachment. I'm not sure what it means, but if anyone can make sense of it, you can.

Caitlin stared at the e-mail, her fingers hovering over the touchpad of her Mac as she debated whether or not to click.

The moms—as they were now officially nicknamed—were in the

kitchen preparing dinner. It smelled delicious. She suspected pot roast. After modeling her new blue frock for them, they'd insisted she wear it to the table tonight. No one ever dressed for dinner around here, and the request had taken her off guard, but she didn't mind humoring them. She knew they'd been bitten by the matchmaking bug, and there was no reason to disappoint. She glanced at her watch. There was still plenty of time before she had to change.

"Spense, get over here and check this out."

The study in her mother's home, plagued by small windows, was an optometrist's dream. *Abandon all hope of escaping eyestrain, ye who enter here.*

She reached over and tugged the cord of an antique brass banker's lamp. Green tinted light shone down onto her hand, making her skin look even more olive and adding a minute amount of illumination to the room.

"Don't open that attachment." Spense squeezed her shoulder lightly.

Her breath caught—like it did every time he touched her. She did her best to ignore his distracting nearness. "I'll do a virus scan first, but did you see the subject line?"

He leaned over her, and she caught a whiff of Old Spice. Funny how a scent that she'd once found old-fashioned and a bit overpowering now sent tingles skittering across her skin and made her stomach feel like she'd just risen to the top of a Ferris wheel. "No, just the sender . . . that is an intriguing subject line. Especially considering the fact no one can raise Cayman at the moment. How do you think *You Don't Know Me8* got hold of your e-mail addy?"

"Came through a contact form on my website. I still have my private consulting site up."

"You should get rid of it."

"Good thing I didn't."

Scanning for viruses complete.

"You want every crackpot on the internet e-mailing you clues to your cases? I'm surprised this is the first time it's happened."

She smiled before clicking on the attachment. "I think I can handle one e-mail without pulling a muscle."

"Suit your—holy mackerel." Reaching past her, Spense used his fingers on the touchpad to enlarge the images. Then one by one, took screen shots, elbowing her in the process.

"Ouch."

"Sorry, I didn't want to take a chance on this vanishing into cyberspace. We should print out all of this stuff."

"You mean all of this stuff you didn't want me to open?" She'd already powered up her travel printer. Less than a minute later, it began to spit out copies of what appeared to be pages from Ty Cayman's passports. Next came an image of Cayman posing in a photo-booth with a beautiful young woman, who looked a little too young to be out with him.

The image was a bit degraded. With her pulse pumping out jets of adrenaline, Caitlin first held the photo far away then brought it closer to her face. "Is that Angelina?"

He wrapped his arms around her shoulders. She gently removed them—too distracting.

"I don't think so, but she's the same type," he said.

The dark-haired woman had laughing, blue eyes. She could've passed for either Angelina's sister, or Laura's or . . . Harriet's.

Caitlin clicked on a file on her laptop and called up images of all three women, lining them up side by side.

Spense covered her hand with one of his while using the touch-pad on her laptop with his other. Her body instantly responded with an ache low in her solar plexus. Her thoughts careened off topic like an escaped grocery cart. She took a deep breath and steered her mind back on course.

Spense minimized the images, navigated to her consulting website then clicked and saved her display photo. "Don't freak out," he said as he maximized the other women's photos. Now they all lined up: Laura, Harriet, Angelina . . . Caitlin.

Her gut tightened, but she laughed off her nerves. "That's coincidence—I mean the fact that I fit the type. But these women clearly *are* a type and that matters because they're all connected to Laura."

"Are they? Or are they all connected to Ty Cayman? When did he come into the picture?"

"*After* the kidnap," she said.

"Unless he was Angelina's boyfriend."

She bit her tongue. "He did lie about Laura having dinner with Ron Saas. And he did disappear with no explanation."

"If we find out that something untoward happened to our new mystery woman—the one posing with Cayman here—it sure will throw cold water on the idea that Laura lost her marbles and killed Harriet in a compulsive re-enactment of an old trauma."

"If something happened to our new mystery woman, then this thing has serial written all over it. Do you want to call Hatcher or should I?" she asked.

Spense paced to the door and back. "Let's hold off. He's not exactly a true believer in our predator theory. I'd rather gather a bit more intelligence first."

"Such as what?"

"Such as who is she, and where is she, and who is *You Don't Know Me8*?"

"The last one seems obvious."

"Not to me," Spense said.

"Our anonymous tipster is Laura Chaucer. She's looking for someone who'll listen without assuming she's gone off her rocker—Grady doesn't fit the bill, and her parents are swayed by his opinion."

"How do you figure it's Laura?" Spense arched an eyebrow.

"I can't be one hundred percent certain. It's a guess, but not a wild or uneducated one. Eight is how old Laura was when she was kidnapped. The 'voice' of the e-mail's author seems feminine, and there's a lot of subtext. If the sender were sitting in front of us, we'd be analyzing her body language as much as her words. So I'm just reading between the lines, trying to pick up the tone of the sender's communication."

He pulled out his cube and tossed it in the air. "I'll play. The e-mail starts by mentioning your father. The subtext could be *your father was railroaded. Please don't let that happen to me.*"

"That's exactly how I'm reading it. And the part about *you're not the type to pre-judge* could mean *you won't assume I'm a lying, crazy murderer just because I wrote that note.* My guess is Laura is trying to defend herself. This is a cry for help, Spense, and I for one do not plan to ignore it."

His back was to her.

"Where are you going?"

"I've got facial recognition software in my suitcase. I intend to find out who our mystery woman is, and what that photograph has to do with Ty Cayman's passport pages."

"He's been traveling with the Chaucer family for over a decade. His room always adjoined Laura's. What if she suspects him of some sort of crime?"

"You mean like murder? It wouldn't surprise me at all to find that this dark-haired, blue-eyed mystery woman went missing in a foreign city around the time Cayman was there."

Her gut was pinging an even louder warning. "The question is . . . how many cities are we talking about? And how many blue-eyed brunettes?"

Chapter 39

Sunday, October 27
7:00 P.M.
Boulder, Colorado

SPENSE SET THE platter containing the standing rib roast the moms had prepared on the dining room table, and a drop of hot grease splattered onto his chest just below his open collar. He felt the pop and smelled the faintest odor of singed chest hair, but better him than his fancy white dress shirt. Looking down, he double-checked, then smiled. No grease stains, just a bright red burn directly on top of his sternal notch. He was good to go.

Only he'd forgotten the matches.

He raced back into the kitchen for them, returned to the dining room and lit two tall tapered white candles. He centered a short crystal vase loaded with red roses between them, glanced up and forgot to breathe.

Caity stood at the foot of the table, her eyes shining like blue diamonds.

"God, you're beautiful."

"Thank you. What's going on?" She pointed to the table, set for two.

"It's a surprise."

She tilted her head back and laughed. "I've had more than one surprise today, and I have to say this is definitely the best of them. Did you do this all by yourself or did the moms help?"

He came around and took her by the hand. In spite of present circumstances, everything felt right with the world when Caity was around. "They made the dinner, but I set the table and arranged the flowers. Does that count?"

She pulled his head down and pressed her lips against his, making his heart skip around in his chest. At this rate, he was going to need a defibrillator before the evening was over.

"Of course it counts. Spense, this is so thoughtful."

"You don't mind that I sent the moms to a movie?"

"No . . . but I have to say, I'm a little confused. I would've thought after your big talk with Agatha today you would've wanted her close."

"I did. Actually, in a way, this was her idea."

A small wrinkle appeared between her eyebrows.

"It was your mother's idea to plan a romantic dinner for me?"

"No. That's not what I meant. I just meant she was eager for you and I . . ." This was getting all screwed up. They were supposed to have a delicious, intimate meal. He was going to loosen her up with a bottle of wine, and then . . .

He dropped to one knee.

"Spense!"

It was too soon. He hadn't warmed her up yet, and he needed to go over his speech a few more times in his head. He stuck his hand in his pocket searching for his Rubik's cube, then pulled it out and looked down at the ring box.

Wrong pocket.

Right woman.

He heard her exhale sharply.

The words he'd been going over in his head suddenly vanished. His hand, always steady with a Glock, trembled as he opened the lid of the jewelry box.

Looking up, his vision was blurry. His tears and the candlelight made it almost seem like Caity was wearing a halo. She looked like a dark angel, beautiful and *sad*.

A warning bell sounded in his head.

Not sad.

He had to be reading that wrong. She was emotional, sure. What woman wouldn't be when the man she loved was on one knee, clearly about to propose? He was emotional, too. He closed his eyes and concentrated until the words he'd practiced came back to him.

Then he looked up and took a big breath so he could get it all out in one go. "Caitlin Cassidy, I've never loved anyone the way I love you. I don't want to go through one more day without telling you that I want us to be together always and forever. I can't bear the thought of ever losing you. Will you do me the honor of becoming my wife?"

The room was so quiet he could hear the clock in the corner ticking down the seconds.

His knee throbbed from being in one position too long. "Caity, hurry up and say yes, will you? My knee is killing me."

"Where did you get the ring?" she asked, her voice hoarse.

Okay. Logical question. He hesitated a moment, because even

to him, the truth made him sound like a lovesick puppy. But then again, if ever there was a time to own up to that . . . "It belonged to my great-grandmother . . ." he started.

"And—and you just carry it around with you all the time?"

"Lately, yeah." By now, his knee hurt like hell, but it was worth it. This was about to be the happiest day of his life. "Mom was keeping it for me. But then when we were working the Man in the Maze case, in Phoenix, I picked it up from her. I've had it with me since then."

"Just on a whim?" Her face flushed.

"Yes. I mean no." He swallowed hard. "You remember the night in Phoenix when I found you huddled in the closet." She'd had a terrible dream about her father, and he'd found her there, shaking and shivering.

Nodding, she bit her lower lip. "You climbed right in there with me and held me all night. We shared our first kiss. I could never forget that, Spense."

"Me either. I—I can't say for certain exactly when I knew that I was in love. But it was that moment, there, in that closet that I realized I wanted to protect you. Always. Anyway, I picked the ring up from my mother's, and I've been hauling it around on all our cases ever since. I guess some part of me knew you were the one even before either one of us was ready to admit it."

"Spense . . ." She grabbed his hands by the wrists and tugged him to a stand. "That's the sweetest, best proposal a woman could ask for." She leaned into him and pressed her face to his chest. He could feel moisture soaking through his shirt.

She was crying.

They must be happy tears.

He flicked his hand across his own eyes. "That's a yes?" Taking the ring between his fingers, he prepared to slide it onto the fourth finger of her left hand.

Her body stiffened, then she backed away, shaking her head. "I'm sorry, but no."

He looked down at the ring, then up at her.

Caity smoothed her palms against her thighs. Her lower lip trembled.

Maybe he hadn't explained it right with all that talk about wanting to protect her and not being ready to admit to himself that she was the one. He should keep it simple. "I love you."

"I love you, too." Her voice was almost a whisper. "Let's sit down and talk about it. I'm open to the idea of getting married, someday, but this doesn't feel right to me."

Heat climbed up his chest, and the grease burn on his neck seemed to catch fire. He tugged at his collar.

She loved him.

He knew that as sure as he knew he would never let her down one single day for as long they lived. But he was ready to answer whatever questions she had. He swallowed his frustration and tamped down his disappointment. "Tell me what's wrong. I want to put a ring on your finger."

She let out a long sigh. "That's part of my problem right there. It seems like you're saying you want to make it legal between us."

"I do."

"But I don't need to make it *legal*. And when you say you can't bear the thought of losing me . . . I don't know where you're coming from. I understand that I seemed upset because of what happened the other night with Grady, but that doesn't mean you're going to lose me."

"So you're not angry about me getting you kicked off the case?"

"Yes, I am. And this seems like a very suspicious time for you to propose."

"Suspicious in what way? Since when did you become anti-marriage? You're the one whose folks were happily married. I'm the one with the asshole father who led a double life and ruined my mother's." He realized he sounded as defensive as he felt.

"That's what I mean about suspicious timing. You just delivered the news to your mother, *today*. Then you drop on one knee and tell me, in different words, but I can read the subtext, that you're nothing like your father."

"Because I'm not." His hands fisted at his sides.

"I already know that, Spense. You don't have to marry me to prove it. I believe in you. I believe in us. But this seems like a dare."

"That's nuts. Yes, I'll admit my mother influenced me a little. She told me not to let you get away. But Caity, this ring has been burning a hole in my pocket since our very first case. The *only* reason I waited this long to ask you to marry me is because I was worried you'd think I was rushing into it. Then, after I talked with my mother, I realized that was wrong. Life is too short. I'm ready to marry you right now. Tonight if you want. To hell with timing and convention."

"I think you're *daring* yourself to get married. You want to prove to me and maybe to your mother that you really are the man you *wish* your father had been. But this won't undo the past. You have nothing to prove. You *are* a better man than your father." She stepped in and met his eyes. "I believe in you. I love you. And I hope someday you'll be able to forgive Jack—for your own sake, because holding onto that anger is going to eat you alive."

He could feel his brain starting to go fuzzy. "This has *nothing* to do with my father. I asked you to marry me because I want to spend the rest of my life with you. I want you to be the mother of my children. And if you don't believe that, then maybe you don't really know me at all."

"Spense, I love you, but . . . it's a no . . . for now."

"For now?" He could hear his voice rising. "A no is a no. This isn't a standing invitation for whenever you get around to deciding. Either you love me, or you don't. So I'm going to ask one last time, Caity. Will you or won't you marry me?"

Her face went ashen. "Are you seriously giving me an ultimatum right now?"

He opened his mouth, but before he could reply, he heard the front door opening and footsteps coming down the hall.

The moms.

"Oh my stars!" The moms bolted in, all smiles. "Agatha forgot her glasses, is it official yet?"

Though he felt as if someone had reached inside his chest and yanked his heart out, he forced himself to smile a greeting at his mother and Arlene. Then he went and sat down at the table. "Not yet. Caity needs some time to think," he said as calmly as *pass the gravy.*

"Well, that sounds reasonable to me." Arlene put her arm protectively around her daughter.

"Of course it does," his mother said. She pulled up a chair next to Spense. "Everyone sit down. I'll be darned if we're letting this expensive rib-roast go to waste."

Chapter 40

YESTERDAY, AFTER KOURTNEY Kennedy had read her note on SLY news, Laura used her loaner tablet and the free Wi-Fi at the Digs to e-mail Dr. Caitlin Cassidy—and that had been no easy task. The wireless service at the Digs was not only slow, it was overburdened by too many users, which meant Laura had been kicked off the internet midtask on multiple occasions. It had taken her all afternoon to get Cayman's passport pages and the fun-booth photo scanned in, and to complete sending the large files.

Today, the internet had gone down completely. Armed with the dates of her travels, she itched to complete an online search for the victims . . . but a blond wig was hardly sufficient disguise for a woman currently headlining every news show in the country.

The Digs were no longer a safe place for her.

She powered up her tablet, took a deep breath and tried once more to connect to the wireless. When the familiar "no signal" light appeared, a tear fell onto her loaner tablet. She slowly set it on the desk in her hostel room, feeling as though she'd just let go of a lifeline, and was now drifting further and further out to sea.

Laura had plenty of reason not to trust the authorities, but at the moment, she had no choice. Cassidy and Spenser seemed her only hope. If anyone was going to put things together, it would have to be them. She could only hope they were as clever as the news stories suggested, and as honest as her heart longed to believe.

It was time for her to go.

Not daring to face the desk clerk, she threw her things into her pack, and left three twenty-dollar bills on the bed to cover her tab. Then she sat down on the floor, drew her knees to her chest, and stared at the wall.

She had to get out of this place, but she had no idea where to go.

There was a bounty on her head . . . call it a reward if you liked. There was nowhere she wouldn't be recognized. She tugged at the sleeves of her jacket and adjusted the pressure of the straps on her pack. Then she looked down at her boots and thought of the code of the hikers:

Take what you need and leave what you can for others.

From her side pocket, she pulled out the map of the Eagles Nest Wilderness. If she caught a bus to Dillon, she could slowly make her way up the road on foot. She could practically hear the mountains calling out to her to come home—to return to the place where she'd been abused, yet still survived. A place where there was evil, but where there was also the promise of good.

And it was that glimpse of the good in others that gave her hope.

Decided now, she stood up and opened the door to her room.

She peeked into the hallway, and noting the coast was clear, hurried out the back door.

Chapter 41

Chapter 41

Monday, October 28
8:00 A.M.
Boulder, Colorado

CAITY RAISED THE blinds in the study letting in a small burst of light. Even in the morning the room was dim.

Over a sip of coffee, Spense nodded at her.

She took a drink of hers and sent back her usual sunny smile.

Just like he hadn't proposed to her last night, and she hadn't turned him down, and afterward they hadn't had the most awkward family dinner ever.

Okay.

If that was how she wanted to play it, he'd go along. If he tried to force a discussion now, it would only give her tinder to fire up that old *our relationship is interfering with our work* argument anyway.

Nope. He had nothing else to say on the matter.

Last night he'd opened up to her, unzipped himself like a winter coat, and she'd just stood there with her arms crossed, unwilling to accept the warmth and protection he'd offered her. And the things she'd said about his father had been like a knife to the gut, which she'd then plunged deeper by her rejection.

One hand tightened at his side, as bile rose in his throat.

Then he looked at her, and regret made his head dip down to his chest. That knife-to-the-gut comparison was unfair of him—he'd taken her by surprise, and she'd had questions. That wasn't exactly unreasonable. He could see the dark circles painted around her eyes, the pale tinge to her skin. She hadn't slept well.

But the bile in his mouth tasted bitter.

He, too, had not slept well—if at all.

After dinner, the moms had pulled him aside and let him know he needed to give Caity *space*. They were sure she'd come around in time. But as far as he was concerned, she'd already had plenty of both—time and space.

Ball was in her court.

Until she came to her senses and figured out what she was missing, he was all business.

Screw this stupid ache in his heart.

"So what if . . ." Spense drained his coffee cup and tossed his cube in the air. He caught it, solved it, put it in his pocket.

Business as usual.

"Awesome, we're playing the *what if* game." Caity finished her coffee and set the cup on the desk, then settled into an easy chair and pulled her bare feet up, hugging her knees to her chest. She had on a white scoop-neck T-shirt and jeans. Luckily, her bent knees covered most of her cleavage, making it easier for him to think about something other than grabbing her and kissing her.

"*What if* the dates in Cayman's passport put him in a certain city at the same time our mystery woman went missing—assuming she did, that is?" he asked.

"Then it doesn't look good for Cayman, but it does look good for our predator theory. Let's cross-reference his passport dates with local newspaper articles. For example, this stamp puts him in Wiesbaden in March, twelve years ago."

They each opened their respective laptops.

Before the proposal fiasco last night, Spense had loaded his up with facial recognition software.

The sound of fingers flying over keyboards filled the silence. A few minutes later, he began to breathe normally again.

He could do this.

In fact he *needed* to do this to prove to Caity that no matter how weird things got between them, they could still take care of business—because their business was really important.

People's lives depended on it.

"I got nothing. No missing or dead women in Wiesbaden in March, twelve years ago," she said.

"If we found her on the first try, we'd miss the thrill of the chase."

"Spense . . ." She had a look in her eyes that wasn't all business.

"Can't go there right now, hon. Let's focus on the case."

She pulled her lower lip between her teeth, and he thought he saw frustration in the gesture.

Good.

Let her get frustrated.

She'd earned a taste of her own medicine.

"There's a long list of dates over the past thirteen years. Maybe we should split them up."

Caity stretched her arms and tucked her chin. "I'll take the first seven years, you take the rest."

He nodded, barely acknowledging her and passed over a copy of the passport pages. "I've got my own—I printed extra last night after you went to bed."

"I didn't sleep all that well."

He retracted his arm and ignored her comment.

All business.

Thirty minutes later, he'd been through several years and as many countries. Whit's life as a business mogul involved a lot of travel. But he still hadn't found a connection to their mystery woman.

"Spense." She looked at him from under those incredibly thick, black lashes, her pupils swallowing the blue of her eyes.

"You got something?"

"I think I found her."

He tapped his touchpad with the intention of minimizing his window, but inadvertently pulled up the next article in his queue instead. "I found her, too. What city are you checking?"

"Amsterdam, seven years ago. You?"

"Huh. Mine is Paris, three years ago. Looks like the same woman, but we can't both be right. Send me your file. I'm e-mailing you mine."

"Got it!" they said in unison.

His heart boomed in his chest.

Two women with remarkably similar looks.

Two cities.

Four years apart.

Both gone missing from nightclubs.

Their bodies later found strangled and stabbed, dumped in wooded areas.

"Which one is she?" Caity put her hand on her heart. "Our mystery woman—the one in the photograph with Cayman."

He ran his fingers through his hair, waiting for his pulse to slow. After all these years, this part of the job—putting a name to a victim, recognizing them for the first time as a real person with a real family—hadn't gotten any easier. "According to my facial recognition software, she's the young woman in the article you found, Stella De Jong."

"It's uncanny though, the way she resembles the woman in the story you uncovered."

"Fabiana Luca, an Italian exchange student, studying in Paris at an academy of arts."

"So we have *two* women, strangled and stabbed in large metropolitan cities at the same time Cayman was there. It could be coincidence, except that Cayman *knew* Stella, and from the looks of this photo, they were on a date. How many dead, dark-haired, blue-eyed women do you think it will take to convince Hatcher?"

"I guess we'll find out when we call him. And Caity, don't freak out."

"Stop saying that. What is it?"

"I'm still looking at Paris, three years ago."

"Did you find another blue-eyed brunette?"

He shook his head. "No. She's blond. I'm sending the file to you now."

He got up and stood behind her, rested both his hands on her shoulders.

She took in a sharp breath. Her body went rigid, then started to tremble.

"*Inga*. Oh, no." She shook her head. "I—I just assumed when Grady said she died in a hiking accident, he meant *here* in Colorado."

The article said Inga Webber fell from a trail while hiking in the French Alps.

"Inga died one week after Fabiana Luca went missing?" Caity buried her face in her hands. "She and Grady must've been vacationing with the Chaucers at the time. If the entourage was there for a week, it makes sense they'd try to fit in a side trip to the Alps. Inga loved the outdoors."

He tried to catch her eye, but she was gazing pensively out the window.

He let her have her moment, then pulled her to a stand and wrapped his arms around her. "I'm sorry, Caity. I know Inga was your friend."

She looked up at him with glistening eyes. "What if her death wasn't an accident? What if she knew something she shouldn't? Grady said her sister, Asta, lives here in Boulder." Her back went rigid. "I'm going to talk to Asta."

That caught him off guard. "When did Webber tell you about the sister?"

She pulled away and went and stood by the window. "I'm not sure. But I remember him saying so. Spense, I believe there's a serial killer out there. Maybe little girls weren't his thing, but now that Laura's all grown up . . ."

"She's his perfect type and perfect age range."

"Do you think he'd risk coming back for Laura after all these years?"

It felt like someone had opened a window, the way a chill went through the room.

He shook his head. "Honestly, I wonder if he ever left her side."

Caity retreated back to her easy chair and pulled her knees up once more. "Remember what *You Don't Know Me8* said in that e-mail about not pre-judging?"

"I do. And it's awfully easy to pin this thing on Ty Cayman."

"Someone had to have known, or at least suspected something if they were living with a serial killer."

"Or vacationing with one. That was a regular traveling circus the Chaucers put together for their trips."

"Maybe I was wrong about the subtext in that e-mail. Maybe the real killer sent it to us in order to pin the blame on Cayman." Caity tapped her chin.

"Maybe. But if Cayman's not our guy, then why is he posing in a photo booth with a dead woman, and why the hell did he disappear?" He picked up his cell and scrolled through his contacts, then he hit the call button. "Hatcher, it's Spense. We've got some information for you, but first I need you to do me a favor. I'm going to fax over a list of dates. I need you to collect the names of each friend or personal staff member who traveled with the Chaucer family for every last one of them. And I particularly want to know if Grady and Inga Webber were along for the ride."

Chapter 42

Monday, October 28
7:00 P.M.
Coffee and Conversation
Denver, Colorado

As it stood, things were tense between Caitlin and Spense—and she was downright miserable about that. He'd laid his heart open when he'd asked her to marry him, and though she'd tried to be gentle, her refusal had hurt him. Now her chest tightened, and her eyes stung as she remembered the look on his face. She'd barely gotten a moment of sleep since then. She kept hearing his words play over and over in her head.

Life is short.

To hell with convention.

I love you.

And he wasn't wrong about life being short. When the Thresher had taken her captive, back in Dallas, hers had nearly been cut even shorter. Since the proposal, she couldn't stop thinking about how she'd felt that day. How she'd been frightened of the horrible death the maniac had planned for her, but even more terrified by the thought of never being able to see Spense's face again, feel his arms around her—missing out on the life she wanted to live with him by her side.

"Caitlin?" Grady broke in to her reverie and brought her back to the moment.

Had she done the right thing by meeting him here?

She'd come alone to Coffee and Conversation to set Grady straight. Even though she'd wanted to tell Spense about what had happened in that dress shop yesterday, she knew that if he found out Grady tried to buy her lingerie, it would only make everything worse.

The last thing anybody needed was for Spense to explode again.

Grady would probably threaten to press charges against him—but she wasn't so worried about that. She had something of her own to hold over Grady this time. Something she could use against him without jeopardizing either the investigation or her ethical obligations.

What did scare her, however, was the idea that next time, Spense might not stop with a one-two punch. And if Grady wound up in the hospital, or worse, that really could spell the end of Spense's career. She took a deep breath and a seat across the booth from Grady. Her skin itched as though bugs were crawling up her arms, but she knew it was in all her head. That was just the skeevies she got whenever she was anywhere near Grady.

"You sure you don't want to go somewhere quieter?" he asked.

"You mean like your place, or a bar? No thanks." Caitlin glanced around the Coffee and Conversation café. Its generous supply of patrons, some with their noses buried in books, some working on their laptops, some slurping and looking around expectantly as if hoping for a chance encounter, made her confident in her decision.

She was safe here.

Grady was far too concerned about appearances to make a scene.

It was the perfect spot to lay down the law.

Grady lifted his arm and motioned the waitress over. "Our beverages must be getting cold by now. Isn't that my order on the counter?"

"Sorry, I just got back from my break. I'll bring them right over, and if they're cold just let me know, and I'll warm them up."

As she hurried away, he returned his attention to Caitlin. "I don't remember you being quite so full of yourself, dear."

The waitress returned just in time to hear Grady's insulting remark. Wordlessly, she set a cup of coffee in front of Grady and a cup of tea in front of Caitlin then hightailed it out of there.

Smart lady.

Caitlin wished she could get up and follow her.

"I ordered you passion tea. As I recall, it's your favorite." Grady clanked his spoon against his coffee cup while he stirred in the cream. "Want some?"

"Cream? Yes." She added the cream and took a sip of the warm liquid, then forced herself to smile. "It's good."

"I know what you like, Caitlin, and I aim to please. I just want you to be happy."

Happy? More like nauseated. But she might as well start out civilly, because things were going to get bumpy soon enough. "Thanks for meeting me."

"When you called, it was a delightful surprise." He reached his arm across the table and opened his hand.

She stared at it a moment in disbelief. Surely he didn't expect her to take it.

"I'm hoping this means you've realized you misjudged me."

"For heaven's sake, you're trying to hold my hand right now. I haven't misjudged you."

"There you go again, misinterpreting."

She leaned forward and met his eyes.

He leaned in, too.

Nobody blinked.

"Grady, this is not a date. I asked you to meet me here because I have something to tell you. I'm no longer your protégée."

"Of course not, dear."

"And I'm neither stupid nor naïve. When a man makes advances, I know it."

He threw back his head and let out a small laugh. "If you're implying that I've made unsolicited advances toward you, you're delusional."

"You might be adept at convincing your patients that they're imagining things, but your tactics won't work on me."

"Aren't you going to finish your tea?"

She picked up the cup, sipping and weighing her words. She needed to be crystal-clear, because she'd be damned if she was going to allow him to continue down this same path. She set her tea down with enough determination to make some of it slosh onto the saucer. "You will not follow me into any more bathrooms. You will not follow me into any more shops. You will not attempt to give me any more gifts."

"The way you're acting . . . I wouldn't dream of it." He made a *tsk tsk* noise with his disgusting lips. "Frankly, I feel sorry for

Agent Spenser. You haven't aged well, Caitlin. You've turned into a bitch."

"Fabulous. Then it won't be difficult for you to stay away from me."

"Not in the least."

"If you step out of line again. If you bring up our past relationship. If you so much as smile at me from across the way, or show up anywhere near me—"

"What am I supposed to do? Follow you around so I know where *not* to go?"

"Not my problem, Grady." She stood up and slapped a ten on the tabletop. "Come anywhere near me again, or try to make any complaint against Spense, and I'll press charges against you for stalking."

"Don't be ridiculous. No one will believe you."

"They will. And I have a witness who heard you sexually harassing me about my breasts. I'm not the least bit intimidated by you. I'll be delighted to be the woman who finally holds you accountable for your bad behavior."

He crossed his arms over his chest. "Don't take this the wrong way, Caitlin, but you could use a little makeup."

Her fists bunched at her sides. Then she relaxed them and touched her hand to her forehead. She was surprised by how damp it felt.

She was perspiring, and a bit dizzy—that's how worked up this infuriating man had gotten her. He wasn't even going to acknowledge her warning. But she knew he'd heard her. His reputation meant everything to him.

He'd never risk it.

"Try something besides Chapstick on your lips, why don't you. You look as though you're auditioning for a part in *The Walking Dead*."

His remarks didn't deserve a reply.

She slipped her purse over her shoulder and walked, with her head held high, out of the coffee shop.

Outside, she paused and drew a few long breaths of the night air.

She patted her stomach—the acidity of the tea disagreed with her.

In fact she wasn't feeling in the least well.

Too bad the parking garage was several blocks away.

She turned onto a side street.

Footsteps sounded behind her.

Her head was swimming from the nausea.

This was more than the effects of hot tea on an empty stomach.

Her gut contracted, and she doubled over from the cramp.

Behind her, the footsteps grew faster, louder.

She jerked her body back to a stand.

It was time to make a run for it.

Chapter 43

Monday, October 28
7:20 P.M.
Outside Coffee and Conversation
Denver, Colorado

BEFORE CAITLIN COULD make her legs move, someone grabbed her around the waist and lifted her off the pavement. The tight pressure of the arm across her upper abdomen squeezed the wind out of her.

She couldn't breathe.

She could only kick her feet, all the while making airless gasps like a fish waiting to be clubbed over the head and gutted. The dim evening turned to blackest night. Pain and confusion blinded her to her surroundings. If only she could catch her breath, she'd scream. There must be someone nearby to hear.

"What the hell is wrong with you, Caitlin?" A man growled the words into her ear.

Grady.

The sound of his voice did wonders for her—it cleared her head and restored her will to fight. His breath stank of booze. He must've been drinking earlier. She butted her head back and felt her scalp bang against his teeth. Her ears rang from the impact.

"Christ, Caitlin!"

Grady's arm loosened, and she sucked in a deep breath. "Put me down or I'll scream." Then reason returned, and she screamed without waiting for his response. "Help! Somebody help me!"

His hand clamped over her mouth. "Shut up, you stupid bitch. *I'm* trying to help you. You're stumbling around on the street like a drunken whore. What the hell are you on?"

She didn't know.

But the way the world was spinning out of control she was definitely on *something*. And Grady sounded . . . pissed off . . . and confused. *Sincere*. For a split second, her body relaxed in his arms, but then she remembered: this was Grady.

Master manipulator.

He could persuade a drowning man to open his mouth lest he die of thirst.

Again, she reared her head back, but the more she struggled the more his grip tightened around her. She felt his powerful fingers digging into her flesh like gloved talons. Again, she screamed, but this time his hand already covered her mouth, silencing her. Somehow, she got one of her legs between his thighs and wrapped one foot around his ankle. He stumbled, and she nearly freed herself.

Her feet touched the pavement.

She pulled in more breaths.

Her vision was blurry, but not as dark now.

Up ahead, she saw a shadowy figure. The walls of an alley

seemed to be closing in on her. Had Grady carried her here, or had she turned into an alley before he came up behind her?

She couldn't remember.

"Caitlin, Caitlin, Caitlin." That boozy breath and the gloved hand suffocated her. "I'm going to remove my hand, but please don't scream. It's *me*. Grady. I'd never hurt you, you know that."

His hand relaxed over her lips.

She bit down hard, tasting leather and reveled in the crunch of his bony fingers.

"Whore!" He dropped her feet fully on the ground and spun her around. His expression was black as the night. He released her waist, drew back his fist . . . and belted her in the face.

Bastard.

She raised her knee and drove it square into his groin.

He grabbed her by the hair. Dragged her down the alleyway.

Her scalp was on fire. She kicked his shins and karate-chopped his hand.

Whimpering, he released her so suddenly she fell facedown on the concrete. Wet sticky fluid dripped down her forehead, finding its way into her eyes, turning the world into a bloodred haze.

Grady got hold of her ankle.

She saw her shoe, kicked to the ground, and grabbed it. Slammed the heel into Grady's ear.

He yowled then tried to protect his head with his hands.

Now!

She catapulted to her feet and ran like hell.

Chapter 44

Tuesday, October 29
9:40 A.M.
Boulder, Colorado

"It's not Grady." Caity extended her arms and flipped a purple and green mile-a-minute afghan off her shoulders. Her sleeves were rolled up, revealing a number of bruises and some swelling where her stitches had opened.

Spense had to look away to keep his emotions in check. If he got anywhere near Webber, he'd take him apart bone by bone, consequences be damned.

So it was probably good Hatcher had insisted on coming to Boulder to interview Caity in the comfort of her own home, though Spense suspected there was more to it than consideration for her cuts and scrapes. As far as Hatcher's commander was concerned, both Spense and Caity were still blackballed from the case. And after what happened last night, if Grady Webber did turn out to be their UNSUB, neither of them could get near him without jeopardizing the investigation.

Hatcher shoved himself off the couch and climbed to his feet. "Look, Caitlin, I appreciate your input. But, I have to respectfully disagree."

Last night, after Caity ran out of that alley and straight into the arms of a beat cop, Grady Webber had been cuffed and hauled down to the city jail where, after an initial advisement, he was now awaiting his preliminary hearing on assault and battery charges.

But Hatcher had bigger plans for Webber.

When doctors in the ER evaluated Caity, she'd requested a tox screen for date rape drugs.

It came up positive for GHB.

And per Harriet Beckerman's autopsy results, so did hers.

"So suddenly, you're a true believer in our predator theory?" Caity asked Hatcher, her mouth falling into a straight line.

"I don't mind saying when I'm wrong. Who's to say Laura didn't write that incriminating note under duress? Or that Webber didn't invent half of what he'd told us about her. If he's a sexual opportunist, it all fits."

"Look," Spense said. "I'm glad you're coming around to the idea of a predator, because I'm absolutely convinced there's one on the prowl. But Caity knows Webber . . ."

Hatcher waved both hands in the air and interrupted. "I talked to Tracy Chaucer in private already, and when I told her Webber's story about Laura standing over her bed with a knife, she had an apoplexy. According to her mother, Laura never threatened a soul."

"I know how it seems." Caity sat up straight and tugged the

hem of her blouse lower over her jeans. "But Grady doesn't quite fit the profile."

"You mean the one you tried to sell me about a cunning, lying sexual sociopath?" Hatcher said. "Seems to me like he does. And I've confirmed that both Webber, and his wife Inga, were traveling with the Chaucer family in Amsterdam and Paris when Stella De Jong and Fabiana Luca disappeared. Webber drugged you. You're exactly our UNSUB's type—beautiful, brunette, blue-eyed. What do you suppose he had in mind for you last night, if it wasn't . . ."

"That's enough." Spense had to stop himself from grabbing Hatcher by the collar. The detective was talking to Caity like she was an object instead of a person who'd just survived a terrible ordeal.

"What the hell, Spense? Caitlin, I can see. She's still recovering from a bump on the head, and she has a history with Webber." He reached for his coat and turned to Caity. "I can understand why you don't want to believe that a man you've been intimate with in the past is a serial murderer. But it's my job to be objective where you cannot."

"He's right on that count," Spense said. "You're not thinking clearly about this. We're looking at an UNSUB who thinks of himself as a pillar of society, someone who uses drugs to control women and believes that's his right. Someone who's educated and entitled and thinks the rules don't apply to him. If Webber's our man, he'd be very motivated to get you out of the way."

"Why me more than you? You're the official FBI profiler. You're the one who punched his lights out," Caity replied.

"Because you're the one who rejected him." Hatcher jumped into the mix. "I'm no shrink but I know these serial murderers usually have a primary—someone who becomes an object of their compulsion. Maybe *you're* the dark-haired blue-eyed girl he's really after and the other women are all surrogates."

"Knock it off." This time Spense couldn't help himself. He got up in Hatcher's personal space and poked him in the chest. "Thirteen years ago, when Laura Chaucer and Angelina Antonelli were taken from the family home, Caity and Webber hadn't yet met. Use your head before you open your fucking mouth again."

Hatcher stepped back and threw his hands up in apology. "Okay. Sorry. But I'm just the messenger in this scenario. Caitlin should watch her back."

"*I'm* watching her back," Spense ground out.

"Then where were you last night, buddy?"

All his blood rushed to his head. One hand curled into a wrecking ball.

Most people had *fight or flight* buttons inside them, just waiting to be pushed.

Spense just had the one—and it was programmed to fight.

Dammit.

This was exactly why Caity hadn't confided in him about Webber.

He counted to ten.

Inhaled.

Exhaled.

Worked his cube.

"Point taken—but watch the way you're talking." He'd barely managed to keep the fury out of his voice.

Caitlin offered a conciliatory smile. "It's okay, guys. I know you both have my best interests at heart. And it's true I'm our UNSUB's type, and that I tested positive for GHB. Grady did grab me outside that coffee shop." She shivered and pulled the afghan around her again. "But I don't see how he could've put anything in my tea. I saw the barista set our drinks out on the counter. At no point after that did Grady leave the table. I didn't have my eye on the drinks the whole time, but I did have my eye on *him*. Anyone could've slipped something into my tea between the time the barista put it out and the time the server came back from her break and delivered it. Have you guys found Cayman yet?"

"No," Hatcher said.

Spense ran a hand through his hair. "GHB messes with your memory, Caity. You probably don't fully recall what happened, but I'd still like to hear you out when you say Grady doesn't quite fit the profile."

"There are profiles, and there's evidence." Hatcher had his coat on and his hat in his hand. "Evidence beats profiles like a royal flush beats a pair of deuces. As much as I'd like to stand here all day and listen to Caitlin explain why the man who drugged and attacked her, who lied to the cops, and whom we can place in the vicinity of every last victim at the time of her disappearance is *not* our guy. But I've got a serial killer sitting down at the jail, and I gotta figure out how to get enough proof to keep him there before a judge decides he's a model citizen with ties to the community and lets him out on bail." Then, without waiting for a response, Hatcher left.

Exactly what Spense would have done in his shoes.

But Caity knew Webber better than they did. He wanted to hear her explanation. "First, I wanna say I'm sorry you didn't feel safe telling me about Webber and the dress shop."

She pulled her afghan tighter around herself. "I wanted to tell you. I realize now, no matter what, I should've been honest."

He sat down beside her and laid his head on her shoulder. "I can't promise I'll never lose my cool again, babe. But I promise to do better, to try harder, and to learn from my mistakes."

"And I can't promise I'll never get hurt again, but I do promise to do better, to try harder, and to learn from my mistakes."

He squeezed her knee. "I guess we both have a lot to learn. Now, if you wanna explain why you don't like Webber for this, I'm all ears."

"Just in case the moms are all ears, too . . ." She got up, checked the hallway and then closed the door to the study. "I agree Grady's a misogynist. Educated, cunning, feels entitled. He manipulated Laura with psychotropic medication—there's no question about that, but we don't know for what reason—he quite possibly thought it was for her own good. Then there's the fact that he's a hedonist. Whatever makes him feel good, he believes to be morally correct."

"So far, I'm with Hatcher—Grady seems like our guy."

"As much as I deplore the man, Grady Webber, while not above using his position of power to take advantage of women lacks one key element of the profile—he doesn't have poor ego strength."

"You mean he's an arrogant SOB and our UNSUB . . ."

"Many rapists obtain sexual gratification by instilling terror in their victims. But our UNSUB doesn't. He can only get off when there's no threat. No witness to his perceived inadequacies. Think about it. No one is less threatening than an unconscious victim because they can't criticize or fight back."

"And you're sure Webber wouldn't enjoy taking such complete control over a woman?"

"I am. I hate to have to think about my own experiences with him, but based on those, I believe that in the bedroom, Grady needs an audience. He uses intellectual discourse as foreplay, and he needs someone who can appreciate how clever he is."

"Someone educated, like you."

"And like Inga . . . someone *awake* to tell him he's brilliant. Whenever I think about Inga, it crushes my heart. I don't believe Grady's our UNSUB, but I do wonder if he might be responsible for *Inga's* death."

"How long will it take you to get dressed?"

"One minute to put on my shoes. Why?"

"I still like Webber for our UNSUB. But I get your point, and one way or the other, I think a field trip is in order—you said Inga's sister lives in Boulder, right?"

Chapter 45

"Ms. Rundstrom, thanks so much for seeing me." Caitlin had phoned from home and mentioned she was an old friend of Inga's. "I hope you don't mind, but I brought someone with me. This is Special Agent Atticus Spenser."

"Call me Spense," he said.

"Call me Asta." She looked like a worn-down version of Inga—tall with blond hair and blue eyes, but she had smoker's lines around her lips. The sunlight on her makeup-free complexion accentuated a sprinkling of broken capillaries on her cheeks, and the deep creases in her forehead aged her beyond her years.

Caitlin believed her to be only a couple of years senior to Inga.

Asta swung open her front door in invitation for Spense and Caitlin. They followed her through a small foyer into an open family room, graced with natural-wood floors and high ceilings.

Though leaded glass windows and old world architectural style lent the home a certain panache, Caitlin couldn't help noting the place had been neglected. A thick layer of dust coated the mantle on the fireplace. Old newspapers were piled everywhere, and unopened mail had commandeered the love seat, leaving the couch and a rickety wooden chair for seating.

Caitlin took the chair—Asta and Spense the couch.

"Special agent. What is that?" Asta asked, stifling a yawn.

"FBI, ma'am. I hope we didn't wake you."

"I don't really sleep, just snooze a little here and there, when I can."

Caitlin was surprised that Asta's expression remained unchanged. Most people got a little nervous around FBI agents. But from Asta's slumped posture and slack jaw, it seemed as though she didn't care one way or the other who sat down beside her on the couch.

She's depressed.

"We'd like to talk to you about your sister," Caitlin said—still no change in expression.

A long silence followed then finally, "May I offer you a coffee or something?"

"If you're having some, thanks." Sharing a food or beverage put people at ease, though Asta didn't look as though she could be any more at ease if she were curled up in her jammies in front of the tube.

Spense stroked his chin. "Got anything stronger? A whiskey, maybe?"

Asta smiled. "Neat okay?"

"Neat's great."

Good job on Spense's part. Caitlin had pegged Asta for a

drinker, but still, she wouldn't have thought to suggest a cocktail at 10 a.m.

"All righty then, you and me will have an eye-opener and toast my dead little sister and her poor, pitiful, grieving husband."

A glimmer of emotion flicked across her flat eyes.

Clearly Inga's death had affected her sister more deeply than it had Grady. And the sarcasm in her voice was telling.

Asta went into the kitchen and returned with two glasses nearly half-filled with an amber liquid.

Apparently Caitlin would be driving.

Asta looked at her and frowned. "I forgot your coffee."

"No worries, really. I've changed my mind."

"Suit yourself." Asta flopped down on the couch and handed Spense his drink, somehow managing not to spill a drop despite the way the cushion bounced.

"Why don't you like Grady Webber?" Spense didn't beat around the bush.

"Does it matter? Everyone else loved him. My parents, for example, were ecstatic when he married Inga." She tossed back a slug of whiskey. "All that money. Brilliant future. A doctor and what-have-you. You think they even cared that Inga was a doctor, too, and could've had a brilliant future all on her own? Once she met Grady, she barely managed to finish residency. All that work, all that education, and then she just gave up her own career to traipse around the country after that piece of crap. She never got to practice psychiatry a single day."

Caitlin hadn't been aware of that.

"Toward the end, just before her *accident* . . ." Asta continued, ". . . she'd decided to go to work. She was going to try to start her own practice, but Grady didn't like that, because it meant she couldn't drop everything for him and those Chaucer family junkets he was always going on. He called her ungrateful. Implied any wife should want to travel the world with her husband and grovel at his feet while he tended to the mind of that poor little rich girl."

"You mean Laura Chaucer."

"Yes." She tossed her whiskey back again. "That child's been through it, I know. But talk about spoiled. If Laura so much as looked at something in the window, the next day it was wrapped up with a bow waiting for her to open it. If you asked me, that whole family needed better boundaries. But of course no one did ask, because I'm not a psychiatrist. No one listens to anything I have to say about the Chaucers, or about Grady, or about my own sister because what would an uneducated woman who works at the supermarket know that Grady Webber does not. If Grady says he and Inga were blissfully happy, well then, I guess they were."

Caitlin raised her eyes to meet Asta's. "I'd like to hear your opinion. What you think matters."

"Too late now. She's already gone. After Inga's funeral I tried to tell the cops I didn't think it was an accident. She hiked all the time, and she was very careful. I told them I thought Grady might've pushed her off that mountain. And they told me that was impossible because he had an airtight alibi. He was at a symposium with a group of doctors—he's got six witnesses and security cameras that place him at the hotel while she was out hiking."

"But you still believe he pushed her off the trail?" Caitlin asked.

A tear ran down her face. "I don't think all of those witnesses are lying, but that doesn't mean Grady couldn't have hired someone to do the dirty work for him. I don't understand why the police just took his word that they were happy."

"Did she tell you otherwise?"

Asta blew her nose. "Not exactly. And I know he loved her, but in a very possessive way. The day before she died, she called me from Paris and said something was very wrong."

"She didn't tell you what?" Spense set his drink on the coffee table atop an old newspaper. Thus far, he hadn't imbibed.

"No, but she did say this was the last time she'd be part of the Chaucers' entourage, and that Grady was furious with her when she told him so."

"That doesn't seem like the strongest motive. It doesn't make him a murderer."

"It sure doesn't make him a considerate husband. And did you know he was accused of raping a girl in college?"

Caitlin gripped the rails of her chair.

The room seemed to be shrinking. The musty odor of newsprint and the sickly-sweet smell of whiskey and stale cigarette smoke made Caitlin want to bolt from the room for a breath of clean air.

"Grady was here on Sunday," Asta continued. "He won't leave me alone because he says Inga would want him to check on me. He says I'm stuck in the anger phase of grief, and I'm taking it out on him."

"Don't you hate it when shrinks interpret your feelings to their own advantage?"

Spense addressed Asta but sent Caitlin a look as though checking to see if she was okay.

She was. Now that she'd had a minute to process the bomb Asta had dropped.

"Let me ask you a question." Asta's voice turned slightly singsong from drink—this likely wasn't her first of the morning. "If Grady has such a great alibi, and I'm the only one in creation who doesn't believe Inga's fall was an accident, what the hell are you two doing here?"

Caitlin rose and walked over to Asta. "Is there room for me beside you on the couch?"

Asta didn't object so Caitlin folded down beside her and met her eyes. "I came to offer my condolences for your loss. Inga was a good person. I liked her very much. And the truth is, I want to know what happened to her, and I don't trust Grady either. Can you tell us more about this alleged rape in college?"

Asta wiped her dripping nose with the back of her hand. "All the charges were dropped."

"Do you know the name of the woman who accused him?" Spense asked.

"Her name is Lisa Blake."

"I don't suppose you know where she is now? I'd like to talk to her," Caitlin said softly. Asta's resigned, helpless demeanor was cracking her heart open.

"Not really. I do know that after she recanted the rape accusation, she dropped out of college and moved back in with her parents. They've both passed since, but she stayed put. Inga went to see her one time, just before the trip to Paris. Inga said Lisa was living in a spooky old two-story house at the top of a road that leads into the Gore Mountains."

"Not outside Dillon? At the edge of the Eagles Nest Wilderness?" Caitlin remembered a spooky two-story house set back from the road they'd taken up to Frank's Cabin. She'd wondered how the owners got in and out in bad weather.

"I think so. But like I said, that was a couple of years ago. I got no idea if she's still up there."

Chapter 46

Tuesday, October 29
1:00 P.M.
Frank's Cabin
Eagles Nest Wilderness

LAURA HAD NOWHERE else to go.

For three days now, she'd been living in the wilderness. She still had a little food and her jacket to keep her warm, but her water was gone, and she didn't think she could survive the elements even one day without it. She was too spent.

Time to make another decision.

She'd been getting a lot of practice at that, and she was beginning to make better choices. With her heart in her throat, she stared at the map she held.

X marks the spot: Frank's Cabin.

She closed her eyes and tried to wipe away the images of blood and feces on the floor. The silk scarves that had bound her to the chair. The knife at her throat.

Her monster.

Surely the crime scene people would've cleaned and cleared the cabin by now. The road was closed to the public. The hut wouldn't reopen for the season for at least another month. There was fresh water and a cabin full of supplies.

Shelter.

This was no longer her nightmare.

This was the place where she'd found the will to survive.

Here, she wasn't a fugitive on the run from both the law and her monster. She was a free spirit. A wanderer. Come to the cabin for rest and renewal. And like her fellow travelers, she had good in her heart. She not only wanted to live, she believed, for the first time, that she deserved to be on this planet.

Her hand shook as she raised it. As high as her spirits had climbed, there was also trepidation. What if the monster came back here?

She pulled in a breath. Then she would've accomplished her aim. She'd have found him. And that meant she'd have a chance at stopping him. Hesitating only a heartbeat more, she steeled her shoulders and pushed through the door to Frank's Cabin.

And nothing terrible happened at all.

She smiled, sighed, and slipped her pack from her shoulders.

Yes!

The bed was stripped, but clean. The floors scrubbed. Even the cracked glass windowpane had been repaired. The forest service must've come in and fixed the place up after it'd been cleared by the cops. Which made sense since so many hikers relied on it in winter. In fact, the rangers had probably replenished the supplies she'd raided from the cellar. At the very least, she guessed she'd find clean sheets and a blanket. She eyed the bunk bed again.

How wonderful to sleep on something other than the cold hard ground.

Yes, this was definitely her safe place.

No one would ever expect her to come back here.

She crossed to the table and shoved it aside to expose the woven throw. Then she dragged the rug away and bent to grab the handle of the trap door to the cellar. A scraping noise sounded beneath the floorboards, making her shoulders jump. She cast a glance around and saw no sign of anyone else. No jacket cast aside, no cap hanging from the wall hook.

She heard the noise again, and this time, she shrugged off her worry.

Probably a mouse.

After everything she'd been through, she wasn't going to let a mouse keep her from opening that cellar door and climbing down to claim her treasures. Bracing one hand on the floor, she clasped the handle tightly with the other. Suddenly a great force from below pushed the door up.

The hard metal slammed into her face.

She fell back, knocking her skull against the floor.

A sickening crack sounded in her ears as the world began to tilt away from her grasp.

Do not lose consciousness. No way are you taking the easy way out. Not this time.

She blinked hard, trying to bring her surroundings into focus.

Oh, dear God.

No!

Her monster loomed above her, straddling her between his legs.

No! Please, not Cayman!

"Help!" she screamed, but there was no one there to hear.

"Laura, get up."

She cowered away from him, slithering on her back toward the wall. The floor shook beneath her from his footsteps as he followed.

Thud. Thud. Thud.

"Laura, do exactly as I say. And I'm warning you, do not scream again."

She saw, for the first time, the pistol in Cayman's hand.

"Y-yes. Anything you say." She lifted her shoulders off the ground and gathered herself into a sitting position.

"Get up, Laura. I'm not going to hurt you."

That was a lie.

He was a monster.

It was *him* all along.

He'd stayed in the room next to hers on all those trips, and he'd known she was drugged and sound asleep when he went out on his night excursions. Cayman killed those women. He killed Angelina. And now he was going to kill her.

Let him try.

Something deep inside crackled to life, snapping her arms open like her wrists had been zip tied and then suddenly cut loose. "I—I can't stand up. Will you help me?"

He reached down to pull her to her feet.

As soon as she had her balance, she shoved him, hard.

Bam!

A gunshot rang out.

As the stench of gunpowder filled the room, a bright flash blinded her. She touched her forehead—it was wet and warm. She brought her hand in front of her eyes, staring at the blood in disbelief. Her skin had gone cool and numb. She couldn't feel her heartbeat.

Gasping, she collapsed in a heap on the floor.

Chapter 47

Tuesday, October 29
1:00 P.M.
Borderline Road
Edge of Eagles Nest Wilderness

SPENSE COULD TELL it had irritated Caity when he'd insisted on driving. But he hadn't imbibed so much as a drop of whiskey back at Asta Rundstrom's house, and the road up to the Eagles Nest Wilderness was closed to the public for a reason. It was soupy and icy and he was the one with experience in tactical driving. At times, he'd struggled to keep the four-wheel drive Jeep they'd rented upright and in forward motion, but they'd made it to the top, and now here they were.

No mistake, this was the place.

The stone house had been built on two different levels to accommodate the mountainous terrain. Its gothic gables and flying buttresses, meant to guard against the heavy winter snows, lent the house a medieval tone. *Spooky* was an apt description.

Caity let out a low whistle as he helped her down from the Jeep. She'd been banged up enough already. He didn't want her slipping in this mud.

"This place is something." She gazed up as if expecting bats to fly out of a belfry.

"Agreed." The house looked more like it belonged in Transylvania than at the borderline of private land and public wilderness in the state of Colorado. He pressed the bell, and it chimed out a few bars of "Edelweiss"—ah, much more Rocky Mountains.

The door opened, and he heard a quick intake of breath from Caity when she took in the woman in front of them. Her jet-black bob framed a heart-shaped face. Her unadorned lips were full, her eyes . . . columbine blue.

"Ms. Lisa Blake?" he asked.

She nodded.

He flashed his creds. "I'm Special Agent Atticus Spenser—I go by Spense. This is my partner, Dr. Caitlin Cassidy. May we come in?"

She didn't unlatch the storm door.

"We just have a few questions for you."

"Sorry, but I don't have any answers. As you can probably tell by where I live, I like to keep to myself."

Caity stepped forward. She shed her outer jacket and pushed up her sleeve, revealing her battered arm. She tucked her long hair behind her ear and turned a bruised cheek toward Lisa. "I'd like to talk to you about Grady Webber."

Lisa touched her fingers to her mouth. "Grady did that to you?"

"He did. May we come in?"

"I—I'm sorry about whatever happened to you, but like I said, I can't help you."

"Lisa." Caity's tone was sympathetic and firm at the same time. "If this wasn't important, we wouldn't be bothering you, but we're here on a matter of the utmost importance. So let me come straight to the point. We've been told that you once pressed rape charges against Grady Webber."

"I dropped them."

This was a good start. Lisa still hadn't unlatched the door, but she had answered a question. Spense kept quiet and let Caity take the reins. He could tell she was already developing a rapport with Ms. Blake.

"We'd still like to ask you a few questions. We're investigating the case of a missing coed, Laura Chaucer," Caity said.

Lisa's face drained of color.

She opened the door with a shaky hand.

He and Caity exchanged a glance. Lisa had seemed much more affected by the mention of Laura Chaucer's name than by Grady Webber's. And that was a surprise—after all she had a very real, and very troubling connection with Webber. She'd no doubt heard about Laura on the news, but it wasn't as if she knew her personally—at least not as far as they were aware.

They stepped through the doorway. Inside, Lisa Blake's home was every bit as imposing as outside.

"You have a gorgeous house." Caity continued with the rapport building, not commenting on Lisa's obvious reaction to the mention of Laura's name. "Did you decorate it yourself?"

"I helped my mother before she passed." The color returned to Lisa's face and the composure to her voice.

"Well, it's very impressive. Do you have professional training—as a decorator, I mean?"

"I studied interior design in college."

"Before you dropped out."

Lisa crossed her arms over her chest. "I thought this was about Laura Chaucer, and it seems you already know the answers to the questions you're asking."

"Look." Caity touched Lisa on the shoulder. "I appreciate your straightforwardness. I'd like to be straightforward with you, too. Is that okay?"

Lisa's eyes lowered. "Please." She uncrossed her arms and led the way into a living area.

Spense sat down in a sturdy chair that looked like it had been used in the Spanish Inquisition, leaving the sofa and love seat for Caity and Lisa.

"I'm afraid these questions are going to get personal, but, as I mentioned earlier, they're important," Caity said.

"Will they help you find that missing coed?"

Lisa now referred to Laura as a coed, like she couldn't even remember her name. Yet Spense was becoming more and more certain that she not only knew Laura's name, she must have some personal connection to the young woman—a connection she wasn't eager to volunteer.

"I want you to be honest with me, so I'm going to be honest with you," Caity replied evenly. "I can't say if your answers will help find Laura or not, but they might. I won't know until I hear them. Now, if you're ready, I'd like for you to tell me everything you remember about the night you were assaulted at an off-campus fraternity party."

Lisa's jaw relaxed out of its clenched position, her eyes opened wider, and her gaze softened. It took Spense only a moment to understand why. With that one simple question, Caity had made it perfectly clear that she didn't doubt that Lisa had been raped. She was ready to take her at her word—a decency not always afforded women who were brave enough to come forward and report a sexual assault.

Lisa brushed her hair back and lifted her eyes to meet Caity's. "I'm ready."

"Just start at the beginning, and we'll interrupt with questions, if that's okay."

But Lisa didn't seem to know where to begin. So Spense decided to get her started. He could back off and let Caity take over anytime, if needed. "You told the police you'd been raped by Grady Webber."

She rested one hand on top of the other. "Yes. But I made a mistake. Grady never hurt me. That's why I dropped the charges."

"You don't seem like the kind of person to make something up out of spite," Spense said, knowing it was common for victims to recant their stories for a multitude of reasons. "So maybe go back to the beginning and tell us what actually happened that night. We can take a break anytime you want."

"I won't want a break. I just want to help. And it's better to get it over with."

"I'm sure it's not easy for you to talk about this, Lisa," Caity said.

"It's not." She straightened her back. "I—I went to a frat party with my boyfriend. Only he wasn't my boyfriend at the time."

"That was your first date with Grady."

"It was our first date, but Grady wasn't my escort, his best friend was. But Grady was there. It was a double date. Nothing bad is supposed to happen on double dates, right?" One corner of her mouth lifted wryly. "Anyway, there was a lot of drinking at this party and some drugs. I had too much alcohol, and I passed out.

Later that night, I woke up in the basement of the house where the party was taking place. My panties were missing, and I was bleeding. I—I was a virgin." Her voice went quiet. "I knew I'd had sex, only I didn't know with whom. The next day Grady called me. He was very solicitous, kept asking how I was feeling, and if I was okay. I just assumed that since Grady knew something was wrong, it had to have been him. How else would he have known? And the boy I went with was my dream date, I didn't believe he would hurt me in a million years."

"Seems logical," Spense said.

"So I went to the police. They took me to the hospital, and the doctors did an exam and collected some swabs and a blood test, they checked my body for hairs and fibers and used some kind of special light on my skin."

"Did they call what they did a *rape kit*?"

"Yes. After the cops interviewed Grady, they came back and told me he'd denied everything, but it was my responsibility to press charges against him, so I did. I also wrote an article for the school newspaper warning other women to watch their drinks at parties."

"I'm confused," Caity said. "I thought you said you drank too much and that's why you passed out."

"I did drink too much, but the tests showed I had other stuff in my system—Quaaludes."

"And you dropped the charges because . . ."

"The rape kit showed the presence of semen. But it wasn't Grady's. They ruled him out because his blood type didn't match. Grady Webber did not rape me."

"But, someone did," Caity said.

"Yes." She pulled her shoulders up. "Someone did."

"I could use some water." Spense offered, because whether she said so or not, he could see Lisa needed a break. She had tears in her eyes, and she was wringing her hands raw. "I can find my way to the kitchen. Anyone else want something?"

"Might as well bring water for everyone," Caity said.

Lisa didn't object.

Spense took the opportunity to wander the house a little in his search for the kitchen. He ventured into a room with more comfortable décor, a piano, and what he presumed to be family pictures atop a mantle. He spied photos of an older couple, and some that looked to be Lisa as a child. He picked one of them up, and even before his brain could process the information, his chin snapped back. He'd seen this exact photograph, of a dark-haired blue-eyed little girl eating a wad of pink cotton candy before . . .

In the war room.

He went for his cube. As his fingers worked furiously to sort the puzzle, the room disappeared around him. He closed his eyes, forcing himself to focus on the image of the little girl. He imagined the sweet smell of spun sugar, the sticky feel of it beneath his fingertips. The girl smiled at him and asked: *Do you see, now? It's so simple.*

The puzzle solved, he put his cube back in his pocket. He did see, and the implications made his heart sting like it'd been hit with a Taser. He opened his eyes, and looked around the room, concentrating on the solidness of the work they had yet to do.

It had taken him years to learn not to bury his feelings, because emotion and instinct often helped solve a case. The hardest part was acknowledging those feelings, and then getting straight on with business. The cube helped—not only to clear his head, but to slide his emotions into a safe slot.

He found the kitchen and took three glasses of water into the living room, passed them around and sat back down in the uncomfortable wooden chair. "Lisa, why didn't the police pursue your rape case further?"

"Because by then, I didn't want them to. By then, I knew who'd raped me . . . only at the time, I didn't believe it was really rape."

A familiar refrain, even now, when date rape awareness was much higher than then. "Because he'd been your date?" Caity asked.

Lisa nodded.

"Whit Chaucer," Spense said.

Caity's eyes widened. She hadn't seen what he'd seen.

Lisa's gaze darted all around the room then found Spense again. She gripped her hands together tightly in her lap. "Yes. But if you ask him now about that night, he'll not only tell you he didn't rape me, he'll tell you he wasn't even my date."

"Why would he deny that he was your date?"

"Because he's a liar. He lies about things even when *he knows you know* they're lies. He'll look up at a clear blue sky and tell you it's raining and somehow, he can get you to believe it."

"What did he get you to believe?" Caity asked.

"That I said *yes*. He made me believe I asked for it." Lisa's mouth quivered, and she quickly looked away.

No one pressed. He and Caity simply waited for Lisa to regain her composure. He suspected Caity might need a minute herself. She identified with Lisa. He could tell by the way Caity's posture mimicked the other woman's, by the way her eyes glistened with empathy, and by the way he itched to put an arm around her shoulder to shore her up.

After a couple of minutes, Lisa looked up and started talking again. "When I found out the semen wasn't Grady's, I confronted Whit. He admitted he'd had sex with me that night, but he said it was consensual."

"You were unconscious, Lisa. You can't give consent under those circumstances," Caity said.

"Whit said I was high, but willing. They were passing around Quaaludes at the frat party like candy, and he said I asked him to get one for me so that I would be brave enough to lose my virginity. I told him that was impossible, because I didn't do drugs. Then he said that I did do drugs when I was drunk."

Blood surged to Spense's face. He wanted to punch a wall, or better, Whit Chaucer. But there was work to do. He put his hands on his knees and leaned forward, concentrating on what Lisa was telling them.

"Whit said that I came on to him. He claimed that I begged him to take my virginity. He said he really didn't want to, and that he was doing me a favor."

Spense didn't think he could speak and keep his cool at the same time. Best to let Caity take that one.

"Why didn't Whit come forward with his version of events *before* you filed charges against Grady?" Caity asked.

"He said he knew the charges against Grady would be disproven, and he didn't want anything spoiling his reputation, or his family's."

"Earlier, you called him your boyfriend, but you said he wasn't at the time. Does that mean you continued to see him afterward?" Spense found his center again.

Lisa averted her gaze. "I was so stupid."

"This isn't your fault, Lisa."

"No. It's his fault—it took me years of therapy to really accept that. Sometimes I fall back into my old mindset, but I don't let myself stay there." She let out a slow breath. "Anyway, Whit was very handsome, and to say he was a 'big man on campus' would be an understatement. I was infatuated with him. When he said I asked for the Quaalude, I thought, maybe, I really did. I didn't believe that a guy like Whit Chaucer would rape me. He was president of his fraternity, *and* an academic all-star. He was even a youth leader at church.

"And after the incident, he was a perfect gentleman to me. He said we would wait until I was sure I was ready to fool around again. I *wanted* to believe him. So I continued to date him, and I didn't say a word to anyone."

"Why did you finally break things off? Or did he?"

"I did. Because it happened again. I still didn't understand that it was rape, but I knew I wasn't in control of what was happening to me, and I didn't want it to continue."

Spense forced himself to breathe slowly and keep the expression on his face neutral.

"There's a cabin about a mile from here—a forest service hut. I woke up with him there one morning. We were both naked." She laughed—a nervous laugh. "Whit acted like nothing was wrong. *Hey babe, where do you want to go for breakfast? Was it as good for you as it was for me?*"

Caity looked like she was going to leap from the couch directly onto the chandelier, but Spense stayed on point. "And you couldn't remember anything, could you?" he asked.

"Not a damn thing," Lisa said. "I was so confused. He insisted it wasn't rape. And even though it felt wrong, I knew I couldn't go to the police for help. I'd already filed a false complaint against Grady Webber, and I'd continued to date Whit for several months after the first incident. He was a golden boy, and I was just some slutty dropout who drank too much and took Quaaludes. Who would believe me if I didn't even believe myself?"

Caity locked eyes with Lisa, "This is not your fault. But I am wondering why now, after so much time has passed, and you understand what really happened to you, with Whit so much in the public eye, why haven't you come forward?"

Spense had been waiting for the right moment to confirm his suspicion—and this was it. "For Laura's sake," he answered the question for Lisa. "She's your daughter, by Whit Chaucer. Isn't that right?"

Lisa opened her mouth and closed it again. A gurgling sob came out of her throat. Caity, looking nearly as flustered as Lisa, got up and handed her a tissue she'd pulled from a pack in her purse.

Wiping her tears, Lisa said, "Whit and Tracy adopted Laura when she was six months old. Neither Tracy nor I knew it, but he'd been dating Tracy the whole time he was seeing me—he said he loved me, but I wasn't good enough for his family, or for his aspirations. He said he and Tracy could give Laura a better life than I could—and they did . . . up until someone kidnapped her, and I could hardly blame them for that. But now, she's missing again, and they're saying awful things about her on the news."

Caity's mouth parted in seeming disbelief. "Lisa, help me understand. Whit was the father, but you said he *adopted* Laura. Walk me through how that came about."

"You mean walk you through how I could ever give my daughter up to a rapist?"

The silence in the room was mercifully short. Lisa rushed to fill it. "Believe me, I've asked myself the same question just about every day for the past decade. But the truth is, I did the best that I could for Laura at the time." She let out a long, shaky sigh. "I was a basket case. Literally. When I found out I was pregnant, I was terribly confused and depressed. I wanted to give the baby up for adoption, but my parents didn't want me to make a decision while I was in that state of mind." She offered a weak smile. "I guess parents don't always make the right decisions for their kids, but mine had my best interests at heart. They convinced me to wait until the baby was six months old and then revisit the idea of adoption. They hoped I'd be well by then, and that I would have bonded with the baby."

"But that's not what happened?" Caity asked gently.

Lisa shook her head. "No. I didn't get well. I got worse. And I didn't bond with Laura. My doctors said post-partum depression compounded a pre-existing mood disorder. I tried to kill myself more than once. I was in and out of hospitals for the first six months of Laura's life while my parents took care of her . . . and then Whit stepped in.

"At the time, my parents and I believed he really wanted to take care of his daughter. Now I think he just wanted her because she was *his*. You know, like a possession—but back then, I still blamed myself more than him for what had happened. My parents thought he was a good guy, and that I was confused and ill, which I was."

"But if Whit was the father, he didn't need to adopt Laura."

"He said that was the best way to handle things since his name wasn't on the birth certificate. His parents and Tracy didn't know the baby was his, and he wanted to keep it that way. He wanted a closed adoption so that Laura would never know about me, and neither would Tracy. I was to sign over all my rights. If I didn't, he said, he'd deal with his parents and Tracy, make a paternity claim in court, and he'd win because of my mental instability. He said I was too fragile for a court battle. The kicker was he promised to send pictures of Laura to my parents, and to pay my medical bills, which were bankrupting them."

"That must've been a terribly hard decision for you to make," Caity said.

"I was confused, medicated, and I didn't want my parents to suffer any more than they already had for my mistakes. I knew Tracy would be a far better mother to Laura than I could ever be." She dabbed her eyes and met Spense's gaze. "The god-awful truth is that although I wanted what was best for my child, I wasn't capable of bonding with her. Not back then."

"What about now?" Spense asked. "You keep her pictures out. Have you followed her life over the years?"

Lisa lifted her hand to brush away a tear. "Yes. I'm better now, after what seems like a lifetime of therapy. I no longer blame myself for the past, and I'm content with my life. I'd like to have a relationship with Laura, but she doesn't know she's adopted, and I never wanted to disrupt her life."

"So you're still looking out for her the best way you know how," Caity said. "But knowing she's in trouble, now, I wonder why you haven't gone to the police with this information."

"I don't see how it will help. And the cops never get anything right anyway. When Laura was kidnapped, and her poor nanny was murdered, they screwed everything up royally. But I've heard about you two before, and you seem like two people who know how to get things done, so when you said you need me to answer your questions . . ." She blew her nose. "I'll do anything I can to help. I told Laura's bodyguard, Ty Cayman, too. He was here just a little while ago, looking for Laura."

The hairs on the back of Spense's neck raised. He exchanged a glance with Caity. The missing bodyguard, the last person to see Laura before she disappeared had come here before them looking for Laura.

"Why would Cayman come here? Does he know you're Laura's biological mother?" Spense asked.

"Yes. They've all been friends for years. I don't think Ty knew about the rape, but he said he knew I was Laura's mother. He thought maybe Laura found out the truth, and that she might've come to me for help." She wrung her hands. "If only Laura *had* come to me. I want to help her so badly."

There was no time to render comfort to Lisa. They had to find Laura, and quickly.

"What do you mean by *they've all been friends*?" Caity asked.

"Ty and Whit and Grady. They all pledged the same fraternity back in college, and they've remained friends ever since."

"Did Cayman say where he was going next?" Caity was on her feet.

"He said he was going to Frank's Cabin, to have a look around and see if he can spot something the cops missed."

"How far is it to the cabin? I assume you have to go on foot," Spense said.

"You have to take the trail, but you can get there on an ATV in just a few minutes."

"Is that how you get down the road in bad weather? Do you have an ATV we can borrow?" Caity asked.

Lisa went to the window and pulled the curtains back.

Parked in the back drive was a red ATV.

As SHE CLIMBED up behind him, Caity grabbed onto his waist and said, "You thinking what I'm thinking?"

"Depends if you're thinking Frank's Cabin's a test of guilty knowledge. No mention made of it at the press conference. Chaucers weren't informed this time around or last time."

"So how does Cayman know about it? He could be our UNSUB."

"Any of them could be. Webber, Chaucer, and Cayman were all members of a subculture that considers drug-facilitated sexual assault as *not that bad*."

"But which one do you think morphed into a cold-blooded serial killer? I think it's . . ." The rev of the ATV's engine drowned out the rest.

Chapter 48

Tuesday, October 29
1:10 P.M.
Frank's Cabin
Eagles Nest Wilderness

LAURA COULD BARELY see through the red film in her eyes, but she could feel the blessed comfort of someone cradling her head in strong, thick arms. She lay on a mattress with something cool and white pulled over her skin—a sheet.

"Cayman, is that you?" she whispered into the arms. The hairs tickling her nose smelled like gun smoke.

No answer.

Was she dreaming, still?

"Am I alive?" She remembered a gunshot . . . and red on her hands.

"Laura, sweetheart." A fuzzy face bent near hers. "You're awake. It's all going to be okay, darling. I'm with you now, and I won't leave this time—not until you're at peace."

"Daddy?" She sat up quickly, banging the top of her head against the wooden bedrail.

"I'm here, honey."

Her stomach lurched. "I'm going to be sick."

"I've got more pills, but it would be best if you try to keep the ones I've already given you down."

The room cascaded around her in a whirlwind of colors. Her father's face split into a thousand pieces. When he spoke, his voice sounded like it was coming out of speakers in the log walls.

"No, please," she croaked. "No more pills, they're not helping me. They're making me sicker. My mouth is so dry, Daddy."

He propped her up and fed her a sip of water from a tin cup. It was cool and sweet on her lips and went down easy. The water made her feel better. Not clearheaded, but better.

"More?" he asked in that scary, disembodied voice.

"Yes, please." She drained the last drop from the cup in his hands.

The cabin. They were in the cabin.

"Cayman shot me." She needed to explain it to him so he could get help.

"No." He laughed.

Her father was laughing.

She was dying, and he was laughing.

"It was *you* who shot *Cayman*. Then you fainted. He's deader than dirt, just waiting for me to feed him to the cougars."

Suddenly, she couldn't breathe. She grabbed her throat, sucking in painful spasms of air.

Her father put his arms around her and rocked her back and forth. "Shh. Not to worry. I'm not going to feed my baby girl to the mountain lions. Not my Laura."

She shoved his arms away. "What are you talking about? I didn't shoot Cayman. I only pushed him. I don't even have a gun."

"You used his pistol. And now you're going to kill yourself. They've already found your note. They just need to find your body. You see Cayman's been watching you all these years. He suspected that it was you who killed Angelina, and he saw you with Harriet. He knows you killed her, too. He was onto you, so you shot him, and dragged his body out into the woods like you did Harriet's. But then, my sweet Laura, you came back to your senses, and you were so filled with remorse that you took your own life. So you see, there's no reason for Daddy to feed you to the animals. You can die in peace, and we'll have a beautiful funeral. Everyone will understand it wasn't your fault. You're not right in the head."

"I'm not crazy." She gagged on a throat full of bile. "Why are you lying?"

"I'm telling the truth."

"I never killed anyone." She sat up fully and crawled as far away as possible from the man beside her on the mattress. He'd given her pills. The only reason she hadn't died in this cabin last time she'd been given pills was because she'd been lucky enough to throw up. Without hesitating, she stuck her finger down her throat. She wretched, and out gushed a beautiful stream of fluorescent green liquid. She could see bits and pieces of pills floating around in her vomit.

He shouldn't have let her drink so much water.

She was confused, but not too confused to understand that he was lying when he said she killed Angelina and when he said she'd killed Cayman.

She was not a monster.

How could a child have done all those things to Angelina, and to the others? "Dr. Duncan told me I couldn't have gotten Angelina to the mountains when I was just a little girl. What you're saying is impossible. It's crazy."

"No, darling, you're the crazy one, remember? You killed Angelina, and I tried to cover it up to save you. But now I see what a terrible mistake that was."

Her heart pounded in her chest. Her father's lies floated before her in the air, written letter by letter with a bloody finger.

"I want you to be at peace, Laura. So I'll tell you everything," he said. "But then, I want you to take the rest of these pills and lie down and go to sleep like a good girl."

She shook her head. "I won't."

"Yes, Laura, you will. Because that night, thirteen years ago, I heard a scream coming from Angelina's room. I went in, and I found *you* standing over her with a pillow. You smothered her. I wanted to protect you, so I gave you some medicine to make you forget. Then, I wrote a ransom note to cover up her murder and make it seem like a kidnapping. Your mother woke up briefly, but she was so drunk she passed out again, and I didn't even have to drug her. I brought you and Angelina up to this cabin. I left you here while I dragged her body out into the wilderness. She was already dead, but I stabbed her to confuse the police. Then I went home, and your mother and I called the cops."

"Does Mother know what you did?" Laura could feel tears clogging her throat, but she refused to let them out.

"Of course not. She's too stupid to know anything except exactly what I tell her. She thought your birth mother had kidnapped you, and she wanted the police to go out and find her."

Birth mother.

Laura pictured the words written in the air with the bloody finger again. Another lie!

"Oh, honey, don't look at me like that. And don't worry. I'm your real father. I love you, and I just thought you should know . . . before it ends . . . that you have another mother. She's beautiful, and absolutely crazy. Just like you."

"I don't believe you!" But somewhere, deep inside, an ache that had nothing to do with drugs or even fear for her life took hold. "If what you say is true, the police would know about her. *I* would know about her."

"Not so. Only the family attorneys knew about the closed adoption. I convinced Tracy that your biological mother couldn't have taken you, because she didn't know who had adopted you. That was a lie, but it was for your own good. I told Tracy that if the police found out and got a court order to unseal the adoption records, it would be a disaster, and then your biological mother really would know how to find you."

His words were like a grenade, exploding inside her, shattering her heart into a million pieces. She grabbed her chest—it wasn't moving. She opened her mouth and gulped in air.

Breathe!

The oxygen turned her blood cold and her mind hard. She forced herself to look at her father. "People close to the family had to know I was adopted. They would have thought my biological mother was a suspect. They would have said something."

"Cayman and Webber knew. And I appeased them by having Cayman look into Lisa's—that's your birth mother's name— whereabouts the night of the kidnapping. She was in an institution at the time. No surprise there. Like I said, she was unhinged, just like you."

Lisa.

Could it be? Her head was pounding with the lies and half-truths that had permeated her entire life. Tears stung her eyes, distorting her vision. She cupped her hands over her mouth, breathing and rebreathing the same air to keep from hyperventilating. Separating the lies from the truth seemed impossible. Only . . . there was one truth she could cling to.

Something she knew beyond any doubt.

She was not a murderer.

Even if her father was telling the truth about this Lisa, he was lying about Angelina.

He stuck his hand out and opened his palm. It was filled with different colored pills and capsules—a kaleidoscope of death.

She knocked his hand away, and the pills went flying like confetti.

"Liar!" she screeched, surprised by how strong she suddenly felt, as if sheer rage had raised her from the dead. "Angelina did scream." She could *hear* that scream in her head. "But I was the one who ran into her room to help her. I remember! I remember!" The doors in her secret mind began to fly open one by one. "You were on top of her. You had your hands around her throat. I *saw* you!"

He was breathing hard and fast. He looked at her with feral eyes. "I didn't want to hurt you, Laura. You were never supposed to see. I could've killed you, too, right then, and made it seem like an intruder had done it all. But I love you, so I tried to find another way out."

A terrible feeling of dread came over her, but she was finished running. There was nowhere left to hide. "If you love me, for once, just tell me the truth. Don't let me die without it." Though it made her want to crawl out of her skin to touch him, she reached out and rested her hand on his arm. "I'm begging you, Daddy."

"And then will you take the pills? Please don't make me shoot you. I don't think I can bear it."

No! "Yes, but I'll know if you're lying. I remember too much. *You* killed Angelina, and then you set everything up to look like a kidnapping so no one would suspect the truth. But what I can't remember is what happened *this time*—to Harriet and me."

There was something shiny next to her father, an object, partially concealed by the covers. A knife? He must've laid it down when he took her in his arms. She could see the black handle and the edge of a blade protruding from beneath the sheets. Her heart raced as she realized it was within her reach . . . *almost.*

He patted her hand. "You should've stayed my little girl. I tried to keep you with me, always. But you wanted to grow up, and when you stopped taking your medicine, you started to think things through. You became too curious. Even after you went off to college though, I had hope. Tracy and I came down for parents' weekend, just to make sure that you were happy. That was the real reason, I swear." He paused and raised her chin with his finger. "I hoped you could be happy."

She wanted to be sick again, but fought it off.

"What did you do to Harriet?" If she got out of this alive, she wanted to be able to tell Harriet's mother what had happened to her daughter. A mother deserves to know.

"At parents' weekend, I saw your young friend in the hallway of your building, and Laura, I couldn't resist her. I had to take her, and so I did. The girls I claim, they don't feel a thing. I make sure they're fast asleep before I . . . anyway . . . the very next day, you and I had our father-daughter breakfast. Remember that?"

She nodded, too nauseated to speak.

"And you told me you thought someone sick murdered Angelina, but not a kidnapper. You said you'd been thinking about our travels. How sometimes the news would report a woman missing just as we departed. You said the women looked like Angelina, and that someone evil had to be near us. And do you remember what you planned to do about your theory?"

She clutched her throat. If only she hadn't told her father she was going to meet with the newspaper editor, with Ronald Saas.

"Who was the man who bought me dinner?" She forced herself to look him in the eyes.

"Someone I hired. A homeless fellow no one will ever miss— I've taken care of him like the rest. Whose blood do you think was all over this cabin? Not yours. It was mostly his. I'd already cleaned up after I killed Harriet."

"You can't get away with this. When they find the homeless man . . ."

He laughed, seeming genuinely amused. "They'll never find his body. Anyway, I hired him to bring you to the cabin, but I made sure he kept you asleep until I could get here the next day. I wouldn't trust something so important as your death to a bum. But I admit I made my own mistakes. You were barely breathing when I left, and I didn't think it was possible for you to survive, not after the huge overdose I gave you. And I had to get back. The police were waiting to interview me, and I didn't want them to get suspicious. But don't worry." The sincere look he gave her made her blood curdle in her veins. "I'm right here, baby. I won't leave you this time until it's all over."

His shoulders sagged, as though he'd grown weary of conversation. But there was so much more she wanted to know. And she needed more time to gather her breath, to steel her nerves for what was to come. She had to keep him talking.

"Did you shoot Cayman?"

"In the back. He was trying to save you from me—your own father, if you can believe that. Once, I slipped and mentioned this cabin to him. I think he suspected this was where I would hide you."

She forged on, she had to keep him talking. "Why does Dr. Webber think I'm a murderer?"

"Because of all the little lies I tell him. Things like how you have a habit of sleepwalking with knives. I hoped it would never come to this, but I've been laying the groundwork for years, in case I needed someone to take the fall for me. Unfortunately for you, my window of opportunity is closing. I can surely convince the law that you killed Angelina and your friend . . . and yourself. But if they ever catch on to all the others, that would be a hard sell, indeed. So you understand why I had to act quickly, once you said you were going to the newspapers."

The web of evil her father had spun was so elaborate, so sticky—it seemed impossible to escape. Oh how she wished she hadn't confided in him about her theories and told him she was going to take them to Ronald Saas.

Now, with the confessional note, and her death staged to look like a suicide, he might get away with it all. If Cassidy and Spenser didn't put the pieces together, if she died here in this cabin, he would go on killing as he pleased. There would be no one left to stop him. "Water . . . I need water for the pills."

He looked at the empty cup and picked it up off the mattress. "I'll get some, but you have to come with me."

Taking hold of her arm, he yanked her off the bed. No way she could get to the knife, now. Not while he had hold of her. She went as numb inside as if she'd swallowed a vial of Lidocaine, but she knew exactly what she had to do.

Her own father was the monster, and the monster had to die.

He dragged her a step toward the door. Then, from somewhere outside, a mechanical sound whirred, like the noise of a motor sputtering. Growing louder, closer.

Her father froze and turned his face away from her and toward the sound.

Now!

She bit his hand, jerked free of his grasp and lunged for the knife.

THE ATV SCREECHED to a halt. Spense jumped off and raced up the steps to the cabin three at a time. He could hear Caity panting behind him. If Cayman was their UNSUB, he might have Laura with him, or hidden nearby.

"Bitch!" A male voice carried to him on the wind.

Spense's brain and body kicked into auto-mode. He held out a *back away* hand to Caity, at the same instant he drew his Glock and stuck it out in front.

No time to clear the cabin.

He kicked open the door and breached the entry.

Christ.

Cayman lay motionless on the floor, blood pooling around him. Chaucer loomed center stage, pressing a knife to his daughter's throat.

Spense pointed his pistol at Chaucer. "Let her go."

"Lower your gun, and I'll put down the knife. This isn't what it looks like." Chaucer's words were calm, but his face was red. His eyes jerked back and forth between the door and Spense.

Spense sighted his shot. He could take it, but if Chaucer anticipated him, he might cut Laura's jugular before he went down. There wouldn't be time to get her off this mountain before she bled out.

"Laura shot Cayman, and then she tried to stab me with a knife. But I got it away from her," Chaucer said. "Terrible thing. But she doesn't know what she's doing. She's off her medications, so we can't hold her responsible."

Man, he was good. If Spense didn't know better, he might even believe him.

"It's over, Senator." Caity's voice sounded behind him.

Dammit.

She should've stayed back. Chaucer could have a gun on him somewhere. Spense's gaze flicked to Chaucer's pant leg—but he didn't see the bulge of an ankle holster. His gaze darted back up to the senator's face, then back down to Cayman.

A pistol lay just to the side of the dead man.

Caity saw it, too, and before Spense could order her not to, she scooped it up and pointed it at Chaucer's head.

Laura was eerily still, her face a deathly white.

"You're okay, Laura. Just hang in there with me. He's going to let you go, and when he does run straight out the door. You don't have to say anything. Blink twice if you understand," Caity spoke directly to Laura, as if they were the only ones who could hear.

Laura blinked twice.

Caity took a step closer to the senator.

"You crazy bitch." The motherfucker actually laughed.

"Me or Laura? Which crazy bitch are you speaking to?" Caity said, her tone even and calm.

"Drop the knife, and let Laura go," Spense commanded.

"I told you, she shot Cayman."

Laura started to blink rapidly.

"Just relax Laura, remember what I told you. When he lets you go, run straight out that door," Caity said.

"We'll sort it all out at the district." Spense addressed Chaucer. "You can call your lawyer, but right now, anything you say may be used against you in a court of law."

"My daughter's not in her right mind. I can explain all of this."

Laura's pupils were giant pools of black, but she didn't move a muscle.

"You want to keep talking, sir, or do you want to let Laura go so your lawyers can work their magic?" Caity took another step toward the senator and his hostage.

Chaucer's lips snarled. The deadly look he sent them was like bullets firing straight out of his eyeballs.

He and Caity shared a glance. They'd faced down evil before. Spense's heartbeat slowed from a gallop to a trot, and his shoulders relaxed. He trusted her. She trusted him.

Advantage good guys.

"You can't possibly be stupid enough to shoot me, Caitlin. All I want to do is walk out of here with my daughter. Agent Spenser, tell her to put down her weapon."

"No can do." Spense moved in, too.

"I'm not stupid enough, but I just might be crazy enough." Caity took one more step. "My aim's a lot better at close range. Just ask my partner."

"Drop the knife. Let Laura go," Spense repeated. They were within tackling distance of him now. "Two of us. One of you."

"Two guns. One knife." Caity locked her gaze on Chaucer's forehead. "Do the math."

Chaucer's white-knuckle grip on the knife pinked up, his elbow dropped. Caity held out her hand. "Give me the knife."

Chaucer relaxed his hold on his daughter.

Before Spense could move, Laura ripped the knife from her father's hand, whirled and buried it in his chest.

As blood bloomed across Chaucer's shirt, he grunted and stumbled backward.

Laura lowered her arm, and the blade clattered to the floor. While her father coughed and gasped, she stared hollow-eyed at Caity. "The monster had to die."

Chaucer crumpled to the ground, his eyes open and lifeless.

Caity went to Laura and put an arm around her, then walked her over to the bed. "It was self-defense, Laura. Isn't that right, Agent Spenser?"

Spense knelt beside Cayman. His skin had grown cold, and there was no pulse. It was too late for him. "Clear a case as I've ever seen. Your father had a knife on you. You struggled. That's all that happened here. Try to remember that."

Laura nodded, and then she smiled. "That's right. I remember. I remember *everything*."

Chapter 49

Wednesday, October 30
3:30 P.M.
Task force headquarters
Highlands Hotel
Denver, Colorado

A LONE, PEA-COLORED linoleum table and three folding chairs were all that remained in what had once been a decked-out war room. Caitlin, Spense, and Hatcher had gathered here for one last confab, and Hatcher had stacked the contents of the fridge—five ham sandwiches, two beef jerkies, and three energy drinks in the center of the table.

"Anyone want to help me finish these babies off? I hate to see good food go to waste." Good food was a generous assessment.

"It's all yours, buddy." Spense stretched his legs, and folded his hands behind his head.

"What about you, Caitlin?"

"I'm good. You enjoy, Jordan." She smiled at the detective, grateful he hadn't pressed anyone harder for details about the struggle that led to Chaucer's demise. There would be more questions for Laura once she was released from the hospital, but Hatcher had made it clear the higher-ups had no interest in prosecuting the young woman.

"How's Laura doing?" Hatcher asked.

Caitlin and Spense had come here directly from the hospital.

"Well," Caitlin said. After being treated upon arrival with activated charcoal and gastric lavage, Laura was looking good. She'd taken a hit from the overdose, but her liver enzymes were only mildly elevated and on a downward trend. "Doctors anticipate forty-eight hours of monitoring and then release. The other good news is her mother, Tracy, is flying Dr. Duncan in from DC. He'll be here to help Laura deal with her trauma, and he'll be present when she meets her biological mother, Lisa Blake, for the first time."

Hatcher drummed his fingers on the tabletop. "Lisa Blake. I wish we'd tracked her down thirteen years ago."

"Don't beat yourself up," Spense said. "It may seem obvious now that Lisa was the primary object of Chaucer's obsession, and the other women surrogates for his rage after she dumped him, but at the time, I don't think anyone could've put it together. The adoption was closed. Only the parties involved and the lawyers knew about it. There simply weren't enough pieces to complete the puzzle."

"You both agree that Angelina was probably Chaucer's first."

Caitlin folded her hands. "Probably his first kill, but obviously not his first rape. I think you'll find many more women are going to come forward with complaints about waking up confused after an evening with Whitmore Chaucer."

"So what was different with Angelina? What made him snap and go from being a serial rapist to a serial murderer? Not that I buy all this psychobabble crap, but if you had to guess."

"Let's call it more than a guess," Spense said. "Let's call it speculation supported by evidence. After all, we now have Laura's eyewitness account of Angelina's murder."

"Laura recalls hearing Angelina scream, and when she ran into the room, Chaucer had his hands around Angelina's throat. That's the evidence piece," Caitlin said. "The speculative piece is this—Angelina didn't ingest enough of the GHB and woke up during the rape. She screamed, and Chaucer had to silence her—thus the strangulation. Later, when he dumped her body in the wilderness, he stabbed her in a fury. The subsequent rush of endorphins and release of his rage gave him a high he'd never experienced before. His compulsion for self-gratification could no longer be satisfied from a sexual release alone. Thus the transformation from rapist to murderer."

"So he risked everything, his family, his career, and his life to get some kind of high? Stupid bastard. The guy had everything, and it wasn't enough." Hatcher let out a breath. "Speaking of stupid bastards, that brings me to Grady Webber. It seems that although he did follow Caitlin outside of Coffee and Conversation, and though he did grab her and punch her, it was Chaucer who most likely dosed her tea with GHB—unbeknownst to Webber. A waitress identified the senator as having been in the coffee shop at around the same time. He was wearing a red toupee, but she still recognized him. If Webber hadn't stalked Caitlin outside, Chaucer may have . . . anyway, we wanna work with Webber. We're hoping Caitlin won't mind dropping the assault charges in exchange for his full cooperation in an ongoing investigation."

"No way." Spense slammed his fist on the table.

"He may not have known about Chaucer's murderous habits, but he's been with the man for most of his travels. He could be a tremendous help when it comes to the other murders."

"Of course." Caitlin touched Spense's arm. "Think about it. Grady's going to get his license pulled, undoubtedly. His reputation will be ruined. And Tracy and Laura are planning to file a malpractice suit—so he's going to pay with his pocketbook, too. With Cayman gone, Grady's the best source of insider knowledge about the senator."

Spense relaxed his fist and took her hand. "It's your call, Caity."

"I'm fine with that," she told Hatcher. "Do we have any more information about Cayman?"

He nodded. "The bodyguard kept a journal. We found it in a safety-deposit box. It seems he'd been on edge about Chaucer ever since Inga's 'accident.' According to his journal, Lisa Blake told Inga to rest easy, that it hadn't been Grady who'd raped her. Inga already had suspicions about Chaucer, put two and two together, and confided in Cayman. She'd seen Chaucer sneaking in and out of hotels in the wee hours, and once she'd seen him in the company of a young woman Cayman had dated. The woman later turned up missing—I believe that will prove to be the woman he was with in the fun-booth photos."

"So Chaucer pushed Inga off a hiking trail because he realized she was getting close to the truth," Spense said.

"Cayman sure seemed to think so. It's one of the many threads we're going to need to follow up. And we don't think Cayman lied about Laura's dinner with Ronald Saas. Cayman had information that Laura was meeting with the editor of the *Mountain Times*, so when a man showed up at the appointed time and introduced himself as Saas, Cayman simply assumed that's who he was. It looks like Cayman really was trying to protect Laura—but he didn't have any proof to back up his suspicions about Chaucer. That's why he dropped out of sight and started snooping around on his own." Hatcher ripped a bite of ham sandwich off with his teeth, chewed and swallowed. "I've got some more news, but first I wanna say it's been swell working with you two, and I hope the Interpol folks don't turn out to be a bunch of dicks. Pardon my French."

Caitlin had to shake her head at that apology. If she took offense at every off-color remark, she'd be toast, considering she spent her days working in the trenches with special agents and cops. "No worries. Let's hear the news. You said, Interpol, so I assume you're going to be putting together an international task force."

"Correct. Search of the Chaucer home in DC turned up these." Hatcher laid several photographs on the table, adjacent to the beef jerky.

Caitlin stopped breathing for a few seconds.

"Son of a bitch," Spense said low and hard.

The photographs showed a collection of newspaper clippings—stories of young women gone missing or found dead all across the globe, as well as rows of locks of dark hair tied with pink ribbons.

"How many locks of hair?" Spense asked and looked away, but not before Caitlin saw the moisture in his eyes.

"Including the two Chaucer planted on Laura, which we believe belonged to Angelina and Harriet . . . thirteen," Hatcher replied.

One for every year.

Chapter 50

THE SUN COMING up over the Sangre de Cristo Mountains was one of the most spectacular events Spense had ever witnessed. Even after the sun had risen, the soft hues of the morning light enhanced the brown earth, green trees, and blue sky on the road to Taos. At first, he hadn't been able to figure why Caity had wanted to roust the moms out of bed while it was still dark out, just so they could leave Boulder by 4 a.m.

But the magic show the light created made him glad she'd insisted.

Surprisingly, the moms hadn't uttered a single grumble over the early departure.

Spense thought it might be nice to stop at the hot springs, but then Caity and the others announced they were on a tight schedule. Apparently that meant a side trip to the Great Sand Dunes was out of the question, so he didn't bother asking.

The only reason he could think of that the ladies might be so anxious about the time was if they wanted to tool around Taos, then score a nice long nap before the gallery opening tonight—the only planned event for the day.

Get up early.

Drive like hell.

Take a nap.

Women.

He whistled at the wheel, while the ladies sang "Ninety-Nine Bottles of Beer."

He wanted to participate, but was enjoying the sound of their feminine voices too much to drown them out with his loud, out-of-tune bass.

Luke Jericho, a well-to-do rancher that he and Caity met as a result of the Santa Fe Saint case, had just added a new venue in Taos to his string of New Mexico art galleries. Tonight's opening gala promised paintings on loan from the Georgia O'Keeffe museum, as well as the best of the local artist community. Both Caity and her mother were big fans of O'Keeffe and of her colorful flowers in particular. Caity's love of flora had come directly from her mom.

He'd never known two people more enthralled by botany.

Would his kids inherit their mother's affinity to flowers?

His grip on the steering wheel tightened, and he reminded himself they weren't a family—even if it felt that way sometimes. He was supposed to be giving Caity space, so he damn well better keep his mouth shut about their hypothetical offspring. Caity had given him no indication she was ready to revisit the subject of marital bliss. And the ball was still in her court.

"There!" The moms leaned into the front seat, pointing. "You're going to miss the turnoff."

Steering with one hand, he slowed up and checked the map. "No, this is the right way."

"But we want to see the Rio Grande Gorge Bridge," three voices clamored at once.

Women.

Still, it was early. There was plenty of time, and he was more than familiar with a woman's prerogative. "I'll turn around."

Twenty minutes later, they arrived at the Rio Grande Gorge.

Everyone piled out of the rental car.

"Let's walk the bridge," Caity suggested.

"Mom's afraid of heights," he said, gazing up at one of the tallest bridges in North America. The last time he was at the Grand Canyon with Agatha, she'd puked over the South Rim, and when he'd taken Caity to Griffith Park Observatory, she'd had a panic attack climbing the stairs. The Rio Grande Gorge Bridge, with its narrow walkway and heavy traffic, was far more intimidating than either of those.

"I most certainly am not afraid," his mother retorted.

But her face was flushed and apprehensive.

He glanced at the side of the road, lined with denizens selling jewelry and purses out of their cars. "Let's think about this a minute. We can check out all this loot, and then, if everyone feels up to braving the bridge we'll all go together. If not, I'll stay behind and make like an ant along with anyone who might be having second thoughts."

All three women shook their heads.

"Not one of you wants to shop for trinkets?"

"Don't worry about me, Atticus." His mother tiptoed up and gave him a peck on the cheek. "I'm going to walk the bridge. This is once in a lifetime, and I don't want to miss it."

"Me either." Arlene hooked her arm through Agatha's.

"If you're sure." He made eye contact with his mother, then Arlene, then Caity. "But we can turn around anytime you want. No shame in that."

In truth, he was itching to get up on that skywalk. It just surprised him . . . in a good way.

Caity led the way at a brisk pace.

Today must be the day for setting aside fear.

Arm in arm, the moms soldiered on, but slowly. He turned to check on them. The wind blew their hair back, showing off their shining faces. They looked like happy campers to him, so he hurried to catch up with Caity.

Her complexion had paled and the skin encircling her lips was tinted blue.

He pulled her up short. "You sure you want to do this?"

Crowds and heights weren't her thing, and it seemed like she might be doing all this for his sake. He loved the adrenaline rush of peering down over rocky cliffs and crashing waves and Caity knew it—she'd heard his Acapulco cliff dive story enough times.

"Never more sure of anything in my life."

"Okay." He couldn't quite read her face. Either she was terrified or excited . . . or maybe both. "But I have a feeling there's something you're not telling me."

"That's because it's a surprise."

He glanced back over his shoulder. The moms weren't far behind, and they had their heads together.

Coconspirators?

"We didn't come to Taos for Luke's gallery opening?"

"That's not until tomorrow."

"So why all the rushing around today?"

"Do I really have to define the word surprise for you, or will you, please, just shut up and trust me?"

THIS WAS ONE of those plans that seemed like a great idea on paper. But that was before Caitlin stepped onto the 565-foot-tall Rio Grande Gorge Bridge. As traffic whizzed by, the wind lashed against her skin like a cat o' nine tails, and flapped her hair into her face, nearly blinding her. She pulled a scrunchie out of her pocket, secured her long tresses in a ponytail atop her head, and voila, the least of her problems was solved.

Her palms were damp, and her heart was keeping time to a punk rock drum beat.

Then Spense moved in close, shielding her from the punishing wind, and she remembered why she'd come up with such an extreme scheme.

She loved him.

Here was a man who'd saved her from a mountain lion, risked his career for her, and complimented her mother's cooking. The same man who'd helped clear her father's name, then adopted a star in his honor. Now, anytime she needed her father, all she had to do was look to the night sky.

This was the least she could do for Spense.

Up ahead she caught sight of their destination, a small platform cantilevering out from the main bridge over the Rio Grande River.

She grabbed Spense by the hand, sucked up her courage, and said, "Come on."

Together, they stepped onto the platform and peered down into the gorge. From this height, the river looked like a sliver of broken mirror coursing through a bank of green wool.

"Do you remember the first time we made love?" she asked.

"Hmm. Let me think." He grinned big, and then said, "Sorry, but what kind of question is that?"

"A rhetorical one."

"Baby, never ask a man a rhetorical question about sex."

"Spense, be serious. Remember how we wanted to take that Tahitian vacation, and we kept waiting and waiting for the perfect moment to make love?"

"And then we realized that perfect moment was up to us to create."

"At a budget motel, you turned the night into something special and made me feel like the most loved woman in the world."

"You are the most loved woman in the world." He grabbed her by the waist and pulled her against him.

She could barely breathe, but she needed to get this out. "I know you're struggling right now to make sense of what happened with your dad. When you asked me to marry you the other day, we'd just gotten kicked off a murder case, and I'd just had a creepy encounter with Grady Webber. It wasn't by any stretch the perfect time for you to propose. I thought we weren't ready, that it was too soon. But I was wrong."

"What are you trying to say, Caity? I'll wait for you, however long it takes. I never meant to make it seem like I was giving you an ultimatum. Marry me or else is not exactly a woman's dream."

"I'm saying that just like there was never going to be a perfect moment to make love for the first time, there isn't going to be a perfect moment to propose marriage. I love you so much it makes my heart pound like I'm in a free fall off this bridge—and it terrifies me. Then I think about the time you dove off the cliffs in Acapulco, how you said it was one of the most exhilarating moments in your life, and that you'll always be glad you took the chance."

He broke their gaze, looking past her, over her shoulder. She turned to see what he saw.

They were here.

Three guys, two of them carrying harnesses and cords, all of them wearing red shirts that read *Bungee Dream Adventures.*

There was no more time to waste. If she was going to do this, and she was, she'd better get to it. She waited a few more beats for the moms to catch up. She gave them the thumbs-up, and they stepped onto the platform with Spense and her.

She dropped to one knee. "Marriage is a leap of faith. But sometimes when you're scared, you just have to jump."

"Caity, you don't have to do this for me. I want you to feel safe and happy. You have nothing to prove. I love you, but I want you to be sure."

"I'm sure of this. You are the love of my life. And I'm ready to take that leap of faith whenever you are." The wind buffeted her about, and she gripped the fence for dear life with one hand and extended her other up to Spense. "Atticus Spenser, will you marry me?"

"Oh hell yes." He pulled her up and into his arms. With his body he shielded hers from the wind. His feet planted wide, he became a wall protecting her from wind and traffic and any trouble that might pass by—no—they became a wall protecting one another. His lips found hers, and he coaxed her mouth open, kissing her thoroughly and shamelessly, right in front of the moms and the Bungee Dream Adventures guys and the tourists and the good lord above.

They finally broke apart, and the crowd let out a cheer. Or maybe they'd been cheering all along, but she'd been too caught up in the kiss to notice.

Spense was her world, and he was all she ever wanted.

"We're still going to Tahiti, right?" he asked.

The bungee guys were setting up. The sound of harnesses rattling shook her to the core.

"Stop stalling." She grinned. "Of course we're going to Tahiti. But not next week, for goodness sake. I need time to plan a destination wedding. We'll invite Gretchen, and Enrique, and Dutch of course . . . all of our old friends, maybe even Hatcher . . ."

"Now who's stalling?" the head bungee man asked.

She looked at Spense. Her entire body was trembling.

He took her hand, turned her palm up and kissed it. "Only if this is what you really want."

In answer, she nodded and opened her stance. An adventure guide rushed to help her into her harness and fasten the safety belts while another guide helped Spense. Behind them cars sped by, and people stopped to gawk and whoop. The guides took plenty of time going over instructions and safety rules.

Then together, she and Spense stepped out onto the edge of the platform.

She took a huge breath and climbed atop the railing a safe distance from Spense.

Below them the Rio Grande River raged.

Ahead of them, their life together waited.

"I'm going to count down from five," a guide said. "Five."

She squared her gaze with Spense's. "I'm so scared."

"Four."

"Me, too," he said. "Isn't it great?"

"Three-two-one," shouted the guide.

Jump!

And then they were flying.

Acknowledgments

THANK YOU READERS! I am so grateful that you take time out of your busy lives to read my books. I really hope you enjoy them. I love hearing from you, so don't hesitate to e-mail me. You can find my contact information and sign up for my newsletter at www.CareyBaldwin.com. I welcome your feedback and appreciate your reviews.

As always, I want to thank my family, Shannon, Erik, Sarah, and Bill for putting up with me and loving me. You guys are my everything.

Thank you to my wonderful friends Leigh LaValle, Lena Diaz, Tessa Dare, Courtney Milan, and Brenna Aubrey for your support. I couldn't do this without you.

K and T ladies: Sarah Andre, Diana Belchase, Manda Collins, Lena Diaz, Rachel Grant, Krista Hall, Gwen Hernandez, and Sharon Wray—you rock! I am blessed to have you in my life.

Carmen Pacheco, what can I say? You have been such a wonderful friend and beta reader and I am truly grateful for you.

I'd like to thank my amazing editor, Nicole Fischer, for her brilliant insights and her unflagging patience. And finally, a huge thank-you to my fantastic agent, Liza Dawson for taking me on and believing in me, and to Caitie Flum and everyone at Liza Dawson Associates for all your help and support.

About the Author

CAREY BALDWIN is a mild-mannered doctor by day and an award-winning author of edgy suspense by night. She holds two doctoral degrees, one in medicine and one in psychology. She loves reading and writing stories that keep you off-balance and on the edge of your seat. Carey lives in the southwestern United States with her amazing family. In her spare time she enjoys hiking and chasing wildflowers. Carey loves to hear from readers so please visit her at www.CareyBaldwin.com, on Facebook https://www.facebook.com/CareyBaldwinAuthor, or Twitter https://twitter.com/CareyBaldwin.

Discover great authors, exclusive offers, and more at hc.com.